WANT YOU BACK

RIVER LAURENT

WANT YOU BACK

ISBN: 978-1-911608-45-5

CHARLOTTE

I woke up with a jolt as a movement to my left roused me from a deep, sound sleep. It took a moment for my surroundings to make sense. I was on a train, headed home and the guy next to me had shifted his weight to get off the train. At that realization, I peered out the window and let out a cry. That was my stop!

I scrambled to my feet and dashed out of the train, jumping out seconds before the train doors closed. I stood on the platform congratulating myself.

"Hey!" a voice called from the train window of the moving train.

I looked up to see the breathtakingly gorgeous, big guy I'd noticed on the train, before I dozed off. He was waving at me frantically from the window.

"You've left your bag!" he shouted, holding up my brown bag.

For a precious second, my brain couldn't compute and I looked down stupidly at my shoulder where the strap of my bag should have been.

"Oh God," I cried. How could I have been that careless? I broke into a cold sweat as I thought about the contents of my bag. It had my whole life in it.

A laptop which I'd waitressed for months before I could afford to buy it, my apartment keys, my wallet, my cell phone, all my recipes… panic seized me as the train started moving. I jogged along with it.

"Want me to throw it?" the breathtakingly gorgeous guy shouted.

"No, no, please don't do that," I yelled back in a panic, thinking of my precious laptop.

"I won't," he reassured quickly. "I'll keep it safe and wait for you at the next stop."

I almost wept with relief as I ran out of the platform. He waved and ducked his head back into the train. I stood watching the train disappear out of sight. I hoped I wasn't wrong, but there was something solid and trustworthy about him. Maybe it was his deep, authoritative voice or the fact that he wore a fncy, obviously expensive suit, or the smile he flashed me.

I had to wait a good fifteen minutes for the next train, all the while shifting my weight from one foot to another impatiently. By the time it came and I got on, I was sure that the gorgeous guy, as nice as he was, would not be there. I had taken too long. He looked like a busy, successful guy.

My only hope was, he'd left my bag with the train station officials. Knots of anxiety twisted in my stomach. I couldn't lose that bag. I was barely making ends meet with my job and combined with school, I couldn't squeeze out more time to get another job. If I did, I would definitely fail my exams. I was in my last year and no way did I want to compromise that.

I squeezed my hands into fists. Digging my nails into my skin, I made promises to God as the train inched slowly to the next station. I would never fall asleep on a train again. I would never be so careless again. Never. My throat thickened with unshed tears.

Up until that point, my schedule was a nightmare. I never stayed still except during class and when I finally got to lay my head on my pillow. I was always on the move but I told myself I only had to do it for less than a year. Then I could start the career I'd always dreamed of ever since I accidentally walked into a posh restaurant when I was ten years old, in search of my mom.

It had been a few minutes to four when I walked into the restaurant, one of the older establishments and they'd been setting out four o'clock tea.

I'd stood there gaping at the arrangement of cakes and the tiniest sandwiches I'd ever seen. My stomach had growled with hunger, but that was nothing new and I'd ignored it, as a tall, proud man, decked out in a white apron strode into the room.

He issued instructions importantly, and everybody scurried to execute his instructions. Looking through me, he'd walked back out. And at that moment, I'd decided I wanted to be just like him. I wanted to be a chef.

Now my dream was close and I couldn't afford to lose my bag. I needed those recipes. Well before the train ground to a stop, I was already at the doors waiting to get out. Before the doors were completely open, I had leapt out and was heading towards the station offices when...

"Hey!"

CHARLOTTE

I whirled around at the deep, familiar voice, and saw him. Emotion swirled in my chest when I saw my bag, overwhelming me. I burst into tears. Great, big, humiliating dumb tears.

I covered my face with my hands as sobs wracked my body. Big, strong hands wrapped around me, pulling me against a hard body. I lay my head on a solid chest as big hands gently stroked my hair and back.

"Hey, hey, it's okay," he said over and over again.

I lost track of time as I stood there clinging to him. When my sobs subsided, I pulled away and let out an embarrassed laugh.

"You probably won't believe this, but this is not something I do often," I said with a laugh.

He chuckled. "That makes two of us. Here is your bag." He handed it to me the way officials at the Olympics handed out medals, draping it over my head.

“I don’t know how I can ever thank you,” I said with feeling, while I stroked the rough material of my bag.

“You could start by telling me your name,” he said, his stunning cobalt blue eyes twinkling.

I stuck out my hand feeling a little foolish for offering to shake his hand when I’d been clinging to him like a limpet only minutes earlier. “Charlotte Evans.”

He enclosed my hand in his massive one. Heat enveloped my body from that simple point of contact.

“Alex Turner.”

“I can’t tell you how grateful I am.” I held my bag tighter. “This bag has my whole life in it.”

He grinned. “I guessed that much.” There was something playful and fun about Alex. Like nothing fazed him.

“Can I buy you a drink?” I asked on a whim. I was only asking him out for a drink to thank him, nothing else.

My life was carefully mapped out and having a boyfriend was not part of my plans. The only way I’d made it this far in my life was by making plans and sticking to them. That was not to say that I hadn’t ever had a boyfriend. I had, but I always ensured that my relationships, if you could call them that, remained casual.

“I’d love that, but I’ll do the buying,” he said.

Grantsville was a small college town in Ohio but one thing that was plentiful was a choice of bars and restaurants. As we walked downtown, I stole looks at Alex. There was something terribly upmarket about him. Perhaps it was his posture or the way he walked. Like he had known wealth all his life.

Other than that, he was easily the sexiest man I'd ever gone on a date with, even though technically, it was not a date. Still, I couldn't help wonder how it would feel to be wrapped up in his arms… without clothes between us.

A familiar ache grew between my legs. For a variety of reasons, it had been months since I'd had sex. One of which was my crazy schedule, another was a scarcity of men that I found attractive enough to go to bed with. Other reasons included immaturity, selfishness... come to think of it the list was quite long.

I stopped in front of one of my favorite joints, a cocktail bar where the crowd was less student-like and the décor was upbeat and modern.

"I'll get the drinks," he said. "What would you like?"

"A Clover Club would be awesome," I said, citing my favorite cocktail, which I treated myself to once every three weeks, or when I'd had an unexpected big tip at work. "I'll grab us a table."

It was six in the evening and the bar was almost full but my favorite table at the corner had just become vacant and I made a beeline for it. I shrugged out of my coat and sat down.

Alex made his way through the crowd to the table carrying our drinks. It gave me a chance to covertly study him. He was definitely over six feet and he worked out, or did some form of exercise. That was a seriously ripped body he had under his clothes.

"Here you go," he murmured, sliding a frothy drink towards me.

"Thank you," I said and waited until he sat down with his beer before I took a sip of my drink. I closed my eyes as I took a sip. Gin, raspberry syrup, and lemon juice, made for a heady combination and I moaned as the taste exploded in my mouth.

Alex's chuckle roused me from my state of pleasure. "I'd be happy to buy you a drink everyday just to see *that* look on your face."

I laughed. "Could you tell it's my favorite drink?"

"Even a blind man couldn't miss it."

I tried to look sophisticated and worldly as I took another delicate sip. "I've been super busy and haven't been here in a while so this is nice."

"Are you a student here?"

"Yes, at the culinary college. What about yourself? Wait, let me guess. You're in law school."

He slumped his shoulders dramatically and made a disappointed face. "Is it that obvious? And all this time, I thought I carried an aura of mystery."

I giggled. "The jacket gave you away, and the walk. All law students walk fast."

"We're used to rushing from the library to class," he said with a laugh.

I loved how he laughed and how he smiled. It lit up his face and converted him from a solemn looking young man to a playful, handsome one. Okay, he was more than handsome. He was sex on a stick. The thick, devil may care, dirty blonde hair gave him a sinful appearance.

"Culinary, huh?" he asked, staring at me as if trying to read my very soul. "What drew you to it?"

I contemplated my answer. "To be perfectly honest I fell in love with the chef's uniform."

"Funnily enough, I can see you in a Chef's gear. And it suits you."

I told him the tale of me walking into a posh restaurant hotel, but refrained from telling him the real reason why I had stumbled into the restaurant. "What about you, why did you want to be a lawyer?"

He shrugged. "All the men in my family are lawyers, from my grandfather to my own father. My great grandfather was a clerk in a law firm eons ago."

A stab of envy went through me. He said it so casually. His grandfather, father, and even great grandfather. I couldn't imagine how awesome it must be to be able to trace your family three generations back. To know your family so intimately.

"It never crossed my mind to be anything else," he added.

I don't know whether it was because it was Saturday, and I didn't have to go back to school or work until Monday, or I was just enjoying male company for the first time in many months. I downed my cocktail faster than I normally did, and before I knew it there was a new one in front of me.

Alex matched me and soon our voices grew louder and we laughed more. He felt like an old friend, but a super attractive one. I found myself fixated on the movements of his mouth. He had the most sensual lips I'd ever seen on a man.

Full and utterly suckable. At least that's what my drunken brain told me. It had been so long since I had let loose and I was loving it. The last call for drinks rang out.

"One more?" Alex asked.

I shook my head. "No thanks, I've had enough." Something strange had happened to me. Something that had never happened before. EVER. My thoughts had shifted. As if a switch had been turned on in my brain.

All I could think about was sex. The ache between my legs grew with every passing second, and I had to resist the crazy urge to touch myself. Unbelievable. In a public place. What was going on with me?

"Shall we leave?" Alex suggested, his voice husky, his eyes veiled.

"Yes," I said quickly, and stood. I was a little unstable on my feet, but my little apartment was only a five-minute walk away. I lived in a cute place above a toy store right in the middle of town, and I loved the convenience of it.

College was within walking distance and so was my regular job. The only time I ever left town was for special event gigs, which paid more, like the one I had worked that afternoon.

As Alex helped me into my coat, the brush of his hands on my bare skin made goosebumps erupt on my flesh.

ALEX

I'd never met anyone who lived smack in the middle of town. It was pretty cool actually. A door on the street led up a flight of stairs and then to a small landing and another door, which was her front door.

"Welcome." She pushed the door open and stepped in. She flicked a switch and the small seating area was flooded with light. Her furniture was scanty, but I guess as a student, she needed very little.

Not that I was interested in her surroundings. As soon as she shut the front door, I took her hand and gently tugged her towards me. She was petite and I was hard for her.

The women I usually gravitated towards were a different breed from Charlotte. They were tougher, less sweet. They understood that it was going to be sex and nothing else. With Charlotte I would have to be gentle.

She came in a small but voluptuous package. The moment she removed her coat in the cocktail bar, a dark hunger for her had consumed me. For the period we'd been in the bar, all I had thought about was what it would feel like to cup her full breasts and flick my tongue over her nipples and hear her moan and beg for more.

She walked into my arms as naturally as though she had been doing it for years. She placed her delicate looking hands on my chest and parted her lips.

With a groan, I swooped down and crashed her lips with mine, forgetting the promise to myself to be gentle. There was no hesitation and no teasing around. The kiss deepened from the moment our lips touched. Our tongues swirled together creating beautiful music.

My erection pushed against her belly, and for the first time in my life I worried about the size of my cock. I was a big guy and my cock was, well, big. She was so small, what if she was not able to take it all. But already my body was bursting with need. A need to see her naked and kiss every bit of her skin came over me.

"Where's your bedroom?" I asked, breaking the kiss.

Both our breaths came out fast and rugged, as if we had been running for hours. In answer, she took my hand and led me down a small hallway and through a door. The window was curtainless, flooding the room with moonlight.

She made as though to turn on the light.

"Leave it," I ordered, I wanted to see her in the moonlight. Like some kind of goddess. "Take off your clothes."

Wordlessly, she did as I asked. Never taking my eyes off her, I quickly removed my clothes, except for my boxers. Then I grabbed a condom from my wallet and lay on the bed watching her. My cock jutted out of my boxers in an almost obscene way and I hoped she wanted me as badly as I wanted her.

She reached behind her back and snapped off the clasp of her bra and it popped off, revealing the most gorgeous tits I had even seen. A growl escaped my mouth. I wanted, no, needed to taste every part of her body, skin, memorizing every curve and contour.

"You're so beautiful," I whispered huskily. "Come here."

Her eyes widened when she caught sight of the bulge in front of my boxers. Instead of being turned off, she seemed to be fascinated by the size of my cock.

"Are you hiding a twelve inch subway sandwich in your pants?" she teased, as she got on the bed and straddled me, her wet pussy rubbing against my belly.

My breath caught in my throat as I looked at her. She was the most perfect woman I had ever seen. I caressed her bare shoulders as I stared greedily at her beautiful body. I moved my hands to cup her breasts and she trembled. "So perfect," I muttered as they filled my big hands.

I rubbed her nipples with my thumbs and was rewarded with a soft moan. She placed her hands on my chest and caressed me. Rolling her nipples between my fingers, I sat up to take one hard bud into my mouth. I sucked them both, one after the other, until she was writhing and rocking over my cock, her soaked lacy panties rubbing on my stomach.

I raised my head and captured her mouth in mine. The taste of her cocktail had faded and she tasted of something sweet, like sun-ripened fruit. She moaned into my mouth, driving me crazy. There was nothing that could beat a woman who responded without inhibitions.

I wanted more. "I want to taste your pussy."

"You don't believe in being subtle," she gasped.

"Not when it comes to the important stuff," I said and gently turned us over so she was lying with her back on the bed. I took a moment to admire her naked body again before ducking between her legs. I slid her panties down over her shapely thighs and legs, dropped them on the floor, and turned my attention back to the gift that lay in front of me. It glistened in the moonlight. I nudged her thighs apart, then lowered my head to her dripping nectar.

Her sweet musky scent wafted up my nose. I placed my hands on the sides of her pussy and opened it up. Her arousal gushed out of her and I lowered my head and swept my tongue over her slit.

She let out a gasp of surprise.

"God, you taste so fucking good," I growled. Then I teased her clit mercilessly until she was on the verge of an orgasm. She pushed my head and I gave her what she wanted thrusting into her with my tongue.

When she came, it was with a series of whimpers, and a vice like grip of my hair. I gave her pussy one lingering last lick before I lay on the bed and pulled her into my arms. Slowly, her breath returned to normal.

"That was fuck-tastic," she declared, and we both laughed.

"I'm happy to be of service," I said.

"Oh yeah," she whispered, as she rolled over me and planted kisses on my neck and chest.

"Oh yeah," I rasped.

"I love how muscular you are," she whispered huskily.

I reached out to play with her nipples. "Thank you."

Her trail of kisses went all the way from my navel where she spent a moment teasing it before she took my boxers between her teeth and pulled them down with her teeth. When my cock was free, she let out a gasp.

"Holy hell, that's better than a 12 inch subway. That's gorgeous," she said, wrapping her dainty hands around it. She even forgot about my boxer briefs and I quickly yanked them the rest of the way.

"Think you can handle me?" I asked.

Instead of answering my question, Charlotte lowered her head and licked the head of my cock. I let out a groan at the velvet brush of her tongue. She licked and stroked it excruciating slowly, but even though I was so turned on and so horny, I was fighting to keep myself from coming, I was not going to rush her. I didn't want the night to end. I clenched my jaw and let her tantalizing tongue tease me.

"He looks angry," she said, what seemed like eons later.

"He wants you," I said. She'd teased me long enough with her mouth.

"Then I'm ready," she said simply.

I reached for the condom packet that I'd placed under the pillow and tore it open with my teeth. With Charlotte's help,

I rolled it on, groaning when she deliberately lets her tongue touch my cock.

I held my cock at the base as Charlotte straddled me and positioned the slick entrance of her pussy above my cock. It jerked and pulsed against the folds of her sex, impatient to be encased in her wet heat.

I wanted to impale her on me with one violent thrust, but I let her take the lead. She gently pried my hand away and replaced it with hers. Inhaling deeply as if bracing herself, she brushed her soaking wet slit with the tip of my cock. A deep groan escaped my mouth. I longed to thrust it between those sweet lips, but I restrained myself.

"You feel so good, Alex," she said, throwing her head back.

I liked the sound of my name falling from her lips especially in the throes of passion. It came out like a soft moan.

"So do you," I said, placing my hands on her hips lightly. "You're hot."

She had a wild and abandoned look, with her hair framing her face and her bow shaped lips slightly parted. She caught my gaze for a few moments, and something intense passed between us.

Then, slowly, bit by excruciating bit, she lowered herself down on my shaft. I watched it disappear into her body. Her eyes widened as my cock filled her up completely, stretching her pussy walls as far back as they could go.

"You're so tight," I said hoarsely.

"And you're so damn big," Charlotte gasped, her face contorted into an expression of a mixture of pleasure and pain.

"Am I hurting you?"

"No," she said. "I love it, but I just need the ache to go."

"Fuck." My cock threatened to come at that very moment. I forced my mind onto other things. College. Places. Anything but the longing to let loose and allow myself to come. My muscles tensed with the strain of keeping myself from coming prematurely.

She started to whimper and she was only halfway down. Instead of going all the way, Charlotte eased herself from my cock, and then lowered herself again to the halfway point. She did this several times, each time taking more and more of me.

Finally, I was buried to the hilt, and it was pure heaven. I distracted myself by reaching for her hard peaks and pinching and pulling them, watching them fall back into position when I let go.

"I want you on top," she said and I was only too happy to oblige.

I turned us around, carefully and slowly, keeping my cock inside her pussy. I kept my weight off her, holding myself up by planting my hands on either side of her.

"How do you want it?" I said to her, pumping slowly in and out as her pussy expanded to accommodate my size.

"Hard and fast," she said immediately.

All the blood in my body dropped to my cock as it swelled more, if that was even possible as I began to furiously plunge into her. She felt and looked so good. Her full breasts jiggled as I increased the pace of my thrusts even more. Her hands went around me to grasp and squeeze my ass.

We were so good together in bed. Compatible, as if we had been two missing pieces of a puzzle that had come together.

Too bad we could only be a one-night stand. I'd vowed not let myself get involved in a relationship while I was in college. In fact, I'd even applied to a college in Ohio, away from my hometown of New York, and more importantly away from my friends.

My friends would have distracted me from my studies and I intended to be the best lawyer that ever graduated from the College of Ohio. I did not need a distraction, especially when I was so close to reaching my goals.

Charlotte was beautiful, fun and hot, but one night was all we'd ever have, but I intended to make the most of it.

CHARLOTTE

"Oh, I'm going to come again," I cried out as Alex took me from the back. I'd lost count of the number of times we'd had sex throughout the night.

We had fallen into a pattern where we fell into a light sleep, woke up, had sex and fell into another light sleep, and the pattern was repeated so many times I'd lost count. This was the night of many firsts. Starting with bringing a guy back to my place on the first date all the way down to the number of orgasms I'd had in one night.

Alex made me insatiable.

I couldn't get enough of his big, gorgeous cock. I'd never seen anything like it and never had a clue what I'd been missing. With a cock like the one he wielded, I was willing to break a few rules. Like see him a few more times, just for the sex, mind you.

"Wider, Charlotte," he commanded.

I liked that he called me by name during sex. A couple of men I knew had reverted to 'babe' and it made me think that they'd forgotten my name. I also liked that he was a selfless lover. He made sure that I'd orgasmed first before taking his own pleasure.

There was a lot I liked about him. Alex Turner was dangerous. He was a man that a woman could easily fall in love with. If only we had met at the right time. Years from now when I'd smashed all my career goals, and I was ready to settle down. He would have been perfect.

All these thoughts flitted through my mind before the swirl sensation radiating from my stomach grew too big and too explosive. In seconds, I was moaning and writhing and fisting the sheets as I climaxed.

Alex gripped my hips as he rammed into me. Deep groans emanated from his throat. Then he grunted, and I knew that he was coming. After that round, I wondered if my second box of condoms had any more left.

"What are you laughing about?" he asked as we lay on the bed, too wired up to fall back asleep.

"I was thinking we might not have any more condoms left," I said.

He chuckled. "You're right. We'll just have to do other things."

"Other things? I've never had so much sex in one night."

He turned to his side and faced me. "I feel like the luckiest man on earth tonight. That's the best sex I've ever had."

Heat enveloped me. I was glad that it was a mutual feeling. "Me too."

He pulled me closer and draped his hand around my waist and I lay cuddled up to his chest. We drifted off to sleep like that.

Dawn light woke me up. I was used to it and had deliberately left my bedroom windows without curtains so that I could wake up early every day. Besides, the view from my bedroom was beautiful and it gave me a great start to the day every day.

I lay still staring at the brilliance of the sun, hidden behind the skies, its colors splashing brilliant orange hues on the horizon. For me, watching the day unfold signaled a new beginning. The worries and exhaustion of the previous day extinguished.

Behind me, Alex breathed deeply and heavily. *What a night!* And all of it stemming from leaving my precious bag behind on the train. Not the best way to meet a man, but it had worked. The chances of meeting someone like Alex were non-existent in my normal life.

His college was a town away and the guys who went there rarely ventured to our town. They socialized with each other, which made sense as the college was one of those that attracted classy, wealthy people. Another reason why it could only be sex between us.

I didn't have to know the details of his home life to know that we were worlds apart. I had no business with a man who could trace his family back several generations. Pangs of regret came over me, but I shrugged them off. That was how life worked and the sooner I accepted it, the less heartache I would suffer.

My stomach rumbled, reminding me that we had not had a proper dinner. We'd munched on snacks in the bar and drank too much. I inched out of bed before another rumble from my stomach woke Alex up.

Quietly I pulled out some panties and a pair of shorts and pulled them on. Then I found a shirt and put it on, not bothering with a bra. I liked to stay braless when I was home and it being Sunday, I had no plans to leave the house.

I threw a glance at Alex. I hoped he would stay for breakfast… and lunch. Just for one day. When Monday rolled around, it would be back to my normal hectic life, but I wanted to enjoy this one day. Make memories that I could reach into, in days and weeks to come, when I was alone.

I padded out of my bedroom and headed to the bathroom to freshen up. Several minutes later, I went to the kitchen.

One advantage of living in a small town was that rent was fairly cheap and I could afford to live in an apartment with a great kitchen. It was the thing that had made me decide on this place.

It was big with lots of modern equipment, including a dishwasher, as well as an old-fashioned table in the middle that could seat four people. I flung my fridge door open and contemplated what to make for breakfast.

As tempting as it was to make a fancy breakfast, I settled for good, old fashioned bacon and pancakes. Fancy breakfasts were reserved for when you knew a person more intimately, and knew their likes and dislikes. My fancy breakfast had backfired a couple of times over the years.

I hummed as I cooked, feeling amazingly fresh despite the active night I'd had. My clit felt swollen and heavy, but it was worth it. All the tension of the week was gone and I looked forward to the rest of the day.

Alex appeared just as I was piling our breakfast onto plates.

CHARLOTTE

I looked up at the sound of heavy steps and when he emerged, my heart did flip flops in my chest. He was a beautiful man with a handsome face, a messy shock of hair falling over his forehead, and a body that oozed masculinity.

He was dressed only in his boxer briefs and my eyes remained glued to his chest. In the daylight, he looked like an Adonis, huge with a perfect body.

"Good morning, Gorgeous," he said with a smile that lit up the room. He came to me and kissed me lightly on the mouth.

"Good morning," I said, feeling a pang of shyness.

"I hope you don't have a roommate," he said, his eyes twinkling.

I laughed. "It's a little too late to worry about that. But no, I don't. Breakfast?" I slid the piled high plate on the table in front of him. "I figured that our bodies might need lots of sustenance after last night."

Alex laughed. "This looks delicious, thanks Charlotte. I can't remember the last time a woman cooked me breakfast." He sat down and eagerly dug into his food.

I found myself wondering things about Alex as we ate. The reference to a woman cooking him breakfast. How many did he have in his past? Was he currently hung up over a woman? A man as hot as Alex could not be unattached. There had to be someone waiting in the wings.

Besides, what did it matter? Today was our last day together then we would both go back to our lives. His private life was none of my business.

"Mmmm… that was delicious. Thank you. I can see now why you're in culinary school," he said after he'd finished his food.

"You're welcome." Why did his compliments please me so much? Both of us were passing ships.

Alex pushed his chair back, and I experienced a moment of panic. Was he leaving already?

"I'll clean up," he said and carried the dishes to the sink.

"I have a dishwasher," I told him.

"Nice," he said. "I'll stack them up then. What are your plans for the day?" We sounded like a couple, having a morning conversation.

"I like to walk along the river bank on Sunday mornings," I told him. "Do you want to come?" The words left my mouth before I could stop them. I held my breath as I waited for his response.

It would be better if he said no. That he had to leave.

"I would love that," he said.

Relief flooded me. I would have him a little longer. I grinned like a love-sick fool. "I'll go grab a shower."

"Wait," he said. "Come here." He leaned against the kitchen counter and faced me.

With my heart pounding hard, I closed the distance between us and stood close to him. So close that my breasts were touching his chest. Without warning, Alex gripped the hem of my t-shirt and pulled it over my head.

I caught my breath as I stood half naked, with my breasts bared for him. My whole body heated under his lust-filled gaze. Then he growled. It was the sexiest sound I had ever heard. Unconsciously, I arched my back, pushing out my chest some more.

"They're as beautiful as I remembered them last night," he said. "I had to see them again this morning. Just to be sure."

Alex in bed and Alex out of bed were two different men, I was discovering and I found both sides of him fascinating. He was sensual and dirty, and wild, and I had a feeling that he was reigning himself in. The out of bed Alex was playful and interesting to talk with.

A strange thought clicked into my head: I wanted all of Alex. I pushed it away with steely determination. Someday, some woman would be very lucky. What I did know was that I was not going to be that woman. My dreams and goals were too important to me.

Alex brought his mouth to one of my sensitive, still swollen peaks and hungrily sucked it. I threw my head back and let out a moan. Exquisite. Heaven. There were no words to describe the pleasure that flooded me from the things he was doing to my nipples with his tongue and teeth.

He shifted from one breast to another, showering each with attention. When he'd had his fill of my breasts, he trailed kisses down to my navel, kneeling in front of me. He pulled my shorts down, leaving me in my panties.

"Open your legs for me," he said and I moved my legs, which had turned to jelly, apart.

"I love your scent," he said as he brought his nose close to my pussy and sniffed it.

"Oh," I said, shocked that he would do such a thing in the harsh light of the morning. He ran a single digit over the swell of my pussy. He gripped my thighs, brought his mouth between my legs, and nibbled my pussy over my panties.

I inhaled sharply. I was going to come before he even removed my panties. He dragged his finger up and down my covered slit, teasing me, making me ache for him shamelessly. My soreness was forgotten as I rubbed myself against his finger.

Alex licked and kissed along the hem of my panties. Everywhere but where I needed him.

"Alex. Please," I begged.

"Patience, my love."

My heart lurched. Had he just called me his love? *Stop it,* I told myself. They were just words spoken in the heat of the moment. I'd heard of love at first sight, but I didn't really believe that such things happened in real life. Definitely not to me, especially not with a guy like him.

I soon forgot the war waging inside me as he pushed my panties to one side and his heated breath fanned my soaking wet pussy. I gasped when he dragged his tongue over my pussy.

"I need these gone," he said and pulled down my panties.

I kicked them out of the way and spread my legs without being told. He returned to his earlier position and teased my clit with the tip of his tongue. I gripped his head and held it firmly in place.

His hands circled my body and he gripped my ass cheeks with his big hands. I was a curvy woman and he seemed to love it. I had no issues with my body but it felt good to meet a man who enjoyed the extra flesh.

He licked my clit and drunk up the juices leaking from my pussy noisily. My fingers dug into his head and I hoped that I was not hurting him, but I had a need to anchor myself to something. I felt as if I was flying as Alex's tongue took me to places that I'd only ever fantasized about.

"Fuck, fuck, fuck," I moaned as I felt an orgasm coming on.

Alex increased his movements and licked me faster and faster until I exploded. My body shook with the intensity of the orgasm and Alex stayed in his kneeling position as he lapped up all my juices, licking my pussy clean.

ALEX

"Who knew that such a peaceful beautiful place existed so close to me," I commented as we walked along the river bank.

A slight breeze blew, riffling the leaves of the trees near the river and keeping the heat of the sun bearable. On a whim, I took Charlotte's hand. She looked up at me and smiled.

God, she was beautiful.

What if I could make it work and not let the relationship interfere with my studies? What was going on with me? I was in my last year of law school and the workload was crazy. The last thing I needed was the commitment of having a girlfriend. Relationships needed time and nurturing.

Time that I didn't have.

But the thought of never seeing Charlotte again brought a bitter taste in my mouth. So many what ifs formed in my mind. What if I never saw her again and we were meant to be? I'd never felt for another woman what I already felt for her.

And it wasn't just about sex, though that was out of this world. It was the full package. I sensed that underneath all the sexiness, she was a good, honest person from a hard background. It had given her a backbone and a quiet confident strength. And there was also the fact that she was hilarious when she was drunk. If only I could find a way to make it work.

"You sighed," she said. "Why would anyone sigh on such a beautiful day in such gorgeous surroundings, hmm? How about we go sit on that rock and you tell me all your problems. These shoulders are stronger than they look."

I laughed. "Okay."

I helped her up the boulder that sat next to the river bank. The river was so clear that I could almost see the rocks embedded at the bottom.

"Do you come here a lot?" I asked.

"Almost every Sunday." She wagged a finger at me. "You're not going to distract me. Tell me what's on your mind. My friends tell me that I'm pretty good at solving problems."

I glanced at her and decided to come clean. "I was trying to figure out how to make us work. I want to see you again Charlotte."

A guarded look came over her features. I wasn't the only one who had a problem with a relationship. Instead of making me feel relieved that she wasn't interested in a relationship either, it made me frantic.

"Look, Alex," she said and twirled her fingers. "You're an awesome guy, believe me, you're a god in bed, but I can't do relationships right now."

That sounded like something I would say. It wasn't very nice when the tables were turned on me. "Me neither," I confessed. "Let's compare notes on why we can't. I'll go first. I have big plans and all of them depend on me doing well in my end of year exams."

She nodded.

I carried on. "I don't have the time for a relationship and I can't let anything get in the way of my dreams. I've worked too hard for it. Your turn."

"It's uncanny," she said. "That could have been me speaking. My reasons are exactly the same as yours. My career is very important to me. I don't want any distractions."

I leaned forward and kissed her lightly on the mouth. "You're very cute when you're serious."

She made a stern face. "You were being serious too, but I'm glad we're on the same page."

"Except for one problem. We're so good together. I've never felt the way I did with you during sex."

"Sex doesn't make a relationship," she pointed out.

"It's a good start," I said quickly. I'd had great chemistry with women in the past that did not translate to great sex. So yeah, I may sound like I ranked sex too highly in a relationship. That's because I did. I loved women's bodies and I loved sex. One woman at a time though.

"Let's just enjoy what we have today and move on with our lives," she said.

I didn't want to believe she didn't want us to try and make a relationship work. "Do you want to hear my reasons as to why I think we would work?" I asked her.

She shrugged, but her lips curved into a smile. "If you insist but I'm not going to change my mind. You're wasting your time."

"Counsel, your objections are noted. However, there are a few pertinent facts you have failed to take into consideration," I said, adopting a formal court tone.

She giggled.

Good. I needed her to be relaxed and happy to convince her that we were perfect for each other.

"One, I think you're the most beautiful and sexiest woman I've ever met," I said.

"I beg to interrupt, Your Honor," she said, smothering her laughter. "but, that is not a valid reason."

I raised my hands in mock surrender. "God, you're picky."

She laughed. I could get used to the melodious sound of her laugh. I wanted to know everything about her.

"I'll start again. We both want the same thing. To reach the peaks of our careers. Which means that we'll give each other the space we need," I said.

She contemplated me. "You'll make a great lawyer."

Lightness came over my chest. "Does that mean what I think it does?"

She seared me with a look. "No, it means that you're convincing, but not enough to sway me."

My face fell.

"Maybe." She paused. "I'll think about it."

ALEX

I knew then she would come around. I inched closer to her and leaned forward to kiss her. I captured her lower lip between my teeth and nibbled it softly. Charlotte deepened the kiss and our tongues twirled together. I forgot where we were as I lost myself in the softness of her mouth.

I reached out and cupped her breasts over her t-shirt. She moaned into my mouth as I teased her nipple and felt it harden under my touch. My cock swelled in my pants. *Fuck!* Charlotte was a walking, breathing sexual fantasy and if I played my cards right, I wouldn't lose her.

"Let's go home," she said, pulling away. "If we stay here a minute longer, we'll be arrested for indecency."

"Good idea," I said, my cock as hard as wood. I couldn't wait to get back to her place for some relief.

I took her hand as we walked back. It was a ten-minute brisk walk to her house. By the time we got there, I couldn't wait anymore. I took her into my arms as soon as she shut the front door.

"I can't get enough of you," I told her before our lips crashed together. I kissed her with everything I had, hoping to convince her that we deserved a chance.

I broke the kiss to unbuckle my belt and pull down my pants. While I did so, Charlotte stared at me hungrily. As if she was desperate for it. *Fuck.* She could make a man fuck her in public without a care for what the rest of the world thought.

I pulled down my pants, setting my cock free. I was glad that I had gone boxer free after my shower. This time, I undressed her while my cock bobbed up and down.

When she was free of her tank top, bra and panties, I dipped my hand between her legs. I groaned as I ran my hand over her slippery pussy.

"You're so wet," I said.

"I want you," she said, looking up at me with those gorgeous liquid brown eyes. She rocked her body against my hand. "I want you so badly."

Fuck. I guided her to the back of the couch and had her stand with her legs apart, gripping the top of it. Then I pulled her back, so that her round full ass was pointed in the air. I stroked her lower back before dropping my hands to cup her ass.

"So soft," I murmured and slid a finder lightly over the crack of her ass to her pussy. She was even wetter than she was a minute earlier.

"Please," she said and any ideas I might have had about taking it easy vanished.

I spread her legs further apart and plunged my throbbing cock into her pussy. She screamed and for a few seconds, I froze, not sure whether it was pain or pleasure. It was pleasure, I decided when she wriggled her ass, impatient for more.

I held her hips and fucked her hard, deep, and fast. She called my name over and over again. I wanted her to whisper it even after I left. I wanted to make her mine permanently.

That thought startled me. I'd never had such strong feelings of possession over a woman. She was mine. Charlotte was everything I'd ever wanted in a woman but never knew.

"More," she said and pushed her ass back.

"Fuck woman," I said. "And you expect me to walk away?"

My thrusts became more forceful. My control slipped just as she screamed my name.

"Yes, yes, yes!"

I fucked her through her orgasm and after it was over, my control slipped completely and I felt myself coming. I remembered in time that I was not wearing a condom and I pulled out and came all over her back.

"Fuck," I said. "Your back is a mess."

She laughed. "I don't mind. I'll smell of your cum for the rest of the day."

I took her hand and we went to the bathroom where I grabbed some tissue and wiped her down with it.

"I'm safe," I told her. "I have regular checks and I haven't had sex in almost six months."

"Me too," she said as we went to her bedroom.

I wasn't finished with her. Not by a long shot. I laid her on the bed gently, and arranged myself between her legs.

"You're not serious," she said.

"I am," I said. "If this is the last day we are going to be together then I intend to make full use of it. Unless you have objections?"

She cupped my head and said softly, "None at all."

This time, I ate her pussy luxuriously, the intention being to learn her body. By the time the evening was over, every crevice of her body would be seared into my memory. And hers. I was going to make it impossible for her to say no to me.

"Did you know you have a tiny red mole on your clit?" I asked her.

She laughed. "No, I don't. How come no one's ever told me?"

Something hot burned my chest. The thought that another man could possess Charlotte the way I was did not go down well. I swallowed my jealousy. "I'll show you." With the tip of my tongue, I grazed over the tiny spot at the side of her swollen clit. "There."

"Mmmm… show me again, please?" she instructed throatily.

I narrowed my eyes. "Show it to you with my tongue?"

She stared back at me with innocent eyes. "Of course, how else?"

With a laugh, I went back to my task. Before too long, Charlotte was moaning and writhing on the bed and crying for more. I finished it off by fucking her while she was lying on her side, facing her curtainless window.

CHARLOTTE

"Miss Evans, could you explain to us the answer that Miss Jonas gave?"

I'd need to have heard the answer that Miss Jonas had given so as to explain it, and since I hadn't, I opted to play dumb and look stupid. I let out a sigh, and the lecturer gave up and turned to someone else.

It had been happening the whole week. I knew the reason for that of course. A six foot three, sexy hunk of a man. After the weekend Alex and I had spent together, I had stuck to my guns and told him that I wasn't interested in a relationship.

To my surprise and a bit of disappointment, he had agreed, albeit reluctantly but if he'd coaxed me, we might have reached an arrangement. Instead, he had walked out of my life and that was the last time I saw him.

Today was merely Friday and I was more exhausted than usual. Most of it had to do with how much energy I was using on trying not to think about him. It was for the best.

Maybe if I told myself that enough times, I would start to believe it.

I was relieved that classes were over for the day. Amy, my best friend and I walked out of class together.

"Did you notice the Prof. checking me out?" Amy asked me.

"Professor Mulberry?" I asked, surprised. Amy had wild and varied tastes in men, but Mulberry was nerdy and too serious to be anybody's type.

"Yes," she said. "I think he likes me and I find him extremely sexy."

I shook my head in disgust. "You're sick."

"I'll tell you something you might not know. Those nerdy looking ones, they're the kinkiest in bed."

I laughed. Amy loved men the way men loved women. And they loved her right back. Since we met, three years earlier, she'd had close to ten boyfriends. What really impressed me though was how she remained friends with all her exes even after they broke up.

Plus, she had no particular bias. She loved them tall, short, slim, plump. As long as he had a cock between his legs, he was a candidate for Amy's attention. I wasn't surprised when she ground to a halt and whistled.

I knew that whistle. It meant that she had spotted a hot guy.

"Now, that is what I call a sexy man," she said.

I looked and spotted him. My insides turned to water. I blinked in disbelief. Alex. Suddenly, I couldn't breathe. He looked so hot, and yet so innocent and proper, leaning against the notice board, wearing a pair of chinos and a button-down shirt.

I blushed as I recalled the things he had done to me in bed and the dirty words that flowed easily from his mouth. He spotted me as I stood rooted to the spot and came towards us.

"Do you remember the guy I told you about?" I said to Amy. It had been a nice change to tell Amy a wild story for once. She was the one who lived the wild life and had all the stories.

I'd been sure that Alex and I would never meet again and I'd not spared her any details.

"The one who fucked you from here to Timbuktu with his big cock?" she asked a little too loudly.

"Hush!" I said, as Alex reached us. I hoped he hadn't heard Amy.

He smiled and my heart lurched. "Charlotte, how odd to run into you here."

I cleared my throat. "Hi." Unexpected shyness came over me.

Amy thrust out her hand. "Hey, I'm Amy, Charlotte's best friend."

"And I'm Alex. It's a pleasure to meet you," he said, then swung his gaze back to me. "I missed you."

Just like that. As if it was normal to tell someone you barely knew that you had missed them.

"That's my cue to disappear," Amy said, her eyes widening at me. "Talk to you later," she said and left us in a hurry.

My stare focused on his lips. The lips that tasted so good and did all those indescribable things to my mouth and pussy. Heat enveloped me. Seeing him again was not a good idea. "Alex," I started to say.

He closed the distance between us and brushed his lips against mine.

"I have to go home, shower, then go to work," I said weakly. That was the reality of my life.

"I'll walk you there," he said and took my hand.

It felt so right to be holding his hand. My legs trembled slightly as we walked from college to my place. I should have told him to go away. To leave me alone. That we were right for each other, but we'd met at the wrong time.

However, my mouth refused to form the words and I found myself opening the street door that led up to my apartment.

"I meant it," I told him, shutting my front door. "I can't be late to work and I need to shower first."

"I don't want you to lose your job," he said. "Go and shower."

"Okay," I said and went to my bedroom. I stripped, grabbed a fresh towel, wrapped it around me and padded to the bathroom.

It was while I was lathering shower gel over my body that the bathroom door swung open and Alex entered. He started removing his clothes. I slid the shower cubicle door open a crack. "What are you doing?"

CHARLOTTE

"What does it look like I'm doing?" he asked. "I just realized how badly I need a shower as well. I smell of sweat."

I covered my mouth to stifle a rush of desire. "No, you don't. You don't smell of sweat at all. You smell of heaven." I moved back as he entered the shower cubicle.

"I'll do that." He took the bottle of gel and poured a generous dollop on his cupped hand.

I wasn't going to say no to those skilled hands on my body. On his first touch, I let out a moan. He lathered it on my breasts, rubbing it on my nipples until they were hard peaks. Unable to resist, I poured some gel on my hands as well and rubbed it all over his jutting cock. Alex groaned as I stroked its long length and thick girth.

"I've missed this so much," he said, dipping his hand between my legs to stroke my aching pussy.

"Me too," I moaned.

"I would spend more time but I don't want to be responsible for you losing your job," he said.

"I have some wriggle room," I muttered. I was too aroused to leave the shower cubicle.

"Good," he said and in one movement, he'd slipped his hand under my hips and hoisted me up.

He held me up against the wall and supported me with one hand, he used the other to guide his cock to my pussy. I wrapped my thighs loosely around his waist as the tip of his cock touched my pussy.

I moaned helplessly.

I was dizzy with need and I couldn't wait for his big cock to impale me. His cock pushed its way in my pussy, and I rocked my hips in an effort to take more of him faster.

"Yes, Alex. Yes," I cried, losing control of my mouth and thoughts. All I wanted was to be fucked.

He drove every perfect inch of his cock in me. I threw my head back and let out deep guttural moans of exquisite pleasure. I dug my nails into his shoulders. My orgasm built up fast. In seconds, I was screaming it out and clinging to him.

Alex followed, hissing in pleasure as he emptied his essence into me. He lay his head on me as our breaths returned to normal. I cradled his head against my breasts.

After a moment, I started giggling. "That was… super fast."

He raised his head, his brow creased with concern. "Was it good for you?"

"Oh yes," I said. "I came in the first thirty seconds."

"Awesome," he said and carefully lowered me to the ground.

We rinsed off and then dried ourselves. We dressed and left my apartment in three minutes. We held hands as we strolled towards the bakery where I worked as a junior chef.

I loved my job even if it did little to expand my knowledge in terms of variety. We specialized in specialty sandwiches, and sometimes it seemed as if the whole of our town ate at our sandwich shop.

One of the reasons I'd been drawn to it was because I dreamed of having my own bakery in the future. A place where I could bake my own bread, and experiment with all kinds of soft mouthwatering sandwiches. You couldn't go wrong with a sandwich shop as long as the filling was good.

"How has your week been?" he asked.

"Honestly?"

"Of course."

"Miserable."

His eyes glittered. "Why?"

"I'd hoped to have you out of my system by now."

He squeezed my hand. "I'm glad you haven't. I've had the longest week of my life, and even got told off by one of my favorite lecturers for lack of concentration."

"I'm sorry," I said, feeling responsible for his lack of concentration.

"It's okay," he said, and then to my surprise, he changed topics. "What kind of a place do you work at? A restaurant?"

"No, a sandwich shop," I said and then told him my dreams of opening my own place someday. I'd never shared that dream with anyone.

"You can do it," he said. "You're focused and hardworking and you'll get there."

His words of confidence filled me with pleasure. "Thank you. Nothing will stand in my way."

Not even a man. The words sat between us unsaid. But I'd started to change my views. I'd missed Alex so much that my school work had also suffered. It seemed that if I hoped to keep my grades up, I needed Alex in my life. But he hadn't brought it up and I didn't want to pressure him.

"This is my stop," I joked when we reached the rear of the sandwich shop.

Alex stooped to kiss me. "Okay. Have an awesome shift. I'll see you tomorrow. Same time."

Before I could answer him, he had walked away.

I watched him until he disappeared, then I entered the shop through the delivery door. I switched my mind to work, but I had a big dopey smile plastered on my face as I changed into my white cook's uniform.

My insides stiffened as I entered the kitchen. The chef's mood dictated how the rest of the evening would go.

"Charlotte," he boomed cheerfully, and I let out a sigh of relief. He was in a good mood. It was going to be a good shift.

"Hi Jack," I said, moving toward the backroom to get the vegetables to slice up. I usually spent the first hour of my shift slicing and dicing and the next hour, preparing sandwiches.

Would it be so bad if Alex and I hooked up? People balanced school, work and relationships every day. My work would not suffer. It would probably even improve as I would be more relaxed.

The evening rush kept me from brooding too much but at the end of my shift, later in the night, I'd come to a decision. I would keep him. If he wanted me, that is.

Excitement coursed through me as I thought about the implications of my decisions. Fear tried to push its way in but I firmly pushed it back. I wasn't getting married to him for goodness sake or signing over my whole life to him.

I was just allowing him into my life. I'd worked hard for the last three years and I deserved to let loose and have a bit of fun. Alex and I had exchanged numbers and as soon as I got home, I found a message from him. I checked the time.

He'd sent it at eight.

Alex: Text me when you get home.

Me: I'm home.

Alex: Good.

Me: I've also made a decision.

Alex: Yeah?

Me: I want to see you again. And again. And again.

Alex: I'm hyperventilating.

I laughed. I'd made the right decision.

CHARLOTTE

Saturday evenings were turning out to be my favorite days. After my shift, I quickly changed out of my work clothes. Alex was waiting for me and we'd planned to spend the weekend together until Monday. I loved the weekends.

Two weeks had zipped by since we made it formal. We were dating and exclusive. The fear that had held me captive for days after we agreed to that had dissipated the more I got to know Alex. He was the real deal. A good guy. Toss in sexy and dirty, and he was my dream man come to life.

"Bye," I called to my colleagues, changing unhurriedly. I didn't see Alex at first when I stepped out. A hoot blared and when I checked, it was him.

He came out of the car and came around to give me a hug and a kiss. As always, the kiss went on a lot longer as he deep kissed me and stole quick feels under my sweater.

"Every time I see you, it feels like the first time," he said.

"You're too good to me," I said.

"You deserve so much more and one day I'll give it to you," he said, his features solemn.

I smiled, stroked his cheek, and turned my attention to the sleek car. "This yours?"

"Yeah," he said, but he looked uncomfortable. "I thought we could go to my place this weekend."

I cocked my head. "We're moving to the next base," I teased.

I expected Alex to laugh but he didn't. Instead, he opened the car door for me and I slid in. I wasn't worried about his odd behavior. I trusted him implicitly. Something was obviously making him uncomfortable but whatever it was, we'd figure it out.

"I love your car," I said when he entered the driver's side. I didn't know much about cars but I did know an expensive car when I saw one.

Alex smiled. "Glad you like it."

I had many more questions, like when did he get it? How could he afford such an expensive car? I held my tongue for as comfortable as I was with Alex, there was a side of him that was very private.

His home life, for example. He rarely talked about his family except for the comment he'd made about his grandfather and father being lawyers.

Oh yes, and he'd grudgingly told me about his married older sister. I hadn't pressed for more, for the simple reason that I did not want him to ask me about my family either.

We talked on the way to his place but as we neared, I grew quiet and took note of my surroundings. We'd driven into a gated posh neighborhood made up of high-end apartments.

"You live here?" I asked as the gate automatically shut behind us.

"Yes," he said.

I was at a loss for words. He navigated the car into a parking lot surrounded by other expensive cars. The kinds you see as centerfolds of magazines. So luxurious, they were given the central spot.

I swallowed hard as the car came to a stop. I got out of the car stiffly. I felt grossly out of place with my jeans, top and sweater. The complex reminded me of places I had seen when growing up. Places that belonged to other people, not us. Places that made me feel small.

We walked into the sleek building and made for the elevators. Then Alex inserted a card and the elevator started moving. That's when I realized that we were headed to the penthouse.

The elevator itself was made entirely from glass and had panoramic views of the surroundings. It came to a stop and Alex and I got out. We hadn't exchanged a single word since leaving the car, which was odd for us as we never ran out of things to say to each other.

He slid a card into his door and held it open for me. I stepped into a living room. The first thing that hit me was how much glass there was. And the views. I thought back to how proud I was of the view from my bedroom and instantly cringed. I'd even mentioned it to Alex.

Had he been quietly laughing at me?

From the impossibly high ceilings hung a glittering chandelier, the likes of which I had only seen in hotels, not a private home. Cream leather seats were arranged around a glass coffee table and underneath a thick white carpet covered part of the floor. The rest of the floor was gorgeous dark wood.

I could honestly say that I had never been surrounded by such opulence.

CHARLOTTE

"Welcome to my home," he said, his tone coated with misery. That made the two of us.

So many things made sense. Alex came across as classy and now I knew that it was because he was. I shuddered as I imagined the kind of family that he came from, and his friends.

It was glaringly clear. Alex and I were from two vastly different worlds and we did not belong together. He knew it too. That was the reason it had taken him so long to invite me to his place.

"What's wrong, Chaz?" he asked coming to me. He had taken to shortening my name to Chaz. I liked it.

I brushed my tears away from my eyes and turned to him. "We're from two different worlds Alex."

His eyes narrowed. "What do you mean?"

I gestured around me helplessly. "Look at all this. How you live. Compare it to my poor little apartment above a shop."

"Don't call it that!" he said harshly. "It's your home and I love it."

I folded my hands across my chest. "Fine, but you know what I mean. You weren't eager to show me your place because you knew it would prove that we don't belong together."

"I don't know what you're talking about," he said, his eyes flashing with anger. "But you're right about one thing. I didn't show you because I knew your views about kids born into wealth. Trust fund babies. Isn't that what you called us?" He was angry and rightly so.

Shame flooded me as memories of that day came to me. I'd indignantly shared my views and my anger for kids who were born with silver spoons in their mouths. "How can we make this work?" I finally asked.

"We'll laugh together and we'll let our bodies do the talking. That's how. I have more fun with you than I've ever had with anyone else, male or female. And we'll push each other to be better people," he said, his voice shaky.

He was right. Alex was good for me. In the three weeks we'd been together, I had not missed work once and we even studied together. Alex was not the problem, I admitted to myself. I was. And I was frightened of his family and his friends back home in New York.

"What if your family hates me?" I asked him.

He looked at me incredulously. "Why would they hate you? You're awesome! Besides, I'm a grown man Chaz and I get to decide who I'll marry."

My eyes nearly popped out of my head. "Marry?"

He stared at me for a few seconds without speaking. "Yes. Did you think this was it? That after the year is over, we'll go our separate ways?"

I nodded numbly.

"I fell in love with you on that first day I saw you on the train Chaz. Dozing on a stranger's shoulder like it was a pillow," he said.

I let out a shaky laugh. "I did not."

He ignored what I'd said. "Then you woke up abruptly, peered out the window and saw that the train had stopped at your station."

I laughed at the memory. It seemed so long ago and yet it was almost a month now. I felt as if I had known Alex all my life.

"Then like lightning, you bolted out of your seat and before I could tell you that you'd left your bag, you were off of the train," he said.

I grew warm all over at the memory.

"I remember how frightened you looked when I showed you your bag through the window and then I yelled that I'd be waiting at the next station and your lips curved into this smile. A smile that did things to me. A smile that I intend to see all my life," he said.

"The next train took forever but you never left. You were waiting," I said as tears fell from my eyes.

"I'll always wait for you Chaz, no matter how long I have to wait," he said and I knew that he meant every word.

We stood staring at each other, until Alex made the first move. He took my hand and led me to a bedroom that was as big as my whole apartment and gently laid me on the bed.

"I should shower first," I said, as he covered my body with his.

"You're obsessed with showering," he said. "You showered before work."

I wrapped my hands around his neck as he looked down at me. "I love you Chaz."

"Oh God," I said. I did love him. I was pretty sure I did. Joy exploded in my chest. I'd never once thought that I'd find love primarily because it was something I saw in movies. I've never seen it in real life.

My memories of my mother were hazy but I recall seeing a variety of men coming to our two-bedroom house. They would drink, growing noisier by the minute and then disappear into her room. Those were the good days.

On the bad days, she resorted to taking drugs, injecting herself with a syringe and slumping on whichever chair she happened to be on. Those were the times when social services would get me and put me in foster care until my mom changed her ways again.

I wouldn't have recognized love if it smacked me in the face.

Alex brought his sensuous mouth down to mine and kissed me. He took my lower lip into his mouth and sucked on it before doing the same to the upper. His play on my lips sent tingles down my spine.

I scraped my fingers through his hair as his tongue skimmed the hem of my mouth. His hard cock pressed against my thigh before Alex broke the kiss and lowered himself until he was above my chest. He popped open the buttons of my blouse and kissed the valley between my breasts. I arched my chest wanting to feel his touch and mouth on me. In my lust filled bubble, I realized how right Alex was.

We belonged together. We were perfect for each other. Which in itself was an accident of chemistry considering how different we were.

I let out a moan when Alex pulled down the cups of my bra, and took an aching, aroused nipple into his mouth. He palmed the other one, and then flicked each of them in turns with his tongue. Wetness dripped into my panties and I was sure that it was soaking wet.

"I need the bra to go," he said and I raised my back and unclasped my bra. He pulled it out of the way.

"Yes, that's better," he said, his voice thick with passion. He kissed every part of my breasts before turning his attention back to my nipples. I writhed on the bed, desperate for more.

Before I could ask, Alex knelt between my legs and pulled down my pants.

"I want you," I said, my voice raspy.

When I was naked and all spread out for him, Alex got off the bed and stripped off his clothes, all the while, staring at my sodden pussy.

"You make me happy," he said, the words simple but loaded with so much promise.

"You make me happy too," I said.

He crawled back between my legs. "And now I'll make you even happier." He flashed me his boyish smile before disappearing between my legs.

I trembled as his tongue teased my folds before moving to my clit. Alex knew all my buttons. Within seconds, I was a writhing mess, crying out his name and flailing my arms about like a wild woman.

I didn't care. He loved me as I was and I loved him back. When I came, I said words that I'd never said to a man, in and away from the throes of passion.

"I love you Alex," I cried as the orgasm tore through me.

ALEX

I had everything planned out as I made the call home. It was April and I'd finished my exams. Charlotte had a free weekend before her exams and she planned to relax and take it easy. I'd come up with the idea of flying home to New York on Friday, spending the weekend with my family before returning to Ohio.

It was time to introduce her to my family. There was so much planning to do. Charlotte and I had discussed it all and we planned on getting married and settling down in New York near my family.

My sister was married to a great guy named Richard Everest, a lawyer as well, who worked for his family firm. I couldn't wait to introduce everyone to Charlotte. I knew they would love her as I did.

I made the call while Charlotte was in the shower getting ready to go to work. I'd pestered her until she had agreed to move in with me but she'd refused to give up her job or her apartment. I'd have been happy to support her as my monthly allowance was more than enough for both of us.

The phone rang once before Nina, our housekeeper picked up the phone. We exchanged a few pleasantries then my mother came on.

"Alexander, is that you?" she asked, even though I'd heard Nina tell her it was me.

"Yes Mother, it's me," I said, pleased to hear her voice. We didn't speak a lot on the phone as she had a busy social life and I was also busy with school and now Charlotte.

"How nice to hear your voice," she said. "Tell me you're coming home. Your sister and Richard have some news for us. It would be nice if we were together as a family."

I laughed. "I think you see into the future Mother. That's the reason I was calling actually. I'm coming home on Friday."

"Wonderful. We're having a family dinner on Friday," she said.

"I'm bringing a guest," I said. "I've been seeing this girl. She's wonderful Mother. You'll all love her. I want her to meet my family first and then I'll propose."

There was silence from the other side. "A girl? That's interesting. Abigail has been asking about you."

My body tensed. As much as I loved my mother, she annoyed the heck out of me. She had very firm beliefs on how my sister and I should live our lives and for the most part I went along with it.

But choosing a woman to love and marry was definitely not one of the things I was going to compromise on. My mother was not going to pick my wife for me. Coming to Ohio for college had opened up my eyes to a lot of things. Separated from my circle, I had come into my own and figured out what I wanted to do and who I wanted to be.

I still wanted to work in my father's firm but I wanted to be taken on merit. I was determined to work as hard as anyone else entering the firm who was not the partner's kid.

I was proud because I had several offers from law firms in Ohio. I'd worked hard for it and now the future looked even brighter with Charlotte by my side.

"You two were so close growing up," my mother continued, ignoring my silence. She liked to ignore things which were not to her liking.

It was true that Abigail had grown up in the same circle as me. Her parents and mine were good friends and in addition to attending the same school, we saw each other socially.

We'd even dated at one point, but I quickly realized we were not cut out to date. Abigail asking about me was not in any way romantic. It was just an old friend asking about another. Both sets of parents had been disappointed when we stopped dating and reverted back to friendship.

"Mother, did you hear what I said?" I said, my tone harsher than I intended. I softened it. "I'm bringing the woman I'm going to marry home."

She sighed. "Okay then. I'll have the guest room ready."

I ignored her lack of enthusiasm. That would change when she met Charlotte. "Thank you."

We spoke some more as I caught up on everyone. My father was busy in the law firm as usual. From my mother's tales, my sister Mary had grown into a carbon copy of my mother. She filled her days with charity work and lunches with her friends.

I shook my head and failed to understand why she would choose that kind of life when she was so bright. She'd been accepted to the bar three years earlier and worked for Jack's family firm before she abruptly resigned. If I got a chance, I would talk to her.

When I disconnected the call, it was to find Charlotte leaning on the doorway, a worried look on her face.

"I didn't mean to eavesdrop but I walked in and you were on the phone. I couldn't help but overhear. Are you sure that it's okay that I'm coming home with you?"

The naked vulnerability on her face tore me apart. "Come here."

She padded across the room, and sat down on my lap. I wrapped my hands around her waist protectively.

"I promise Its okay. Right this moment, Mother is getting the guest room ready for you," I said, worrying about how much of the conversation she'd heard.

She let out a sigh and the worried look left her face.

"They'll love you," I said. I had no doubt that once my family met Charlotte they would love her as much as I did. How could they not? She was kind, gentle, funny and loyal as hell.

I kissed her deeply and then patted her ass. "You'll be late for work."

She cupped my face and kissed me. “I love you.”

“I love you too,” I said.

When she left, I fished out my laptop and bought two tickets to New York. We would arrive at five in the evening. Perfect time to freshen up and socialize before dinner.

CHARLOTTE

"Hey, relax, you'll break the arm rest," Alex teased as the plane cruised down the runway ready to take off. "It'll get easier once we're in the air."

I relaxed my grip on the arm rest and shot him a reassuring smile. I wasn't worried about the plane falling. My source of nervousness was the frightening fact that I was going to meet Alex's family in the next hour and a half.

It had been just the two of us for so long. Of course there were friends but those were people Alex had met in Ohio, not his circle at home. Nausea swirled in my stomach. If it were up to me, we'd not have left Ohio.

Which was wistful thinking. Love required that you meet your boyfriend's family and get on like a house on fire. The problem was that I'd never played families except with a doll I'd been given by one of my favorite foster mothers.

I didn't know what families did or how they related to each other. In a moment of inspiration, I turned to Alex. "Can I ask you something?"

He covered my hand with his. "You can ask me anything, you know that."

I inhaled deeply. It was a stupid question to ask. "How do people act in a family?"

He stared at me blankly. "I don't understand."

I swallowed hard. I'd told Alex about my background, but I don't think he understood it. How could he when he'd grown up surrounded by people who loved him.

"As you know, I didn't have a sibling." Lack of a sibling was the hardest thing I faced when growing up. I'd always thought my life would be perfect if only I'd had a sister or a brother.

"It was just mom and me." And most of the time, she was so out of it, she even forgot who I was. I remember once, we were on the couch and she'd been dozing.

Then she'd woken up, startled by something and stared at me, as if shocked to see me there.

"Who are you?" she'd said and before I could answer, she fell back asleep.

"I know Chaz," he said.

"And I never spent enough time in foster care to find out how real families behaved."

Alex looked thoughtful. "You mean like what people do on a day to day basis?"

"Not really, no." That was part of it but there was more that I couldn't put into words. "What binds you together?" I watched movies and TV and I knew that families shared meals, their days and stuff like that. Maybe what I wanted to know was what made them a family.

"That's a difficult question," he said. "Shared dreams and goals, a love for each other, support. I'm not sure if that's the kind of thing you mean."

I nodded but was a mess inside. I felt even more of an outsider. I took a deep breath. With time, his family would be mine too. Didn't in-law relationships work like that?

It would take time, but I would work for it, I told myself. I would do everything in my power to get along with them and spend time with them. These thoughts calmed me down. I felt as if I had a purpose.

By the time we landed at LaGuardia, I was ready to meet my future family. We took a cab from the airport to Manhattan where Alex's parents lived. Alex hadn't been home in the year we had been together and his attention was on the passing landscape.

Guilt flooded me. I'd been selfish and hadn't encouraged him to go home either. Well that was going to change.

Less than fifteen minutes later, the cab stopped in front of what could only be described as a mansion, set back away from the road. After paying the cab, Alex and I hopped out. As he went to the trunk to fetch our bags, I looked up at the massive house and a knot of anxiety formed in my stomach.

"Let's go," he said and shot me a reassuring smile.

I smiled back but I was sure that my smile was a grimace. Alex walked me up to an imposing huge, curved wooden door. He placed our bags down and rang the bell.

My heart felt like a fist pounding the inside of my chest. We stood for a few seconds and then the heavy door was opened. A plump woman with a smiling face and a black apron over a white dress, stood there smiling.

"Alex, you're finally home!" She stepped forward and Alex bent his head to kiss her cheek.

"It's good to be home Nina. I've missed you all," he said. He turned to me. "This is my girlfriend, Charlotte Evans."

"It's a pleasure to meet you Miss Evans. Come in. I'll take those," she said. "Everyone is in the drawing room having pre-dinner drinks. You know that's your mother's favorite time." She winked at Alex and they shared a laugh.

Pre-dinner drinks? I'd never heard of those in a private home, but then again, how many private homes had I ever been in?

ALEX

As soon as we stepped into the drawing room, voices rang out as Alex's family all stood up to welcome him back home. I stood apart to give them time to greet each other. It also gave me a chance to observe them for a few seconds.

Mr. Turner was a big burly man and clearly the main donator of Alex's big guy genes. He had a loud boisterous laugh but an intimidating presence nonetheless. He clapped Alex hard on the back and said how he couldn't wait for his son to join him at the law firm.

I tried to imagine how it felt to have a job in your father's firm waiting for you, and failed. I was proud of Alex though. He studied harder than anyone I knew when he didn't really need to. It wasn't like his dad was going to withdraw the offer if Alex didn't graduate with honors.

His mother was one of the slimmest women I'd ever seen, with a stylish bob that fell to the sides of her face. She was clearly ecstatic to see her son and she seemed to disappear in Alex's huge arms as he hugged her.

His sister, Mary, was a carbon copy of her mom. Her bob was shorter, younger but she had the same oval face and brilliant blue eyes. Her husband, Richard was dark haired with an easy smile and manner, and clearly, he and Alex were good friends.

When Alex had done the rounds of hugging his family, he beckoned me over and draped a protective arm around me.

"Everyone, I want you to meet someone very special to me. This is my girlfriend, Charlotte Evans. Chaz, this is my father, James Turner."

I smiled and struck out my hand. He enveloped mine in his huge one, reminding me of Alex's handshake.

"It's a pleasure to meet you Miss Evans," he boomed, scrutinizing me.

"This is my mother, Patricia Turner," he said and I turned to his mother and took her small hand into mine.

"It's nice to meet you," she said with a smile that did not reach her eyes.

His sister was just as reserved and she gave me a tight smile but Richard, her husband was friendly enough. We all sat down on the huge cushy sofa that felt as if it could swallow a person.

"Alex, kindly pour some wine for Charlotte," Mrs. Turner said.

I declined and opted for water. Everyone stared at me as if I'd committed a cardinal sin.

“It’s just a glass to relax you before dinner,” Mary said.

“It’s cool if she doesn’t want wine,” he said and fetched me a glass of water. He opted for water as well.

I wasn’t a prude and I loved my wine but there was time for everything and meeting my prospective in-laws was not the best time to drink alcohol. I wanted to keep a clear head and not do something that I would regret forever.

“Alex didn’t tell us much about you,” Mrs. Turner said. “Where are you from?”

This is the part I’d dreaded. But I’d given it a lot of thought and decided that I was going to be honest. If these people were going to be my family, then I had to be honest from the beginning.

“I grew up in Cleveland,” I said.

“Oh,” Mrs. Turner said. “We know a few people in Cleveland. Old friends. Maybe you know them.”

I could have laughed out aloud. There was no way we had friends in common. “I grew up in the poorest part of the city.” Silence followed my pronouncement.

They all stared at me, waiting for me to go on. I ploughed on. “My mother was an alcoholic and a drug addict, and I grew up in and out of foster care.” I glanced at Alex and he gave me an encouraging smile. “I worked hard in school and got a scholarship to culinary school.”

“That’s commendable,” Mr. Turner said.

“Yes,” Mrs. Turner agreed.

"Charlotte goes to school and works too. That doesn't stop her from topping her class year in, year out," he said, his voice brimming with pride.

Surely, they could see that I deserved their son. I was not afraid of hard work and Alex would never have to bear the burden of caring for the family we would have alone.

"Did Alex tell you that after law school, he'll join the family firm here in New York?" Mrs. Turner said.

"Yes," I said and turned to Alex. "I'll be happy to find a job wherever Alex is."

"How sweet," Mary said.

"Yes," her mother agreed but her tone did not echo the words.

I felt as if I'd failed an exam but I didn't know which questions I'd gotten wrong. I knew the importance of maintaining a good posture to show confidence but I felt myself slumping in my chair.

At that moment, the woman who had opened the front door for us came in and announced that dinner was ready. Alex took my hand and squeezed it as we went to the dining room. Warmth swamped me at the contact and I knew everything would be okay.

I was grateful because my training meant that I was at home in a dining room, no matter how posh. I could feel Mrs. Turner's eyes on me. Judging me. Growing up underprivileged as I did, meant that I was highly tuned to other people's reception when they met me.

I knew that she didn't like me. I thought that maybe it was my background that had put her off. I'd believed from Alex's story about how hardworking his parents were meant that they would admire how hard I had worked to get myself an education.

Instead, it seemed to have the opposite effect.

CHARLOTTE

"Richard, Mary, tell us your good news," Mrs. Turner said when we were on the main course.

The food, tender steak sirloin and a variety of vegetables, was superb and as I ate, the knots in my stomach started to relax.

Mary and Richard exchanged a warm look before she started speaking. "Richard and I are expecting a baby. I'm eight weeks along to be exact."

There was silence at first as everyone assimilated that information and then a series of congratulations broke out. I listened as they talked about the baby. Mary's face was flushed and she and Richard kept touching each other.

I'd always wanted children but I'd thought they would come when I was in my late thirties. My grand plan had been to concentrate on my career and then Alex had come into my life and all those plans had disintegrated.

Now, looking at Mary and Richard, I couldn't wait for the moment that Alex and I would announce to his family that we were going to have a baby.

I was thankful that the conversation for the remainder of the evening revolved around Mary and Richard's baby. After dinner, we returned to the living room and this time, Mary declined a glass of wine and I took one. I needed it after the grilling I'd endured.

"What are your plans for the weekend?" Mary asked Alex.

"I'm planning on taking Charlotte on a tour around the city. It's her first time in New York and she'd love to see some of the touristy places."

After my glass of wine, I felt exhausted and was glad when Mary and Richard stood up to leave. After saying goodbye to them, everyone was ready to retire for the night. We said goodnight with Mrs. Turner telling Alex to escort me to the guest room.

The guest room was on the second floor, along with Alex's room and two other extra bedrooms. His parent's suite was on the first floor. The size of the house was mind boggling. Alex showed me the room and kissed me goodnight.

Disappointment flooded me when he shut the door and left. I'd hoped to spend a few minutes with him talking. I wanted to know what his parents thought about me.

We would not be apart for long, I told myself and went to the adjoining bathroom for a quick shower. Afterwards, I slipped into a thick cozy bathrobe and returned to the bedroom. It was a gorgeous room, decorated with heavy drapes and a huge four poster bed as well as pretty rugs on the wooden floor.

As I was drying my hair, a gentle knock came on the door. My heart leaped. I should have known that Alex would come back. I called out for the visitor to enter.

The door swung open and Mrs. Turner stepped in. "Oh, you're in the bathroom."

I looked down at my bathrobe. It was pretty decent. "Its fine, come in." I felt stupid saying that as I was in her house.

"I won't take much of your time," she said and came in and sat on the bed. She patted the space next to her and I sat down.

She smiled at me and hope soared in my chest. Maybe I'd misjudged her earlier. I'd done that in the past. Assumed that someone was judging me when in fact it was their normal modus operandi.

"First of all, I think that you're a wonderful young woman and you have a great future ahead of you," she said.

Warmth enveloped me. I could have hugged her at that moment.

"Just not for my son."

The smile froze on my face. My ears rang with disbelief. I was sure that I'd heard wrong. She couldn't have said that to me. I whipped my head to face her and she met my gaze unblinkingly.

"I'm sorry?" I said.

"You heard me. You and Alexander are from terribly different backgrounds and while I believe that someday, you'll make a young man somewhere a good enough wife, I think you're wrong for my son." She spoke as if she was discussing the weather, not a subject that had a huge impact on my life.

"Alex and I love each other." I hated that my lips were trembling. It was the very thing that I'd had nightmares about.

The Turners had seen right through me. There is a phrase that says, if it looks like a duck, swims like a duck, and quacks like a duck, then it probably is a duck. That was me. No education could cover up the fact that I had been brought up by an alcoholic and drug addict.

I'd come from the gutter and they wanted no association with me.

"Love?" Mrs. Turner said, spitting the word out like it was dirty. "Young people brandish that word around while understanding so very little of what it means. A month from now, both of you will be in love with other people."

I wanted to burst into tears but I wasn't going to show her how much her words were hurting me. I thought of losing Alex and my chest constricted, squeezing my heart. Pain pierced through me. I couldn't bear to lose him.

He'd become my whole world. But who said I was losing him? His mother wanted us to break it off but it didn't mean that Alex would.

I still had some fight in me. I thrust my chin out. "Alex won't leave me."

She laughed. Startled, I stared at her.

"Is that what you think? That I'm stupid enough to think I can convince my infatuated son to leave you by simply appealing to his good sense, which I know is missing right now?"

She paused as if waiting for me to speak before she continued.

"Of course not! His father and I will convince him by what he values the most. His lifestyle and his future. Alex can't wait to join the family law firm but his father will let him know that there's a condition attached to it."

I gasped. "You can't do that!"

She nodded. "Oh *yes* we can. We'll do everything to ensure that Alexander has a good future. If we have to threaten him, then so be it." She stood up and turned to me. "That's not all. From now, henceforth if he doesn't end this silly little dalliance, his allowance ends with immediate effect."

ALEX

A knock came on my bedroom door as I was waiting for a decent amount of time to pass before going to Charlotte's bedroom. No way was I not going to spend the night with my woman.

I opened the door and was surprised to see my father. "Can I see you in my study?"

"Sure," I said and followed him to the first-floor study room. He held the door open for me and shut it behind us.

My father was a formal person and he didn't speak until we were both seated. He, behind the big mahogany desk and me in the spare chair.

"We're very happy to have you home son," he said.

"I'm happy to be home too," I said. "But I go back on Sunday."

He waved a hand. "I know. But it won't be long before you're back home permanently."

"True," I said.

"Your mother says it wasn't a good idea for you to study in Ohio," Father said.

I was puzzled. That was an odd thing to say. I'd sent them all my grades throughout my year undergraduate course and I'd done very well. "Why would she say that?"

"Because the intention had been for you to study and come back to New York where you'd meet a suitable girl," Father said.

My heart fell as I understood what the meeting was all about. Charlotte. They didn't think that Charlotte was good enough for me. If only they knew the truth. I wasn't good enough for Charlotte. She deserved a better man than me.

I kept my cool. Maybe good reason would prevail. My father was a reasonable man. The only problem was that my mother wielded a lot of influence over him.

"I've already met a wonderful girl whom I want to marry," I said.

"We don't think she's the right person for you. You need someone with the right background. Someone who'll fit into our lifestyle. Someone from the right family."

I reigned in my anger. "Father, Charlotte is a wonderful human being."

"No one is disputing that fact son," he said. "But even you can see that her background can become somewhat of an embarrassment."

My muscles quivered. Blood rushed through my brain. I couldn't believe that those words were coming from my father's mouth. I knew that my parents were snobbish but I never thought they would stoop so low as to dislike a person based on where they were born. "To who?"

"To all of us."

Shame flooded me. I had come from these people. "I'm not going to give up Charlotte."

A hard look came over my father's face. I knew what I was up against. He had not built one of the most respected law firms in New York by losing. Unfortunately for my parents, Charlotte was the one thing I was not going to lose.

She made my world go round. She brought joy into my life and made me whole. She brought out the maleness in me and made me want to be a better man for her.

"I was afraid it would come to that. Son, we're not giving you a choice. You must give her up," he said his tone cold.

I knew that side of him. I'd seen him in the courtroom. But he was fighting love, and there was no way I was giving up my love. I couldn't imagine anyone else I would have wanted to marry and have a family with. Charlotte was it for me. The one and only love of my life.

"If you don't, we'll cut off your allowance and—"

"What?"

"That's not all," he said in a cold voice. "The offer to come work in the law firm will be withdrawn."

I stared at him, stunned. "You don't mean that?"

He nodded. "I do. Think about it very carefully and let me know your decision in the morning." He strode out of the room.

My father was ruthless, but threatening to cut off my allowance and withdrawing my job? The one job I'd waited for all my life. I got up and paced the room, growing angrier by the second.

They were pushing me against the wall so that I would dump Charlotte. That wasn't going to happen. I wasn't a helpless little boy. I was a grown man and could take care of myself and mine.

By the time I left the study twenty minutes later I'd made a decision. And the first thing I did when I returned to my room was to book Charlotte and me seats on a flight to Las Vegas.

ALEX

Considering the things that were waiting for me in the morning, I had a pretty restful night. I woke up pumped and ready to start my life with Charlotte. Sure, I had to rethink my grand plan, but I was young and determined and I was going to be a success. With or without my father.

I showered and dressed, packed my stuff, and carried my bag to Charlotte's door and knocked. She called for me to enter. I found her fully dressed and seated on the bed and I knew that she'd had a visit from my mother.

"Good morning," I said cheerfully as if everything was perfect, even though my heart ached at the sight of her looking so defeated. I kissed her cheek and she summoned a smile. "I'm glad you're dressed. We're about to leave. We're going to Las Vegas."

Her eyes widened. "What? What's going on?"

"In my eagerness to marry the love of my life, I skipped a very important step." I went down on one knee and took her hands. "Charlotte Evans, from the first day I saw you dozing on the train and then rushing out like your life was in danger, I fell in love with you. You've made me happier than I deserve to be and I'll spend the rest of my life trying to give you even half of what you give me. I love you Charlotte. Will you be my wife?"

Tears filled her eyes. "Yes, but—"

I placed a finger on her lips. "No buts."

She nodded. "Yes, I'll marry you."

"Let's go. We'll be late for our flight."

She packed her bag and in minutes we were walking down the stairs. I found my parents as well as Mary and Richard in the living room. No one looked surprised to see us with our bags.

Mary was the first to speak. "Don't be a fool Alex," she said. "You're throwing away everything you've worked hard for. And for what?"

"If you ever hope that we'll speak again, I suggest you think very carefully before you speak," I said, grinding my teeth.

"She means well," Richard said. "We all do."

I didn't bother to answer. "Charlotte and I are headed to Las Vegas. In exactly six hours, she and I will be husband and wife."

"You're throwing away your life Alexander," my mother said.

"At least it will be my decision," I said. I stared at my father and keeping Charlotte's hand in mine, we walked out of the home I had grown up in.

Charlotte was teary in the cab on the way to the airport. Only when we were airborne did she start talking. I'd expected it. Having grown up without the security of a family, she valued families above all else. She once confided in me how she looked forward to being part of a family.

Then my family rejected her. That tore my insides but there was nothing I could do to spare Charlotte. All I could do was reassure her that we were going to be a family.

"I don't know if we should do this Alex," she said.

Even if I'd been expecting her to say something of that nature, hearing the words caused panic to rise up my throat. What if I couldn't convince her that I had made the right decision? That no one, not even family had a right to come between two people who loved each other.

"I have no doubt that we're doing the right thing. They'll come around; I promise." Charlotte liked practicalities so I laid it on her heavily. I told her all the things I'd done overnight in preparation for our lives together.

"I've written to the housing agent. I'm giving up my apartment. I've also written to one of the firms in Ohio that offered me a job. I accepted it."

"Oh Alex, but your apartment, you love it," she said, a stricken look on her face that made me chuckle.

"Those are material things. What I love is you in it. We'll move into your place." I was suddenly glad that Charlotte had not given up her apartment.

"I feel bad," she said. "You were going to work in your father's firm."

I shrugged. "And now I'm not, period."

"Are you sure this is what you want? I won't be offended if you want us to break up. I understand. They're your family Alex."

"Families support each other. They do not judge and condemn," I said harshly.

She took my hand and squeezed it. "We'll be okay. We'll work hard and you, Alexander Turner will be a success."

"That's my girl!"

"After my graduation," she said. "I'll be able to get a better paying job."

"We'll be fine, don't worry," I said. I was going to be the hardest working new lawyer the firm had ever seen. And eventually, Charlotte and I would return to New York.

I'd booked the marriage ceremony at one of the many chapels adjacent to the hotel where we would stay for two nights. I managed to buy rings before the ceremony and Charlotte wore one of the pretty dresses she'd planned on wearing for dinner at my parents'.

The ceremony was simple and full of emotion. Our witnesses were strangers provided by the chapel. When we walked out of the small chapel, I felt seven feet tall and my own man. Pride swelled in my chest. I had done the right thing and fought for my bride.

We went straight back to our room where I'd arranged for a bottle of champagne and flutes to be delivered. Despite the humble ceremony, we were happy and excited to know that we were formally husband and wife.

I popped the bottle open and poured each of us a glass.

"To a happy and blessed life together," I said, raising my glass.

"To us," she said, her face flushed. She'd never looked more beautiful than she did that evening.

We carried our champagne to the balcony where we had a dizzying view of the glittering city. Who would have predicted that I'd get married in Vegas? My sister's wedding had been planned months in advance and had been the talk of the town.

I'm glad that Charlotte and I have been spared that circus.

"It looks so beautiful," she said. "You have to be here to experience the magic."

"It doesn't compare to photographs or the screen," I said as we looked out. I turned to face Charlotte. "I feel so happy and settled. How do you feel?"

She smiled. "I feel good too. A little guilty but good. I don't know how I got to be so lucky, but I'll take it."

"It's me who is lucky," I said to her. "And you are not to have any more guilt, and I know just the way to erase it permanently." I took her champagne flute and placed it on the balcony.

Taking her hand, I led her back into the room and proceeded to show her just how special she was to me.

CHARLOTTE

I parked my small Honda in our drive, not surprised to see that Alex was not yet home. He worked long hours at the law firm and never complained. I was super proud of him and how hard he worked for us and our future.

It had been six months now and I still felt guilty especially on the days when Alex worked late into the night. I imagine that it would not be the case if he had gone to work for his father.

He threw all that away because of me. In the first few weeks, I'd harbored the hope that his parents would come around and they'd call us. As the weeks had gone by, my hope had diminished until it became clear that they were not going to back down.

Alex never showed it but I know he had to be missing his family terribly. He'd let it slip the previous week that his family usually spent the summer in Martha's Vineyard where they had a summer home by the lake.

I carried groceries into the two-bedroom single family home we had rented. It was cozy and comfortable and felt like a home. Fridays were my favorite days as Alex nor I worked on the weekends.

Plus, it had a lovely deck off the kitchen where we liked to have our breakfast on Sundays. I carried my shopping to the kitchen, rolled up my sleeves and started preparations for dinner.

I loved the view from my kitchen window. The sun had sunk into the skies, leaving remnants of light in its wake. We had fallen into a nice routine and as Alex had predicted, we were good for each other. We had fitted seamlessly into each other's life as though we had been living for years as husband and wife.

An hour later, Alex's key sounded at the front door and moments later, he strolled into the kitchen. I whirled around and smiled hugely as my world righted. He wore a similar grin on his face as he closed the distance between us and pulled me into his arms.

"This is my favorite moment of the day," he said, kissing my neck.

"Me too," I said and raised my head for a kiss.

I moaned as our lips came into contact. Six months of being husband and wife had not lessened the passion between us. If anything, it had increased and we couldn't get enough of each other.

His lips were firm and his mouth hot. Alex's hands cupped my ass pressing me against his erection, teasing me with it. He lifted me and I wrapped my skirt clad legs around his waist. Then he broke the kiss to carry me into our bedroom.

"What about dinner?" I asked, my voice husky with arousal.

"We'll warm it," he said.

I felt as though I was drowning in his cobalt blue eyes, flaring with passion. In the bedroom he lowered me to my feet and pulled the top over my head and unclasped my bra. My skirt and panties quickly followed, then he laid me gently on the bed and stood over me undressing.

"I've been thinking of you lying in bed like that, ready for me," he said, as he removed his clothes.

I never ceased to be amazed by the size of his cock and how well it fit into me considering my size. When Alex was naked, he came to the bed and draped his body over mine. I rubbed my hardened nipples over his chest and he groaned into my mouth.

"I love your body Chaz," he said and he rubbed his thumb over my nipple with one hand and supported his weight with the other.

"I love this huge sexy body too," I said, stroking his chest and shoulders. "You're—"

He silenced me with a deep kiss that drove all thoughts from my mind. The exhaustion of the day ebbed away as his tongue swirled in my mouth. He moved his lips to my jawline and neck, peppering kisses along my sensitive spots.

I moaned as his hands cupped my breasts and his mouth descended onto my nipples, sucking them in turn. When he descended further down and clamped his mouth on my clit, I lost it completely, screaming his name and gripping his head.

It wasn't long before my legs were trembling as an orgasm rolled from my pussy to the rest of my body.

"Go on your knees Chaz," Alex growled and I did as he said.

I grabbed a handful of the beddings and braced myself as Alex gripped my hip with one hand and with the other, he guided his cock to the entrance of my pussy.

I let out a gasp of pleasure as he thrust his cock into me, his hands gripping my hips hard to keep me in place. He drove so deep, it almost hurt but I was soaking wet from my orgasm and all I felt was a deep sense of fulfillment as his cock filled every space.

"Alex," I said over and over again.

Every time his cock filled me to the hilt, it hit my clit and it wasn't long before an orgasm was rocking me.

"Yes," I moaned as pleasure flooded me.

Alex's thrusts grew faster and harder and, in a few moments, he was filling me with his hot, thick liquid. I collapsed on the bed when it was over and Alex spooned me, with his hand draped loosely around my waist.

"You feel so good," he said. "You make it so tempting to fall asleep."

I laughed and turned around. "You're sleeping," I accused him.

He opened one eye.

"Come on lazy bones, let's jump into the shower. It will wake you up."

He groaned in protest but did as I suggested. We padded into the adjoining shower and enjoyed washing each other. Alex told me about his day and the cases he was working on while I entertained him with stories of the day's happenings.

CHARLOTTE

I'd made pasta with a sauce of hot Italian sausage, pepperoni, and meatballs. Even after a day spent in the kitchen at work, I didn't mind coming home to cook for Alex. He made me want to cook for him.

He made appreciative noises as we ate at the kitchen table.

"I ticked all the boxes on my list for a potential wife when I met you," he said.

"You had a list?" I asked.

"Of course. Picking a wife is an important decision," he said in his courtroom voice making me giggle.

"What was on the list?" I said and forked a meatball into my mouth.

"Gorgeous and sexy," he said.

"That's so shallow," I said laughingly.

Before Alex could respond, my phone vibrated with a call. I picked it up and stared at an unfamiliar number on the screen. I'd saved the numbers of Alex's parents, sister and even his brother in-law Richard. So, it couldn't be any of them and besides, they didn't have my number.

I swiped to answer. "Hello," I said tentatively.

There was silence and then a clearing of the throat on the other end before a woman's voice came on. "Hi, my name is Helen Stewart, I'm hoping this is Charlotte Evans' number."

The hairs at the back of my neck rose. That voice. It sounded so familiar. So eerie. As if I knew the speaker, which made no sense whatsoever. I didn't know anyone who bore that name.

"Yes, this is Charlotte," I said.

Alex raised his eyebrow and I shook my head.

"I can't tell you how happy I am to find you," she said, her voice rising. "I've been looking for you for almost a year."

"Me?" I said. I wracked my brain and couldn't figure out why a strange woman would be looking for me.

"Yes," she continued. "I hope that this is not going to come as a shock to you and that our mother had mentioned me to you."

My blood turned to ice. "I think you're confusing me for another person."

She was silent for a few minutes. "Ah, so she never mentioned me."

As sorry as I was for her, I was growing impatient. "Look—"

"Was your mother's name Mary Anne Evans?" she continued in the eerily familiar voice.

And that's when it hit me who she reminded me of. My mother. The same sweet voice that could coax a rat from a hiding place. "Yes," I whispered.

"I'm your older sister, Helen," she said. "Our mother gave me up for adoption when I was three months old."

I pressed a shocked hand to my chest. My heart thumped against my rib cage. It fought for space in my chest with the air frozen in my lungs.

"Are you okay?" Alex frantically asked me.

"Hold on a bit," I said to Helen and covered the mouthpiece and turned to Alex. "She says she's my sister and that my mother gave her up for adoption when she was three months old."

"Do you believe her?" he asked.

"Her voice. She talks just like my mother," I said and then put the phone back to my ear. "Sorry about that."

"It's okay, I know I've just dropped a bomb on you. I would like to meet you," she said. "I hired an investigator to look for you and coincidentally, I live in Ohio as well. I'm in Cleveland."

My heart would not stop beating fast. It was beginning to sink in. I actually had a sister. An older sister. The one thing that I'd longed for all my life. It was as though my subconscious knew that I had a sister somewhere.

"Oh," I said. "I'm free tomorrow."

"I can drive down tomorrow," she said, her voice shaky.

"Okay," I said. "There's a park near my place. I can send you the address."

"Thank you for agreeing to see me," she said, her voice cracking.

How could I not? After my mother died, I'd resigned myself up to the reality that I would never have another human being related to me through blood. And now this? Excitement coursed through my veins.

"Thank you for looking for me," I said.

We said goodbye after agreeing that she would drive down at noon. When I disconnected the call, I turned to Alex in wonder. "Who would have thought?"

"Did your mother ever mention another child?" he asked.

I shook my head. "No. But you couldn't really have a conversation with her. She was never herself." I refrained from telling Alex that she usually woke up high and continued that way for the rest of the day.

"How do you feel?" he asked, staring at me curiously.

I contemplated his question. "Still shocked but excited and curious. I wonder if she looks like me and whether she likes the same things I do."

It was possible that we'd been sired by the same man. I wonder if she knew anything about our father.

"I wonder why your mother gave her up for adoption and kept you?" he asked. "That's got to be hard to deal with, for her."

I hadn't thought about that. While it was true that I'd had a pretty shitty childhood, at least I never had to wrestle with questions of identity. I knew exactly who I was.

I was the child of a drug addict. My heart went out to Helen. It was a harsh reality to know that your mother gave you up for adoption but chose to keep your sister.

Anxiety settled in my stomach.

"Do you want me to go with you tomorrow?" he asked.

I shook my head. I needed to meet Helen on my own "Thanks, but I think I'd better meet her alone first."

CHARLOTTE

I arrived at the park fifteen minutes earlier, wanting some time to compose myself. I chose a bench that gave me a view of everyone entering the park. I fidgeted every few seconds, unable to sit still. Several people strolled into the park but none could have been Helen.

A mother holding two children's hands, which made me wonder whether Helen had kids. A young couple with only eyes for each other. An older woman holding a walking stick out to enjoy the summer day.

And then I saw her stroll in. There was no mistaking Helen. I could have been looking at myself. She was a brunette, like me, and wore a similar style to what I usually wore. Pants and a blouse though her clothes and shoes looked expensive.

She also had more jewelry than I usually wore. As she got closer to me, I stood up on shaky feet.

"Charlotte," she said in mom's voice.

I'd been ten years old when she died but I still remember her distinct voice. Helen and I fell into each other's arms in a hug that came naturally. I couldn't believe that I was twenty-three years old and hugging my sister for the first time.

"I prayed for a sister all the years I was growing up," I told her. Tears spilled from my eyes and I saw that she was also crying.

"Me too," Helen said. "Let's sit down. There's so much I want to know about you and our mother."

We sat on the bench side by side and held hands.

"We look so alike," I said. "How old are you?"

"Twenty-four," Helen said and we did some calculations.

It turned out that our mother had given her up for adoption when Helen was three months old and mom was about six weeks pregnant.

"Why do you think she did it?" Helen asked, her voice catching.

"Probably because she couldn't cope with two kids. She couldn't cope with one kid either. Tell me about the people who adopted you. Were they kind?"

Her features softened and she smiled. "My parents are wonderful people. I was an only child and sometimes I think they might have spoilt me a little."

"Really, how?" I asked greedy for information on a normal childhood.

"Well, I was the only one amongst my friends who got a birthday party every year and a visit to Disneyland since I was six years old," she said in a laughing tone. "They'd tried to have a baby for many years before settling on adoption."

Feelings of envy came over me. I'd worried that Helen would have issues on being the one who had been given away. Instead I found myself envious of the obvious good life she had lived.

"I wish I'd been the one she had given away for adoption, "I blurted out.

She placed a comforting hand on my knee. "I'm sorry I wasn't there to share in the burden. It must have been hell having a drug addict as a mother. But look how well you turned out?"

I burst into tears. I covered my face as sobs wracked my body. She draped her hand over my shoulders and inched closer. I lost track of time and didn't know how long I sat there crying.

"I know I'll be doing that tonight," Helen said as I mopped my face with a handkerchief that she offered.

"Are you married?" I asked her, glad to talk about her.

"Yes," she said. "I'm married to a wonderful man named Ed, short for Edward and we have a one and a half-year-old daughter."

I grinned, my spirits suddenly lifted. "You mean to say that I actually have a niece?"

She laughed. "Yes, you'll love Kacy. She's adorable."

"I can't wait to meet her," I said and abruptly stopped speaking. I was making a lot of assumptions. What if Helen just wanted to meet me, satisfy her curiosity and move on with her life?

"I can't wait for you to meet her," she said, to my relief.

It was odd to think that the woman seated next to me was my sister and yet we knew so little about each other.

"And Ed too. We're high school sweethearts and we always knew that we wanted to get married," Helen said. She seemed so put together and her life so organized. "You're married too?"

I smiled. Alex was the one good thing in my life. "Yes. His name is Alex and he's a wonderful man."

"The Evans sisters are blessed," she said and it took a moment to realize that she was referring to the two of us.

My chest swelled with emotion. There was something about Helen that made it easy to ask her questions. "What is his family like?"

"My in-laws?" she asked and when I nodded, she continued. "They are the loveliest people you'd ever meet. It helped that we knew each other for years and both sets of parents knew that we were going to get married."

"That's nice," I said and wondered if Alex's parents would have accepted me if I'd been adopted rather than raised by a drug addict.

"What about you? Did you get a whole new family when you and Alex got married?"

I made a face. "I wish. Unfortunately, no. I wasn't the kind of girl they had envisioned for their son, so they more or less cut us out of their lives."

Helen's mouth fell open. "What horrible people!"

"I thought so at first but now I'm getting a better understanding. He's their only son and they had such great hopes for him which included marrying a girl from their kind of world. They probably just hoped to frighten him and when it didn't work, they didn't know how to heal the rift."

She stared at me. "You're a really good person. You raised yourself well."

That made me laugh because it was so on point. I really had raised myself. I worked hard and got myself scholarships. Everything would have been perfect if Alex's family was in our lives.

"They'll come around," she said. "Especially when a grandchild comes along. They won't be able to resist it."

"You think?" I said.

She nodded. "Grandkids are impossible to resist."

CHARLOTTE

Alex and I had started talking about kids. It would be a tight squeeze with his schedule, but I really wanted a baby. A family of my own.

Helen and I talked and talked. I asked her about our father and she too had no idea.

Our stomachs were the first to complain. We got up and walked to a hot dog stand at the entrance of the park. It was fun to realize that we both liked loads of mayonnaise slathered on our hotdogs and no mustard.

We returned to our bench and spoke for a couple of more hours.

"Hey," she said. "Can you guys come over tomorrow for a barbecue. We usually have a barbecue every last Sunday of the month."

"Yes!" I said. "I'd love to meet your family."

"And I'd love to meet Alex. You talk about him a lot. He must be very special," Helen said. "Not to mention a man who chose his fiancée over threats from his family."

"He is," I said. My muscles ached from sitting down for so long. I walked Helen to her car and we hugged goodbye.

It felt good to know that I would be seeing her the following day. Only after she'd gone and I was walking home, did I realize that I had forgotten to take pictures of us to show Alex.

Alex had opted to go to the office rather than stay home alone. I got home as he parked his car in the drive and we walked into the house together.

"How was it?" he asked.

There was so much to tell him. We cuddled on the couch as I told him everything Helen and I had talked about, including the invitation to go to their house the following day for the barbecue.

"What do you think?" I said, looking up at his face.

"We have to go," he said. "It will be nice to have more family. I'm really happy for you Chaz."

I kissed him. "I know."

I kissed him again and it grew into a heavy make out session. We made love on the couch and afterwards, cuddled some more.

~

I loved our lazy Sunday mornings. Alex yawned and stretched and then swung his legs out of bed.

"Coffee coming up," he said, pulling on his boxers.

I loved the five o'clock shadow on his jaw and the untidy mop of hair on his head, giving him a sinful look. Not that I could manage to make love again after being at it most of the night. As he left to make coffee, I thought about a baby again.

When Alex returned carrying two mugs of coffee, I brought it up. "I'm thinking about what we talked about. Having a baby."

He handed me my coffee and sat on the edge of the bed. "I've been thinking about it too. It would be nice to start our family but I worry it might be too much for you. Work and a baby."

I laughed. It was just like Alex to over worry about me. "Millions of women do it all the time. They hold down jobs and raise families."

He grinned. "You're right. I'm good if you are."

"Should I throw away my contraceptives?"

He nodded and raised his mug and I clinked mine with his. "To having loads of fun making babies."

I laughed. "Why am I not surprised that you're more interested in the process rather than the end result?"

"Because you're so sexy and trying to make a baby is going to be a lot of fun," he said. "I can't wait to meet your sister today."

"You'll love her."

After breakfast, Alex and I freshened up and left the house for a morning hike. It was a nice way to get in some exercise and also enjoy the outdoors. By the time we returned home two hours later, we were sweaty and tired, with enough time to shower and head out to Cleveland.

I paid little attention to the landscape as we drove. My mind had switched to Helen's family. I couldn't wait to meet my niece. We got into Cleveland at one thirty and drove to the suburbs where Helen and her family lived.

My first assessment of Helen had been right. They were pretty comfortable, judging from the huge beautiful house that we pulled up to. As soon as we got out of the car and were walking on the porch, the door burst open and she ran out to meet us.

I laughed at the enthusiasm of her hug. "I'm glad you're here," she said. "I've been nagging everyone, worrying that you won't come." She turned to Alex. "And you must be my brother-in-law." In the warm way I'd started to recognize as a Helen way, she pulled Alex into a hug.

He hugged her back, clearly pleased with the reception. "It's a pleasure to meet you," he said, looking from Helen to me. "You don't need a DNA test. You're obviously sisters."

"Yes, I've been boasting to everyone that I have a sister. Come on in."

I wondered who everyone was. I hadn't bothered to ask who would be there when she invited us. All I'd cared about was meeting my niece and brother-in-law.

We entered a foyer and then walked through an open plan living room, an industrial sized kitchen with equipment that made me want to grab an apron and start cooking and then finally stepped out to a garden that stretched as far as the eye could see.

"Gorgeous," Alex said.

I was relieved to see that there were less than fifteen people.

ALEX

I flipped burgers on the grill and kept an eye on Charlotte, but she looked like she was having a lot of fun. She was standing with Helen and her parents. Helen leaned towards Charlotte's ear and said something that made my wife throw her head back and laugh.

Seeing her like that warmed my heart. Her new found family were awesome people and Helen's parents had threatened to make Charlotte their daughter as they'd always wanted to have two children. Charlotte was glowing from the love showered on her.

Then there was her adorable niece Kacy, who was jumping on a small bouncy castle with a paternal cousin. Helen's husband was a lawyer as well and a pretty easy guy. They were a good warm bunch and I felt lucky that we had found them.

"They look so alike," Ed said. "Here, brought you a cold one."

"Thanks." I took the cold can of beer and opened it. I took a swig and sighed as the icy cold liquid went down my throat.

It was the perfect day for a barbecue. The sun was hot but not too hot and a soft breeze blew from the woods behind Ed and Helen's property. The scent of roasting meat was the icing on the cake. Being here with them reminded me of how little we had socialized in the last six months.

Though I couldn't complain. Not when I remembered the enjoyment, I'd derived from peeling the layers back and getting to know my wife more. In and out of bed.

Ed placed fresh steaks on his side of the grill. "I've been wanting to ask you. Are you in any way connected to the New York law firm, James Turner & Sons?"

It took a moment for me to answer. It had been so long since I had heard the mention of my family that it felt like a punch to the belly. "Yes," I finally said. "James Turner is my father."

"Oh, I met him once in a courtroom, he's a beast," Ed said, his voice brimming with admiration.

"Yes, he's pretty awesome," I said, dreading the inevitable question.

"So, what are you doing working in a tiny firm in Grantsville?" Ed said. "Shouldn't you be by your father's side, adding to the billing hours of the company?"

There was no way to explain apart from the truth. "We fell out. They wanted me to marry someone else, and I had set my mind on Charlotte."

Ed's jaw dropped. "People still do that?"

I laughed at his astounded expression. Living out of my family circle in college and now working had also opened my eyes to another world. A world where family members respected each other's independence.

"Some parents do and their children agree. But there was no way I was going to marry a woman based on her family background," I said, still furious they didn't think Charlotte was good enough.

"Good for you," he said, and punched my shoulder lightly. "I can't believe they'd cut you off for such a reason, though."

"They'll come around," I said. Mere words. My father was a stubborn and sometimes ruthless man.

His pride was at stake and he wasn't going to bow down and retract his words. Neither was I for that matter. I'd spoken to my sister twice, and my brother-in-law once in the last six months.

What astounded me was that even after telling them that Charlotte and I were already married, they'd suggested I would divorce her in time. Clearly, I came from a family of mad people.

The afternoon was a success and, in the evening, we left in a flurry of hugs and promises to keep in touch.

"That was the nicest afternoon I've had in a long time," she said.

I glanced at her. God, she was beautiful. Her face was glowing and she had a permanent smile. I couldn't resist the urge to tease her. "You're lucky that I'm not a sensitive man."

She laughed. "I know. That's why I can speak my thoughts honestly. I should have added, minus the time me and you spend together."

"I know," I said.

"What did you think of Helen?" she asked.

"I love that she looks like you," I said. "Including her personality. Ed was awesome too. He and I talked a lot."

"I knew you'd have a lot to talk about when I heard that he was a lawyer," she said.

"That always helps. One thing us lawyers have in common is that we talk too much."

Charlotte was silent for a moment. "He probably knows the family firm."

I was saved from responding when Charlotte's phone vibrated with a message. I didn't want to go down that road as it always left her feeling shitty and guilty.

She typed on her phone and then sighed.

"What's the matter?"

"Amy. She wants to see me. I told her we'll be home in a few," she said. "I wonder what happened now. Things with Simon were going so well."

I tried to call Simon and didn't get an answer. "I can't keep up with Amy's boyfriends."

Charlotte laughed. "I don't blame you. Amy is so pretty, I don't understand why she picks losers for boyfriends."

I glanced at my wife. "It's not easy to find what we have. There's a lot of trial and error."

"I know. I just forget sometimes," she said.

ALEX

We got home and I parked the car in the garage. Amy was parked in the street parking and Charlotte got out and went to her. It happened while she was walking out of the garage. She tripped as she went over the ledge that separated the concrete path and the lawn.

A place where she had passed through countless times. Charlotte went sprawling on the grass, landing face first. I dashed up to her and helped her up.

"Are you hurt?" I asked worriedly.

Amy left her car and hurried to us.

"Just my dignity," she said and giggled, but it was clear she was embarrassed.

Amy kissed her. "Are you drunk? That's the only plausible reason that would make a person not see this ledge."

Charlotte laughed. "I've had a glass of wine, but I'm definitely not drunk or even tipsy. I don't know what happened. It's one of those things, I suppose."

We all walked into the house. I left the ladies in the living room and went upstairs to our bedroom, giving them some privacy. I shut the door and fished out a letter that Mary had forwarded to me.

It was an application form to take the New York State Bar Exam. I wanted to take it so badly, but this was not the right time. My working hours were crazy as one of only two clerks in the firm, there was no way I could take time off to study and travel to New York for the exams.

I folded the form and placed it back into the envelope. There would be time for all that. What was important was to earn a living for us.

Charlotte came upstairs an hour later. She jumped on the bed and bounced on it. I held on to my laptop.

"You look too serious," she said, looking at me as she bounced up and down.

I folded my laptop and slid it under the bed. I lay flat on my back and invited Charlotte to lie on top of me.

"Are you hungry?" she asked, nibbling my neck.

She smelled of the outdoors, as if she had been walking in the woods and rolling in the grass.

"I can't eat anything else after all that meat," I said. "You?"

"I'm full."

"Is everything okay with Amy?" I said and cupped Charlotte's perfect ass.

"Usual boyfriend trouble but she'll be fine," she said as she slowly popped open the buttons of my shirt.

I shrugged out of my shirt when she undid the last of the buttons. She ran her fingertips over the hairs on my chest and then played with my man nipples. I inhaled sharply as jolts of desire went straight to my cock.

My cock swelled and pressed against her thigh as she did things with her tongue. She sat up and pulled her top over her head. She reached at the back and snapped open her bra. Charlotte knew how much I loved her breasts.

"Big and beautiful," I said, reaching out to cup them.

I teased the stiff peaks of her nipples with my fingers. She brought her mouth down to kiss me, teasing my lips before dipping her tongue into my waiting mouth. I ran my hands over her thighs and ass.

"I've been thinking about tasting you all day," she whispered.

I raised an eyebrow. "All day? You naughty girl."

She dropped down my body, leaving heat wherever she planted a kiss. She tugged on my shorts and I raised my hips and helped her pull them down along with my boxer briefs.

She let out a sound that was a cross behind a gasp and anticipation. She took my cock in both of her hands and then rubbed her lips over the tip. I threaded my fingers through her hair as she took my cock into her mouth.

Was it right for a man to want his wife twenty-four seven? She was incredible. In and out of bed. It was inconceivable that anyone would tell me to divorce her. Charlotte was my everything. My one source of happiness. She made my life meaningful.

My cock hit the back of her throat and I let out a loud moan. It swelled in her mouth growing impossibly big and I wondered as I often did how she was able to keep it in there.

“Fuck Chaz,” I said as she swirled her tongue around the crown of my cock. ‘I’m going to come.” I withdrew my cock gently from her hold.

“You never come in my mouth,” she said with a pout.

“One day,” I said. “I like it when we come together. Now, lie on your back and spread your legs for me.”

She batted her eyelids before doing as I said. “I love it when you’re bossy. So different from the normal you.”

She lay on her back and I stood over her and took a moment to admire the swell of her breasts and her curves.

“You’ve spoiled me for any other woman,” I said to her. “I’ll never want anyone else as long as I live.”

“You’d better not,” she said and wagged a finger at me. “You made a vow.”

“I did. The best decision I ever made.” I took her knees and pushed them back to her shoulders, exposing her gleaming, wet pussy to my appreciative eyes. “And now I want to fulfil another vow.”

She giggled. “I don’t remember that one.”

“It was veiled in making you happy,” I said and gripped my cock. I ran it up and down her slit, loving the sounds of pleasure that came from her mouth.

“Oh God, yes,” Charlotte cried softly. “I want you so much.”

"Fuck Chaz, you turn me into a beast when you say that," I growled and prodded the entrance of her pussy with my cock.

"I love it when you're a beast," she said, looking at me with those sexy blue eyes. "Fuck me Alex."

I slid my cock into her pussy and she closed her eyes and let out a long moan of pleasure. I braced my hands on her thighs and thrust in and out, making each thrust long and deep.

"Faster," Charlotte says.

My thrusts became fast, quick jabs. I knew I was hitting the perfect spot when her cries became screams. She threw her hands back to grip the head board as if she was afraid that she'd fly off the bed.

"Oh my God," she cried. "I'm on fire."

"Come Chaz," I urged her.

I tightened my grip on her thighs as they tensed. Then she let out one long cry and I felt an orgasm rocking her body. Seeing her like that, writhing her body, with her mouth half open, set me off and I let go of my control and relief washed over me as I came, emptying myself into the waiting hot body of my wife.

CHARLOTTE

I sat in the waiting room of the ophthalmologist twisting my hands on my lap. It was my second visit and my body was tense with nerves. Added to that was the guilt of keeping something away from Alex.

After that episode when I fell outside the garage, my vision had gotten worse. At work, I'd dropped things more times than I could count, thinking I was placing them on the work top. At home, cooking dinner was becoming a challenge until I'd been forced to accept that something was seriously wrong.

I'd booked an appointment with the ophthalmologist the previous week, and had come in for a variety of tests. The doctor was a solemn older man who said very little. He put some liquid in my eyes and then proceeded to check my eyes through several machines, peering at me and asking me what I could see.

Dr. Martin was his name and he'd told me to return after a week. I was a mess and a part of me wished that I'd told Alex.

But I'd chosen not to tell him as they had a big case coming up at work and he was knee deep in research.

I tried to bother him as little as possible. He had made so many sacrifices for us and he deserved to have a little peace in his life.

A gray haired, bespectacled woman left the examination room. The receptionist stood up and went into Dr. Martin's office. My insides turned to jelly. Please help it be something that can be resolved with eye drops.

She returned a minute later. "You can see the doctor now."

"Thanks," I managed to say. My legs trembled as I entered the office.

The doctor was stooped over sheets of paper, which was not reassuring at all. He looked up at me grimly. Or was it my imagination. I didn't know what was real and what wasn't. My imagination had taken over, fear in the driver's seat.

"Hello Charlotte," he said. "Please sit down."

No, it wasn't my imagination. He was definitely more serious that he had been the previous week. My palms grew wet and I rubbed them over my pants. What could be the worst thing that could happen? Maybe an eye surgery, I thought, answering myself.

"So, do I need a prescription?" I said.

He looked at me and nodded his head. "Unfortunately not. It's a lot more serious than that."

My heart dropped to my feet. A truth that had been skirting around my brain came to the forefront. Something I'd feared but told myself it was irrational thinking. Punishment.

I'd not told anyone. Not even Amy but a part of me believed that I would get punished for taking Alex away from his family. I fought down a hysterical sob. I should have walked away from Alex. By now, he'd have been over me and he would have married his family's choice.

Family was the most important thing in the world and I had taken him away from his. I knew that at one point, I was going to pay. That moment had come. I tried to be brave. Whatever the doctor was going to say was something I had brought on myself.

"You have a very rare eye condition known as peripheral vision loss," Doctor Martin said.

I didn't bother repeating the name of the disease. "Is it treatable?" I didn't care about anything else other than whether there was a way out.

He didn't answer for a moment. Panic filled my chest. Was I going to die at twenty-three from an eye condition?

The doctor shook his head. "Not at the moment, no. It is a degenerative disease, which affects your eyesight as time goes, eventually leading to blindness."

Fear clenched a tight first around my chest. Blindness? I glanced around and noticed that my vision had narrowed and I couldn't see as widely as I had seen, say three months earlier.

Tears filled my eyes. I was fucking twenty-three! I was not an old woman. I slumped in my chair and allowed the tears to flow from my eyes. How much bad luck could one person endure in a lifetime?

Just when I was settling into a semblance of normalcy with a great husband and a new family. My very own family. Something I'd never had, and was enjoying greatly. I spoke to Helen at least once every day. And now this?

I felt like smashing something against the wall at the unfairness of it all. My chest constricted with pain. I had so many questions but I couldn't speak as sobs wracked my body.

"Should we call your husband?" Dr. Martin asked.

I snapped out of my misery and self-pity. "No! Please." I fished a handkerchief from my handbag. "What causes it? Are you sure that's what it is?"

He nodded. "We did a myriad of tests. I'm not sure as to what causes it. It has something to do with the deterioration of the optic nerves but we don't really know."

"How long until I go completely blind?"

"Two to five years," he said. "Every patient is different."

After asking a few more questions, I realized that no matter how many questions I asked, he was not going to tell me what I desperately wanted to hear. That it was a mistake and I was going to be fine.

CHARLOTTE

I walked out to my car, entered and sat gripping the steering wheel. Poor Alex. Meeting me had been the worst luck of his life. I'd brought him nothing but trouble. And now illness. As I sat there, the beginnings of a plan started to form in my mind.

The best thing would have been if Alex and I had not met. But we had. The next best thing would be if I disappeared like a cloud of smoke from his life. I thought about never seeing him again and fresh tears filled my eyes.

My heart felt as if it was breaking into pieces. We'd had so many plans for the future. But that meant nothing. I'd taken so much from his life. His family, his career, his friends. It was time to let go of that dream.

People like me, born in the gutter, did not get their happily ever after. I'd lied to myself enough. I couldn't keep dragging Alex down with me. He deserved better.

Without me, he could return to the family firm where he belonged and take his rightful place as his father's heir. He would marry a girl that his family approved off. At that thought, my heart expanded to painful proportions.

I couldn't imagine my Alex belonging to another woman. As long as I never saw it, I would be okay. I cried until I had no more tears. I drove out of the parking lot and headed home. I'd left work two hours earlier and I had some time before Alex came home.

Another thought plagued me as I took a shower. What about my best friend Amy? She'd become a big part of my life. So had Helen and her family. I thought about cutting them off from my life and I started bawling in the shower.

But I had to. Amy was a softie and if Alex pressed the right buttons she would break and tell him where I was and why I'd left. And of course, Alex would come for me and convince me to stay with him by quoting that nonsense we had said in our wedding vows.

For better or for worse. But blindness? That was too much to ask. Not to mention all the sacrifices that Alex had made for me.

As for Helen, I didn't know her well enough to know whether she could keep a secret. What I did know however, was that it would be unfair to ask her to do so. We'd only found each other and asking her to carry such a burden was wrong.

I would write letters to all of the important people in my life, explain to them that I have to go but not tell them the real reason. Alex's was going to be the hardest one to write because I was going to have to lie.

If I wanted him to move on with his life, I was going to have to be ruthless.

"Honey?" Alex's voice called, jerking me back to the present. I'd taken longer than I'd planned in the shower.

I turned off the knob and grabbed a towel. "I'm in the bathroom."

"Okay," he said.

I dried myself and when I padded into the bedroom, he was seated on the edge of the bed, sporting a massive tent in his pants.

I laughed. "To what do I owe that to?"

"Just thinking of you in the shower, rubbing yourself between your legs as soft moans escape your mouth," Alex drawled.

"Not true," I said. "But now that you mention that…" I dropped the towel and sashayed towards him.

I emptied my thoughts of the devastating afternoon I'd had and thought only of pleasuring my husband. I straddled him and rubbed my pussy over the swell of his pants.

"You look hot in a tie," I said to him.

"And you look hot naked, wife," he said.

I bit my tongue to keep myself from bursting into tears. I loved it when Alex called me wife. I covered his body and kissed him, cradling his face as I did so. His hands roamed my back, my ass and my hips.

He patted my thighs and rocked his hips, dry humping me. Some things were so easy to take for granted. Like having a man you loved to make love with. To try out all the crazy sexual fantasies you'd ever had.

"My cock needs to be freed," he said.

"And I need it," I told him and lifted myself off his body.

Alex unbuckled his belt and pulled off his pants. Half-naked, I clambered on top of him again as he held his cock, ready for me.

"Yes," I said as I slid down his thick wide cock. I closed my eyes as I took the full length deep inside my pussy.

I'd become addicted to making love with Alex. What would I do on the days when my body refused to understand that Alex was gone and there was no one to fill that void?

I tried to push away thoughts of an empty, lonely life and failed. There had to be another way out, I told myself. But I was fooling myself and burying my head in the sand, just as I had when I said yes to marrying Alex.

I was doing it for Alex. I was protecting him from any more heartbreak. He was the kindest, sweetest man I knew and he did not deserve any more pain. I hadn't realized that I was crying until Alex stopped thrusting and his firm grip on my hips loosened.

"Why are you crying Chaz? What's wrong?" A shadow of fear took residence in his eyes.

I smiled through my tears. "Just me being weird. I love you so much. These are tears of joy."

"Are you sure?"

"What do I have to be unhappy about?" I said. "Now, fuck me!"

"I love it when you're bossy," he said.

He flipped us around and placed my legs on his shoulders. He made love to me with slow deep thrusts that made me whimper and cry out his name. Heat spread from my pussy, enveloping my whole body.

All too soon, an orgasm built. Alex sensed this and increased the pace of his thrusts and I angled myself so that he hit my clit with every stroke. I closed my eyes as an intense orgasm ripped through me. I bit my lower lip to keep from bursting into tears again.

ALEX

Monday was a bitch at work and I was glad when the day was over and I could go home to my wife. The nights were becoming chilly and I couldn't wait to snuggle up with Charlotte on the couch with a blanket draped over us.

Not that there was a chance of cuddling for long. Charlotte and I were like two explosive devices. One touch and we exploded. Just thinking about my sexy wife made me hard.

One of the advantages of living in our small town was the absence of traffic. In ten minutes, I was driving up our street. It was past seven and lights lit up in the houses I passed before I got to ours.

I smiled as I parked the car. Our house resembled a Christmas tree with most of the lights turned on. I'd stopped asking Charlotte to turn off the lights she wasn't using when I realized that it was baggage she carried from her past.

She was left alone at home when she was a child, sometimes for days. It had torn me apart when Charlotte told me how she would leave the lights on at night to ward off monsters. Despite knowing in her logical mind that monsters did not exist, a part of her felt safer when the house was lit up.

One day, she would feel safe enough to turn them off, in the meantime, I was around to wrap her in my arms and make her feel safe. I turned off the ignition and got out of the car. With long quick strides, I was turning the front door key.

"I'm home Chaz," I called out.

I shrugged out of my coat as I waited to hear Charlotte shout back at me where she was. My stomach rumbled at the spicy scent that filled the air. I kicked off my shoes and made for the kitchen. I peered into the pot on the stove. Chili. Yum.

I scooped a spoonful and shoved it into my mouth. I closed my eyes and sighed with ecstasy. The sound of swallowing echoed back at me. It suddenly hit me how silent the house was.

Chaz was usually in the shower, kitchen or bedroom. I went to look for her in our bathroom. It smelled of her floral shower gel which meant she had showered not too long ago. Where was she?

"Chaz?" I felt silly calling out in what was clearly an empty house. As I returned to the bedroom, I noticed the envelope on the bed. Puzzled, I took it and turned it over. It was addressed to me in Charlotte's small neat handwriting.

A wisp of fear ran through me. Why would she write me a letter when we lived in the same house? With trembling fingers, I tore the envelope and removed a sheet of paper.

I started reading.

Dear Alex,

By the time you find this letter, I'll be long gone. I'm sorry to start off the letter like this but there is no easy way to tell your husband that the marriage is over. Kaput. I hope this doesn't come as a shock to you but I'm sure you noticed that I grew increasingly restless in the last couple of months.

While I do love you (I always will), I'm not cut out for marriage. I feel imprisoned, as if I should be out there doing grand things. That sounds horrible but I don't know how else to explain. I think we got married too quickly without giving ourselves time to experience life before tying ourselves down.

There's also this guy that I like. A lot. At work. We are going away together, to have some fun. To be young again. To be without responsibilities.

I urge you to do the same Alex. Go back to New York. Join your family firm. Have fun. That's what I wish for you.

One more thing. I've signed our divorce papers. They are in the second drawer in the closet. Sign them and both of us will be free. I'm excited about this next phase of life, I hope you are too.

I wish you all the best Alex. You're a good man and I hope you find someone who deserves you.

Please don't look for me. Let me move on with my life. Those are my wishes.

Love always,

Charlotte.

I read the letter over and over again until the words penetrated my brain. Charlotte had left me! I found that part again. She had found someone else. At work.

Nausea rose up my throat. It felt as though I'd swapped lives with someone else. It couldn't possibly be my Charlotte who had written that letter. We were in love! What was she talking about? I couldn't stay still. Maybe it was a prank.

But I knew Chaz. She didn't prank people. Oh God. I was going to be sick. I needed to talk to someone. Amy would know. *Wait.* I went to the second drawer and yanked it open. A bulky legal sized envelope lay on the top. My hands trembled as I fished out the papers inside.

Divorce papers. I flipped to the last one. Signed, as she had said. And it was Charlotte's handwriting. The skin around my face tightened. I felt as if I had endured a bad cosmetic surgery. Nothing felt like mine.

I dropped the papers as the nausea rose up my throat. I ran to the toilet and bent over the bowl and retched. I hadn't had lunch and soon the stench of bile filled the bathroom.

I washed my face in the sink and staggered back to the bedroom. Amy would know. She would have an explanation. I called her and to my relief she picked up the phone on the first ring.

"Alex, did you get a letter as well?" she sounded distraught. My hope sunk.

"Yes," I said dully. "She said she was leaving me for someone else." Those were not words I had expected to ever come from my mouth.

"She said the same thing to me. That she wanted to leave her old life behind and start fresh," Amy said.

I gave her a summary of what Charlotte had written in mine.

"Do you believe that?" she asked.

I stood outside the kitchen window and looked out. She was out there. Probably with a guy.

"I don't know what to believe any more. She signed the divorce papers. Amy, its so clearly something she's been planning for a long time."

"But it doesn't make sense," Amy protested. "I know Charlotte and if she was seeing someone at work, then I'd have known it. She was... is my best friend. I know what she can or cannot do and this falls squarely on the latter."

I contemplated going to her work place. Then I visualized the scenario. None of her colleagues would want to look me in the eye. And no one would admit that they had known what was going on. I'd look and feel like a fool. The guy whose wife had left him for another man. That was one tag I did not want to have.

"We have to find her," Amy said. "Something is not right."

I shook my head. "The Charlotte I know would not hurt the people she loves."

"Exactly! Can we meet, have coffee and figure out what to do?" Amy said.

I glanced at my watch. It was eight. I was usually so occupied in the evenings and now suddenly it stretched out before me with nothing to do. Charlotte was my whole world. Pain stretched my chest. How was I going to continue without her? Who was I without Charlotte?

We said goodbye and I grabbed my car keys from the kitchen counter. We'd agreed to meet in a coffee shop in town. I got there in less than ten minutes. Amy was already there, nursing a mug of coffee. She looked as lost and as sad as I felt.

"Hey," I said and slid into the chair opposite.

"Hey." Her eyes were red rimmed. She'd been crying. If only I could cry. I'd have bawled my eyes out all night, man or not. Anything to get the lump stuck in my chest to move.

The waiter came and I asked for a black coffee.

"Won't you have something to eat? I'm sure you haven't eaten," Amy said.

I remembered how hungry I'd been when I got home. It was almost an hour ago and yet in that short time, my life had changed. For the worse. Food had ceased to matter. So had a lot of things. The only thing that mattered was Charlotte.

"Chaz cooked some chili before she left," I said, realizing how well orchestrated her disappearance had been. A bitter laugh escaped my mouth. "Did she actually think that I'd read her letter while I munched on dinner, thinking what a lovely meal it was?"

Anger was beginning to replace the pain. That was much better. I could deal with anger.

"Alex, don't you think something is going on here?" Amy said. "Charlotte had been withdrawn in the last couple of weeks. I think something drove her to this. She wouldn't do something like this."

My training as a lawyer kicked in. "How long have you known Charlotte for Amy?"

"We met here in college the first day and became instant friends," she said.

"I met her here too," I said. "The point is that none of us knew Charlotte before Ohio. All that we knew was things she had told us. I've never met anyone who knew her in the past. Helen is like us. She met Charlotte the other day."

"Helen!" Amy said, her face lighting up. "She would know. Can you give me her number?"

It was as though she'd heard nothing of what I said. "Sure." I pulled out my phone from my pocket, punched in the screen and read out the number to her.

The waiter brought my coffee and I gratefully took a sip. I mused over what I'd said to Amy. Charlotte had been raised in very traumatizing circumstances. She'd been neglected and unloved. She'd never seen a therapist as far as I knew. What had that kind of upbringing done to her?

Maybe she couldn't handle long term commitment. Looking at it like that, I realized that anything was possible with Charlotte. I had possibly even joined a queue of broken hearts she'd left in other places.

From listening to Amy's conversation, Helen had received the same type of letter. Saying goodbye and explaining nothing.

I didn't care what reasons or issues Charlotte had. You didn't do something like that to people you loved. We had made vows to each other for fucks sake! Who walked out of a marriage that was less than a year old because they wanted to live a little? What had we been doing, acting? What sort of fucked up reason was that?

"Helen is devastated," Amy said. "I caught her minutes after she'd come from reading her letter."

We drank our coffee silently.

"What are you going to do now?" Amy asked.

A new wave of anger came over me. She had no right to do this to me. I'd had my whole life mapped out. With Charlotte by my side. Now, I had to go back to the drawing board and figure out what to do. One thing was for sure though, I was not going to sit around moping for her.

She was not worth it. I'd sacrificed everything for love and love had turned out to be a disillusion. "I'm going to go back home. To New York."

Amy's jaw dropped. "You're not going to look for her?"

I shook my head. That chapter of my life was closed. Forever.

CHARLOTTE

I was in a doctor's office. This time, the village General Practitioner. I had seen him a few times when he came into the diner where I worked as a chef, to have his lunch. I'd made an appointment and gone to see him a few days earlier.

My stomach had been a mess for a while now. From vomiting to aching. I'd been sure it had something to do with stress or something bad I'd eaten at the diner. When it persisted, I'd decided to see a doctor.

It brought back horrible memories of the day I'd gotten the news about my eyesight. My peripheral vision was still bad but overall, it had not deteriorated further and for that I was grateful even though I knew it was only a matter of time.

It had been two months since I left my husband, my home, my friends and my life.

It had almost broke me as it was the hardest thing I'd ever done. As I sat in the waiting room, memories of that day washed over me. I'd planned to leave the house at noon but couldn't do it. I'd tried to think of other ways. Maybe Alex and I could divorce and remain friends.

But I'd known that I was clutching on straws. If I loved him, then I had to let him go. I remembered the words I'd written in the letter to him and cringed. The aim had been to turn his love to hate.

Hate would help him leave Ohio and return to his family. Hate for me would make him want to live the life his parents had wanted for him. Had he found someone else already? I pushed away those painful thoughts.

What about Amy and Helen? Did they miss me? Had my flimsy explanation of why I had to leave been sufficient? Maybe for Helen but not Amy. She knew me too well and she had to have suspected that something else was up. I missed them so much.

Every morning, when I got up and found myself in my one-bedroom house, I fought the temptation to go back home. I had to remind myself that I had no home in Grantsville to go back to. That was the choice I'd made to give the man I loved a new beginning in life.

"Daisy Evans," the receptionist said and I stood up.

I'd started using my middle name and hoped that it would throw off anyone looking for me. But then again, I didn't expect anyone to look for me.

"You may see the doctor now."

I entered the inner office. The doctor looked up and smiled.

"Miss Evans, have a seat. I have what I hope will be good news for you," he said.

Relief washed over me as I sat down. I needed good news.

"You're pregnant!"

I gasped. "What?" I couldn't be. I'd left Alex two months earlier. Oh God! That meant that I was more than two months pregnant.

Panic rose up my throat, threatening to choke me. A coldness hit my core as the implication of the news hit me. I was going to have to tell Alex. Everything I'd done to set Alex free had been for naught.

I couldn't think. I looked up and realized that the doctor was talking to me.

"Is the father present?" Dr. Martin asked.

I nodded. Maybe not at that very moment but one thing I knew about Alex was that he would want to be a part of his baby's life. Ten minutes later, armed with a bunch of prescriptions, I left the doctor's office. I'd taken my lunch hour to see the doctor and needed to go back to work.

Woodfield was the smallest town I had ever lived in and I'd purposely picked it for that very reason. I'd debated between moving to a large city but discarded that idea as I needed the warmth of small-town living.

With no family and friends, I craved a close community I could be a part of. I walked back to the diner, my mind a whirl of activity. Where would Alex fit in our lives? Would I have to tell him that I'd lied about having another man in my life?

"You're back early," Michael, the other chef said as I entered the kitchen.

"I finished early with my appointment," I said.

"Have a cup of tea, honey," Beatrice, the lady who washed the dishes said, standing up from where she sat to serve me. "You look like you could use one."

I sank into a chair gratefully. "Thanks." I suddenly longed for Amy… and mostly for Alex. I imagined how he would have reacted to the news if we'd still been together.

He would have slipped his big hands around me and lifted me up high in the air. Then he'd have twirled me around and we would have danced and celebrated.

"That's better," Beatrice said as she handed me a cup of tea. "Nothing like a smile to add cheer to the day."

I blinked back the tears that formed in my eyes. I swallowed hard. I decided to call Alex that evening after work, before I lost my guts. A plan quickly formed in my brain. He could see the baby whenever he wanted but I was not going to be a part of his life.

Then I realized that it would be even easier than I thought. After all, the damage was already done. Alex hated me. He would demand a DNA test when the baby was born. Pain funneled into my heart at the thought of Alex questioning the paternity of the baby.

I could not blame him for it, though it was going to hurt. I was the one who had made the decision to lead him into thinking that I had fallen in love with someone else. An unrealistic thought formed, an tiny part of me had hoped that he would come after me.

That he knew me well enough to know that the things I had written in the letter couldn't possibly be true.

CHARLOTTE

I'd sit in the same position for close to an hour.

Darkness had set in and I hadn't made a move to either turn on the living room lights or make that call. My palms hurt from gripping my cell phone so hard. Beads of sweat poured down my forehead.

My throat had closed up and I was afraid that if I called, I would not be able to speak. But I couldn't stay in the same spot all night. I had to make a decision. I raised my left hand and let it rest on my flat belly.

It was hard to believe that at that very moment a child was forming in my belly. A baby conceived from the greatest of loves. The shock of my pregnancy had worn off and now I felt a glimmer of excitement about the baby.

The future loomed ahead and stopped me from embracing full-fledged joy. I'd heard of women who were blind and were great mothers. But how would it feel to know that I'd never see my child's face as a grown up?

A sob choked me. Stop it, I said to myself. Those thoughts were not helpful at all. One day at a time was going to be my new motto, I decided. The one step I needed to take was to call Alex. I could do it.

I would detach myself. Not think of how much I love him and how awesome his voice sounds. Not miss the protective way he had of wrapping his arms around me.

With trembling fingers, I scrolled down to find his cell phone number, even though I knew it by heart. Any excuse to delay the inevitable. I found it and before I could dilly dally further, I hit call. I held my breath but the phone was silent and then a voice said that the number was no longer in service.

Relief swathed me before I realized how stupid that was. One way or another, I needed to find Alex. I went back to my contacts list and scrolled until I found the house telephone number.

The phone rang and just when I thought no one was going to pick it up, Mrs. Turner's distinct voice came on the phone.

"Hello," she said, her voice cold as ice.

Hearing her voice and knowing that she disliked me, made me freeze. I moved my mouth and no words came out.

"Is there anyone there?" she asked.

I gripped my cell phone and cleared my throat. "Hello, Mrs. Turner, this is Charlotte. I tried to call Alex's cell phone, but it says the number is no longer in service."

Then a horrible thought sprouted in my mind. What if something had happened to him? Like an accident, and all along I'd assumed that he was well?

She did not answer for the longest time and I thought that she was going to disconnect the call. "Yes, he changed his numbers and anything that had a connection to you." Her voice was colder than ice.

I swallowed hard and told myself that was to be expected. I'd wanted him to hate me and I had succeeded. "I understand but something important has come up and I need to get in touch with him."

"You've hurt him enough. He's finally starting to live and is even dating. Let him move on with his life."

I didn't hear the rest of it. Two months and he had already found someone? My chest felt as if it had been ripped open and someone was poking my heart with the tip of a sword, going deeper each time.

I had so many questions that I could not ask because they were none of my business. When I left Alex and divorced him, I had forfeited the right to ask any questions.

But I wondered internally. Did he miss me? Did he think of me at all or had he moved on immediately? Had he suffered as I had or was he thinking that divorce was the best thing that had happened to us? Was he happy to have his old life back?

"There's something I really need to talk to him about. Our marriage is over. This is not what this is about."

Her sharp inhale sounded over the phone. "How do I know that? You've turned out to be a cheat, Charlotte. I think you're just saying that because you've realized what a good deal you had with Alex. Well it's over now. You can't heap whatever issues you have onto Alex. Deal with them yourself."

"Please. It's important," I insisted, tears flooding my face.

"I don't believe you and neither will he," she said.

"Can you just tell him and let him decide," I said, clinging to the belief that I knew Alex. He was a fair person and even though as his mother said, he did not want to hear from me, he would listen.

"I will. If he doesn't get back to you, fill in the blanks for yourself," she said and disconnected the call.

I felt as though a weight had been lifted from my shoulders after making that call. I got up and proceeded to my small kitchen to prepare dinner. I even whistled as I cooked.

Having Alex in my life, even as my baby's daddy and nothing else would be enough. It would give me the security of knowing that if anything happened to me my baby would have a home.

I allowed myself to dream about the future. About Alex coming to pick up our baby to spend a weekend with him. A little boy who looked exactly like him. And suddenly, what lay ahead did not seem as frightening. Not with Alex in our baby's life.

ALEX

Two Years Later

I stood at the periphery of my own party, thrown for me by my father to celebrate the fact that I had officially become a partner. I should have been pleased and proud that my hard work had paid off.

But I hadn't worked for sixteen hours every day including weekends to make partner. I'd done it to exorcise my demons. To forget. It had worked. Now, I could think about Charlotte without bursting into tears like a child. I could revisit the past and search for clues while remaining emotionally detached.

The last two years have been the hardest of my life. I'd accomplished a lot professionally. I'd sat for my Bar exams and passed. I'd applied for and been accepted into various legal organizations that sat well on my resume.

The other parts of my life had stayed stagnant. I thought about Charlotte every day and in odd moments wondered what she was doing. Was she happy? On bad days I wondered if I had even known her.

On good days, I thought there was another explanation for what had happened and then immediately chastised myself for refusing to accept facts. After Charlotte left me and I returned to New York, I'd spent the next six months bawling like a child at night.

I couldn't understand how my life had gotten so pathetic. My wife had left me, I was living at my parents' house and I was working for my father.

"You look like you're having fun," Richard, my brother-in-law said, sidling up to me.

"I'm okay really," I said. "Just thoughtful."

"Congratulations," Richard said. "You've worked hard for it."

"I had no other responsibilities."

He was silent for a moment. "Can I give you some advice, brother to brother?"

"No."

"Look at her," he said, ignoring my response. "She's perfect. She understands our lifestyle and she's been throwing hints at you for two years."

"Hints that I choose to ignore because I'm not interested," I snapped. Abigail did nothing for me. She never had.

"What are you waiting for?" Richard said. "She's gone bro, and from what you told me, she's not going to come back. Move on. Live."

My lungs constricted, making it hard to breathe. I knew that Richard spoke the truth. But it was a truth that I wasn't ready to face. Not even after two years.

"Give her a chance. See how it works out," Richard said.

As though sensing that we were talking about her, Abigail strolled towards us. It wasn't her looks that were the problem. She had dark silky hair that fell to her shoulders and a slim nice enough figure.

Another man would have described her as sexy. Not me. No woman could capture my interest. Unless she was Chaz. I hated the idea, but I couldn't stop how I felt. What man wanted to still be hung up over a woman who had left him for another man?

I hated that I still loved her but I didn't know how to not be in love with her. I didn't know how to move on. I'd wished more times than I could count that there was a button that you pressed when you didn't want to have feelings for someone any more. A stop button.

Abigail reached me and kissed my cheek. She wore a floral scent that strangely reminded me of Charlotte's perfume and it made me feel sad.

"Hi, you look so handsome and mysterious standing here," she said. "Do you want to dance?"

I shook my head. "I'm good."

"It's a party for goodness sake," she said with a laugh.

I was very tempted to walk out of the ballroom where the party was being held and go home.

"I've irritated you," Abigail said, narrowing her eyes at me. "I'm sorry. I didn't mean to but it pains me to see you still so sad."

"I'm fine and thanks for caring. I was actually thinking that I need to move out of my parents' house." I hadn't been thinking about it actively but after voicing it, I realized that I really did need to get my own place.

"Really? That's awesome and I can help with that. I have a friend who sells houses. Shall I call her?"

"Sure," I said, glad that we had switched topics.

"What kind of place do you want?" she asked.

"An apartment." A house would remind me of the life that I'd had with Charlotte. Sometimes it seemed to far removed from my reality that I wondered if it had really happened.

Abigail and I discussed what kind of features I wanted in the apartment and I really got into it. Excitement seeped into me. I couldn't remember the last time I'd felt excited over anything.

"You know, I've never given up on you," she said when there was a lull in the conversation.

I knew then how a gazelle felt when it was hunted.

"We would be great together," she said softly.

I turned to face her. I owed her the truth. "I'm not capable of loving another woman. That part of my life is done."

"I know. I'm not looking for love Alex. Just companionship," she said, meeting my gaze.

I thought of the empty nights that waited for me every evening. The loneliness that came from having no one to share my life with. Abigail's proposal sounded so uncomplicated. Unlike what I felt for Chaz.

She was pretty too and I didn't dislike her company. We'd been friends for a long time. Maybe Abigail was what I needed to move on. To start living again. I couldn't spend the rest of my life nursing a broken heart.

The more I thought about it, the more the idea of dating Abigail became less repulsive. She knew my past and I'd been honest about my emotional state. And she still wanted us to get together.

She wanted companionship. And I wanted to forget Chaz.

"Hey, stop being so serious. We'll just hang out together... maybe have some fun," she said and that was the final push that I needed.

All right, it would be just sex. Nothing like what I had with Charlotte.

ALEX

My phone vibrated with a call as I prepared to leave the hotel in Cleveland for the airport. Being in Ohio had been torturous. It was too near to where I'd left my heart. The previous day, as I'd been driven from the airport to the hotel, I'd kept searching for Charlotte's face.

I knew that she had left the state and gone to start a new life elsewhere, but my brain associated Ohio with Charlotte. Life had been tough then and a real struggle, but it was the period in my life when I'd been the happiest.

I glanced at the caller. It was a new number. I sat back on the bed and answered it. It turned out to be one of the guys I'd met at the legal conference calling to ensure that he'd gotten the correct number. Like me, Andrew worked for his family firm and we'd bonded and agreed to hook up when he was in New York or I was in Maine.

Just as I disconnected the call, another call came in. This time, it was from Abigail. I fought down feelings of irritation.

The promise to keep it just sex had only worked for a few days after which Abigail had become clingy and demanding.

It was only a matter of time before we broke up. I didn't want to be called twenty times a day and having all my time being hijacked. I'd known that Abigail loved socializing but the parties and dinners were too much. I missed my quiet evenings at home with Charlotte.

My time with Abigail was definitely up. In fact, it was a mistake. It was not fair to her. I had nothing to give her. I was an empty shell. Even the sex was not exciting or fun. I was just going through the motions.

"Hi Alex, I just wanted to confirm what time your flight is coming in," she said. "I can pick you up and we can go straight to the brunch I told you about at the museum."

"I'm not going to brunch, Abigail," I said.

"But you promised," she whined, sounding like a petulant five-year-old.

"I'm not interested in these social events, Abigail. It's not me. I work hard and at the end of the day, I just want to put my feet up and relax." Like I used to with Charlotte.

I'd been thinking of Charlotte more and more. I knew the reason for that. It was because I was so unhappy. Again, I'd made a wrong decision. Picked the wrong woman. It seemed as if I was doomed as far as women were concerned.

"Don't be such an old man," she snapped. She'd also grown impatient with me. We were just wrong for each other and one of us needed to put a stop to it.

This had gone on far enough. "We need to talk."

Something in my voice warned her that whatever I wanted to talk about was serious.

"We can talk when you get back," she said quickly. "And we don't have to go for brunch. We can relax at home," she said, her voice dripping with sweetness.

That did not entice me. The thought of relaxing with Abigail was a complete turn off. She did not know the meaning of that word. I needed to talk to her and fast, but a glance at my watch told me that I was perilously close to missing my flight.

"I'm sorry, I have to go, but you have to know that this thing we've got going is not working."

"Look, let's talk when you get back, okay," she insisted stubbornly.

Frustrated, I said goodbye and hurried out. I'd already checked out and a car was waiting for me outside the hotel to take me to the airport.

"It's going to be a close call," the cab driver said. He was right.

"Just try your best."

I glanced out as we headed to the airport. The world was so big and at times I wondered where Charlotte and her boyfriend had made their home. I could think of her and her lover without feeling like someone was stabbing me repeatedly.

One thing gave me satisfaction whenever I thought about them together. They were not married. I'd not signed the divorce papers and the time had elapsed. If Charlotte wanted to divorce me, we would have to begin the process again.

I found comfort in the fact that I was still her legal husband. It was petty but it made me feel damn good.

We made it to the airport a few minutes before the flight. I ran across the terminal but when I got to my gate, it was already closed. I fisted my hand and let out a string of curses. I really didn't want to spend an unnecessary night in Ohio. It had too many painful memories.

I decided to rent a car and drive back. The idea grew more appealing as I walked across the airport to the car rental offices. A long drive would give me a chance to ponder things. Figure out my next move.

Fifteen minutes later, I was driving the rental car out of the airport and headed to the highway. I'd sent a text to Abigail letting her know that I'd be home the next day and we must finish our 'talk' then. Even messaging her had brought out feelings of resentment. I was tired of owing her an explanation.

I'd hoped that working with my father would bridge the gap between us but it hadn't and I knew that was my fault. I hadn't been able to forget the threats that he had issued that had made Charlotte and me have to abandon our dreams to live together in New York.

Maybe then, she would not have left me. But that was fucked up thinking. I couldn't blame my father for Charlotte leaving me. That had been squarely on Charlotte.

After driving for close to four hours, I was nearly crossing into Pennsylvania for the short drive to New York. It was close to five in the evening and I was starving. I got off the highway and followed the directions to a small town called Woodfield.

I spotted a diner on the edge of town. I parked the rental car in the parking lot and headed inside.

CHARLOTTE

"Daisy, can you cover for Lulu for a few minutes. She has to dash home and check on her boy. He wasn't feeling well," Hannah said.

She was the owner and manager of the diner and was particularly kind to us single mothers as she had raised her son alone until she found love in her later years.

"Sure," I said.

"Don't bother changing, they all know you're a chef anyway," she said.

I washed my hands and left the kitchen. Four to seven were our busy hours when everyone in town seemed to come for their dinner. We were also pretty close to the highway and we usually got quite a lot of out-of-town customers.

I knew how lucky I was to still be able to do a job I loved and provide for my son. My vision had deteriorated further and I'd been forced to let Hannah know but she'd been adamant that I continue working.

My job gave Kayden and me, a pretty comfortable lifestyle, for which I was grateful. For more than a year, my vision had not deteriorated further and I clung to the hope that it wouldn't for many more years. Every day, week, month was a gift to spend more time with my son, raising and loving him.

I stepped into the diner and Hannah pointed me to a lone diner with his back to me seated at a booth at the corner. "He hasn't been served yet."

I didn't bother with a pen and notebook to jot down the order as our menu was ingrained in my memory. As I approached him, something about the way he sat and the back of his head reminded me of someone I knew.

As I got near, he turned his head and our gazes caught. I grinded to a halt and clamped down a cry with a hand to my mouth. I blinked rapidly sure that my eyes were playing tricks on me.

Alex. I rubbed my eyes and when I looked again, I was sure. I forced my legs to move. He stood up and stared. He seemed just as shocked to see me.

"Chaz?" he gasped.

My heart melted. I'd not heard that name in more than two years. I moved even closer so that I could see his features better. He looked a little different. His features had hardened.

"Alex," I said.

"I can't believe it's you." He looked away and then swung his gaze back to me as if he expected me to disappear at any moment.

He wasn't wrong. If I could have run, I would have. As the initial shock wore off, my brain scrambled to come up with a plan.

Alex sat back down. I didn't know what to say or do. A million thoughts crowded my brain, top of which was Kayden. I recalled the conversation I'd had with Alex's mother. It was ingrained in my brain.

I'd told her to pass on the message that I urgently needed to speak to Alex. He had ignored me. That memory hardened my heart.

He was not the Alex I thought I knew. This was a man who had rejected me when I really needed him. In essence, he had rejected his son.

"How have you been?" he asked.

"Good," I said briskly, now determined to get him out of my life. "What can I get you?" I handed him the menu.

He opened it and stared at it for the longest time as if he couldn't decide what he wanted to eat.

"How about the day's special?"

"Sure. That would be good."

I took the menu and as I did so, our fingers brushed and sparks leaped from his hand to mine. I snatched my hand away and hurriedly left. I gave my order to Hannah who passed it onto the Chef.

I served a couple and two other people, all the while keeping an eye on Alex. Though I couldn't see him clearly, I could see that he had not moved from his position. Panic filled me as I thought about Kayden. Alex didn't know that he was a dad.

Kayden was a year and three months old and he was a carbon copy of his father. Same sandy colored hair that was a dead giveaway. His dad's cobalt blue eyes and traits that reminded me of Alex all the time.

Even at fifteen months he had a sense of humor. Kayden was an easy child and for that I was grateful. It was easy to make him laugh and when he was sad or he cried, it was never for long.

When Alex's dinner was ready, I carried it to him. I prayed and held my breath that after he ate, like any other out of town customers, he would eat his food and leave.

"Thank you," he said, when I placed his dinner in front of him.

I was relieved when he didn't say anything else. I walked away and continued working. When he was finished with his food, I hurriedly cleared his table. He paid for his dinner and then looked up at me.

"Charlotte, can we talk?"

I felt as if I had been punched in the stomach. I'd been sure that he would leave my life as quickly as he had appeared. That he would accept that we had both moved on with our lives.

"I don't think we have anything to talk about," I mumbled.

His eyes flashed as he narrowed them. "You don't think we have something to talk about after you signed divorce papers and left me without a warning?"

I glanced around us and noticed that his loud, harsh voice had attracted attention. I realized that hoping that Alex would disappear after his dinner was wishful thinking. I considered running away, as I had that first time.

But this time I was not alone. I had Kayden and leaving would require planning. I couldn't just take off with a fifteen-month baby. I closed my eyes for a few seconds. As far as he knew, there was someone in my life. If I gave him a few minutes of my time, he would leave.

"Fine, I finish my shift in fifteen minutes. I'll meet you outside."

Thankfully, Lulu came back and I returned to the safety of the kitchen. When my shift was up, I changed into my street clothes and left through the delivery door at the back. I fought the urge to flee but that would be counterproductive.

Alex would possibly just come back the following day. I sucked in a breath and went around to the front of the diner. It was easy to spot the rented sedan with the driver seated in the front.

I went to the passenger seat, opened the door and got in. Alex didn't turn to look at me. He kept his gaze trained somewhere ahead.

"What's his name?" he asked.

CHARLOTTE

Panic seized me by the throat. Did he know about Kayden? All along I'd assumed that Alex showing up was a coincidence. What if it wasn't and he'd had an investigator following me? Nausea rose up my throat.

"Who?"

He turned to look at me. I was taken aback by the anger in his face. "The guy you left me for."

Relief flooded me. I scrambled for a name. "Kayden." I cursed under my breath as soon as I said my son's name.

He looked at me quizzically. "That's sick."

I didn't understand what he meant at first, and then I remembered. He and I had always said that we would name our child Kayden, if it was a boy and Mia, if it was a girl. So now he thought that I had a boyfriend with the same name.

If the matter was not so grave, I'd have laughed. Instead, I stared out the window.

"When did you start seeing him?" he grated out.

God. I hadn't worked out the details of my indiscretion, after all, Alex and I were not supposed to meet again. My anger had dissipated and to be honest a part of me was happy to see him.

It saddened me that he didn't look happy. Whoever he had hooked up with clearly hadn't made him happy. If they had, he would not have been interested in my life.

"I don't think it's important now," I muttered.

A deafening bang ripped through the air and I jumped before I realized it was a fist to the dashboard of the car.

"Don't fucking tell me what's important and what's not," he thundered.

His eyes bulged and angry veins formed across his forehead. I'd never seen him like that in the years we had been together. I cowered in fear.

"I want to go home," I said, my voice trembling.

Then something happened. Alex slumped in his seat, like a balloon that had been popped. "I'm sorry, I didn't mean to frighten you." He covered his face with his hands.

Guilt flooded me. I shouldn't have been frightened. Alex might have rejected me, but I'd brought that on myself. One thing was for sure, he would never hurt me.

He removed his hands from his face and turned the ignition key. "I'll drop you home."

Panic engulfed me. "No," I said. "I'll be fine."

He stared at me, his expression unreadable. "Why? Will it upset Kayden? Just so you know, I don't give a fuck if he gets angry or not. He stole my wife."

I had no response to his outburst. I fastened my seatbelt. I wasn't too worried about Alex seeing Kayden because he was next door with Mrs. Horace who watched him when I worked.

I'd have to go and pick him up first. What I was worried about was Alex finding out where I lived. But hopefully, he would be on his way back to New York soon.

"When are you leaving?" I asked him.

"I planned to stop briefly in Woodfield and be on my way but it's late and I'll spend the night and leave tomorrow morning. Any recommendations on where to spend the night?"

"Yes," I said quickly. I'd have given him my right hand just to get him to go away. "There's a small B&B in town that is pretty decent." I gave him the directions to the B&B and my rented home.

I loved living on the Horace farm though it was no longer a working farm and only Mrs. Horace lived in the big house. She had had the barn converted into a cozy two-bedroom house and it worked out perfectly for the two of us.

Her husband had died years earlier and her only son had moved to West Virginia where his wife was from. By renting the house to me, she got an extra source of income but more importantly something to occupy her by taking care of Kayden.

She was more of a grandma to Kayden than a babysitter and although she spoiled him terribly, she loved him and we in turn loved her. She'd been a real treasure find when I'd needed help. She had even driven me to the hospital when my water broke.

"Here we are," I said to Alex.

He looked at my home with interest. I was proud of it. I'd done a lot to make it homey, starting with a gorgeous garden that ran all the way round the house.

"Thank you," I said, itching to get away.

"You're welcome," he said and then said, "Are you happy, Charlotte?"

I looked away as tears filled my eyes. How could I have been happy without him? Alex had been my whole world.

"Does Kayden make you happy?" he added, his voice harsh with pain.

I swallowed the lump in my throat and smiled. A genuine smile. I gave him a genuine answer. "He does. He makes me very happy."

A flash of pain came to his eyes which in turn made my heart feel like it was tearing to pieces. Afraid I'd say something that I would regret, I quickly opened the car door.

"It was nice to see you." I smiled as one would to someone who once was a dear friend but was now a stranger. "Have a safe journey tomorrow and I wish you all the best."

He stared at me for a few seconds without responding. Then he nodded. "You too."

I banged the door shut and walked up to the house. I stood at the front door and watched his car pull away, then disappear.

Only then did I move, heading to Mrs. Horace's house to fetch Kayden.

ALEX

I'd had a restless night and when I woke up the following day, I realized that I wasn't ready to go home. Seeing Charlotte had awakened all my intense feelings for her. I had hoped that I'd stopped loving her, but it seemed that my love had been hibernating. One look at her and it was all back.

The pain, the love, the desire, the horror.

I hated myself at that moment. What kind of a man was I? She had left me for another man, whom she now lived with and I still could not stay away. Okay, I would say goodbye and then drive away. Go home where I belonged.

I had breakfast in the dining room and then went to the reception to check out. Instead, I found myself extending my stay by two days. To what end, I didn't know, but I needed to know more. Maybe even see this Kayden. After all, I deserved to see the man who had lured my wife away from me.

The man she thought was better than me. I returned to my room and grabbed my car keys. I was already showered and ready for the day, which was a good thing because I wanted to catch Charlotte before she left for work.

I drove to her house, marveling at the turn of events that had made me run into Charlotte. I wasn't hopeful that she and I would get back together. After all she had a man in her life.

I remembered the expression she had worn when I asked her whether she was happy. Jealousy speared through me a second time. There was only one word to describe how she had looked when she answered my question. Blissful.

But I deserved closure. Maybe after this, I would lodge my own divorce proceedings and she and I would be done forever. I needed to forgive and heal but to do that I needed to understand.

I needed to know why. I drove to the farm and stopped outside the barn house. Charlotte's curtains and windows were already open. No surprise there. She had always been an early riser.

I killed the engine and as I got out of the car, the front door flew open and Charlotte strode towards me with an expression of contained anger on her face.

"What are you doing here?" she asked and then continued speaking without giving me a chance to answer. "We said goodbye yesterday." She folded her arms under her chest and her breasts popped out.

To my shame, my cock swelled as memories of our explosive love life came to the forefront of my mind.

Before I could say a word, I caught sight of an older woman hurrying towards us. I had no idea where she had come from, but I assumed there was another house out of sight.

Charlotte followed my gaze. She dropped her hands and smiled at the approaching woman. "Hello Mrs. Horace."

"Good morning," the woman said, throwing a curious glance at me. "I just came to check on you. You're late and I got worried about Kayden. He had a bit of a diaper rash yesterday."

"He's fine. Everything's okay. I'll bring him over in a few."

"Okay," Mrs. Horace said, throwing another glance my way. Charlotte didn't offer an explanation and she had no choice but to turn away and go back the way she had come.

Then something the woman had said hit me.

...I got worried about Kayden. He had a bit of a diaper rash yesterday.

I stared at Charlotte, stunned. "Kayden is a baby?"

She refused to meet my gaze. "Yes. He's my son."

A coldness hit at my core. Who was this person? I thought I knew Charlotte, but clearly not. Why would she lie about having a baby? I didn't understand any of it.

"And you led me to believe he was your boyfriend?"

She bit her lower lip. I instantly recognized it as nervousness. Was her boyfriend hurting her?

"I didn't say it," she said.

"Don't be absurd Charlotte. You're not a seven-year-old. You know that lying by omission is still classified as lying," I snapped.

She did not respond. My chest felt as if it was burning. Jealousy rose up my throat. She had had a baby with another man. I curled my hands into fists. I wished that I'd not stopped at the diner and I had not seen her.

"Are you still with him, the nameless boyfriend you chose over us?"

She shook her head.

I was stunned. "So, he got you pregnant and left you with a baby?"

"Yes."

I wanted to kill him. Lowlife piece of shit! I clenched my fists and kept my voice normal. "You'll be late to work and we need to drop Kayden at Mrs. Horace's." I strode towards the house.

"Wait," Charlotte cried behind me. "You need to leave. Go back to New York to your own life. Leave us alone."

ALEX

But I was already entering the house. I pushed the door open and stepped into the living room. A cute baby boy sat in a play pen chewing on a toy. He looked up at me and his face crumbled as his lower lip shook. Within seconds he was wailing as if someone had hurt him.

Charlotte hurried to him and lifted him from the play pen. She cuddled him to her and he wrapped his small hands around her neck.

My throat constricted painfully as I watched mother and son. Memories swamped me of Charlotte whispering into my ear about how much she wanted to have our baby. How then could she have gone off and had a baby with another man? I didn't understand any of it. Her betrayal was too big. Too hurtful to comprehend.

Kayden looked at his mother with pure adoration in his face. I swallowed a lump in my throat. Having my child look at me like that was something I would never experience.

A little while after Abigail and I started going out, she started talking about us having a baby. Of course, I said no and forcefully too. I didn't want to have a baby with her. Even the idea repelled me.

I watched Charlotte's features soften as she cuddled her son. "It's okay, darling. This is mommy's friend. His name is Alex."

Kayden's response was to wriggle out of his mother's hold until she lowered him to the floor. I stood watching him as he waddled over to his toys and plopped down on the floor.

Charlotte laughed and so did I. The tension evaporated.

"We'll carry your train to Mrs. Horace," she said, bending to pick up Kayden.

He wriggled and tried to get out of her hold. He was going to grow up to be a person who made his own decisions.

"I'll grab the train and the bags." I grabbed the train as well as the diaper bag on the chair and Charlotte's bag. Kayden was another man's son, but I couldn't help wanting to be part of this little family. It needed a man. I could be that man.

"Thanks," she said. Her gait was slow as she moved to the door and I wondered what was wrong with her.

Worry over her health came over me. Questions whirled in my mind as I followed her to Mrs. Horace's house on the other side of the compound. I stared at her back and marveled that I once thought I knew Chaz as intimately as you could know a person.

Only to realize later, just how little of her I really knew. Mrs. Horace must have been looking out the window because when we neared the front door it swung open.

"Good morning, my little angel," she said, reaching out to take Kayden from Charlotte.

Kayden clearly loved her because he raised both hands and shook them as he laughed as if they shared a private joke. Charlotte gave her some last-minute instructions and then we left.

"I just need to close the door," she said when we headed back. She went to her front door, opened it and took a key from the inside lock and closed it. She hid the key under a rug at the front.

"You realize that everyone hides their key under their rugs, right?" I said, my forehead creasing into a deep frown, as I held the passenger door open for her.

She laughed. "I've never given it any thought. Come to think of it, that's dumb."

"I guess you'll be fine. You live in a small town."

As she entered the car, her sweet musky scent wafted up my nostrils and memories swamped me. As if by the click of a button, an image of a naked Charlotte sprawled on the bed, came to my mind. I immediately grew hard as her sounds of pleasure filled my ears.

"It's safe to close the door now," she said.

"Very funny." I was glad she couldn't read my thoughts. She would think that I was perverted.

She had dumped me for another man and had had his baby and there I was wanting to have sex with her. The memories refused to leave my mind. I rearranged my pants so that she couldn't see my hard on.

In the car, all I could think about was how special and out of this world sex had been with Charlotte. Sex with Abigail was like relieving a bodily function. You just wanted to get it over and done with, fast.

Awareness lit up my skin at Charlotte's proximity. The last time I'd felt attraction that strong and gripping had been with her. A warning stirred in my brain. This woman had caused me so much pain, anguish and humiliation. I needed to be careful. Charlotte was dangerous and not in a physical way.

The drive to the diner was quiet but I could feel her glances a few times. I came to a stop at the entrance and waited for her to get out.

"What are you doing Alex?" she asked.

"Dropping you off at work," I replied pleasantly.

"You know what I mean," she snapped. "When are you going home?"

"I'm not sure. I like it here and I'm enjoying catching up with an old friend."

She stared at me and then without another word, she left the car. Only when she was walking did she look back to shout 'thank you'. I grinned and waved.

The day stretched out before me but I had an idea of how I wanted to spend my day. I drove back to Charlotte's place, and carried my laptop into her house. I placed it on the small kitchen table, rolled up my sleeves and got to work.

I started with the kitchen. The experience of living alone had done wonders for my housekeeping skills. It took fifteen minutes to clean the kitchen and another fifteen to mop the living room and kitchen floors.

I rearranged the living room and opened the windows to bring in some fresh air. The last thing I did was to make myself some coffee, after which I settled at the kitchen table with my laptop to get some work done.

Time went by fast and the next time I checked my watch, it was noon and my stomach was gnawing with hunger. Charlotte's fridge was not promising. I decided to make a grocery run, which I'd intended to anyway, to get stuff for dinner.

For the two days I would be in Woodfield, I would try and help make Charlotte's life easy. Despite the pain she had caused, a part of me still loved her and still wanted to protect her. It was insane and I should have been running in the opposite direction.

She had always had a hold on me from that first moment when I saw her. I wasn't going to fight it. It was only two days after all, and then I would go back to my own life.

I drove to town and parked at the grocery store. There was something homey about the small town. It reminded me of our home in Grantsville. We had known just about everyone in the town.

Charlotte and I had such a good life. How could she have picked lust over that? Clearly, it hadn't been love. You couldn't love someone and then leave them when they got pregnant.

Protective feelings came over me. All I wanted was to take care of her but I knew the danger of that kind of thinking. Despite her gorgeous looks and charming manner, Charlotte was a woman who thought nothing of trampling on someone's heart and leaving without a backward glance.

I had fallen in love with an icy woman. Not that she came across as cold on the surface. On the contrary. She seemed like the warmest, sweetest most loving person. But her actions told a different story. Being the recipient of that, I had no intentions of being hurt again. I was wiser when it came to love.

I picked what I needed for a few dinners, paid and carried them to the rental car. It had been years since I'd felt as carefree as I did at that moment. I even fucking whistled on the drive back to Charlotte's place.

CHARLOTTE

I loved the fifteen-minute walk from work to home. It gave me time to relax and switch from work mode to mommy mode. But I wasn't thinking about Kayden as I walked home. My thoughts were on Alex.

I wanted him to go back to New York but a part of me stupidly hoped he would stay a little longer. With the shock worn off, it felt so good to see him. He was still sexy Alex, even if I couldn't see the details of his face because of my eyesight problems.

But more than that, feelings I'd wrestled with after I left come back to haunt me. I had taken great care to ensure that I left no trail behind but deep down, I'd always hoped that Alex would see through the letter I'd left behind and come find me.

He was a lawyer and a good one at that. Lawyers looked at the evidence and questioned things. The evidence of my love had been there. Our lives had been perfect. Our marriage had been full of laughter and passion. How could he believe that I had fallen in love with someone else?

Why hadn't he realized that it must be something else and given me the benefit of the doubt and looked for me? Alex knew the people to employ to find a person who did not want to be found. If he'd wanted to, he would have found me.

That hurt then and it hurt now. I reached the same conclusion I'd reached two years ago. Alex had been relieved that our marriage was over and I'd given him a way out of it.

Hurt and anger gripped me. I rounded the corner and saw his car. What was he doing in my house? I remembered his comment about the keys. I wanted to march right up to the house but my gait was deliberately slow.

It had taken falling flat on my face to realize that eyesight worked hand in hand with balance. By the time I pushed the front door open, I was boiling with anger. The first thing that struck me when I stepped into the living room was how clean and neat it was.

Not that I was a dirty person but keeping a house in such pristine conditions when you had a toddler and a job, was near impossible. Delicious scents filled the living room, teasing my senses.

I made for the kitchen and that's where I found him, looking at home, as if he lived with us. Pangs of longing came over me. A longing for a life and a dream that I'd left behind.

Alex looked up from his laptop and smiled. "You have very quiet steps. I didn't hear you come in." He forked his fingers through his thick, sandy colored hair.

My fingers itched to do the same. I'd loved touching his hair.

He stood up and then seemed to change his mind, and sat back down again. He grinned at me and I suddenly wished that I'd taken the time to run a comb through my hair before leaving the diner.

I'd not thought of my appearance in a long time. The only man who saw me was my little man and he loved me no matter how I looked. Thinking about Kayden brought reality slamming back into my brain. What was I doing thinking about Alex in that way?

I wanted him to go back to his fancy life and family back in New York. I made myself remember the hurt and rejection I had endured from his family. I tried to hate Alex for it. But my heart refused to cooperate. I couldn't pin that on him.

He wasn't responsible for how his family behaved and he had married me against their wishes. He had never ever made me feel inadequate. In all the years we had been married, he had lavished me with love. But that was the past.

"Hi," he said and then looked around sheepishly. "I made myself at home. I hope you don't mind."

I folded my arms across my chest. "Actually, I do mind. You don't live here Alex. In legal terms, you're trespassing."

He held my gaze and I felt myself drowning in his cobalt blue eyes. "No, I'm not. We're friends Chaz. We'll always be."

As I stared into his eyes, the memory of the first day we met jumped to my mind and I started to giggle. I remembered Alex peering through the train window holding up my bag for me to see.

I had foolishly looked down at my arms as if I had an identical bag and then looked at him, horror stricken when I realized I'd left my bag.

"What?"

"I was just remembering that window on the train when you held up my bag for me to see."

He chuckled. "That was hands down one of the best days of my life." Alex paused for a few seconds before he continued speaking. "And night."

The air became charged with sexual tension in an instant. My body betrayed me by trembling with longing. It had been two years and counting since I'd felt a man's arms around me.

Arousal took over my senses like a sudden storm. Faint warning bells went off in my mind but my body had full control. Alex stood up and as he closed the distance between us, my gaze was drawn to the huge tent at the front of his pants.

That was the last straw for me. He came to me and stood so close that my nipples touched his chest.

"Chaz." He said my name like a moan.

CHARLOTTE

I didn't know who moved first but in the next second, we were in each other's arms, kissing hungrily. Frantic with need, I threaded my fingers through his hair and ran my hands over his back. I couldn't get enough of him.

I moaned into his mouth when his hands cupped my breasts and squeezed them. I almost came when his thumbs found my nipples over the material of my top and thumbed them.

Wetness gushed out of my body, soaking my panties. His hands left my breasts to stroke my back and cup my ass. I'd missed this so much. Reality tried to push its way in. I needed to pick up Kayden from Mrs. Horace.

He would be fine, a louder voice said in my head. Sometimes I was late from work and Mrs. Horace usually didn't mind watching him until I got home.

I lost my train of thought when Alex slipped his hands under my legs and lifted me into the air.

"Where's the bedroom?" he asked, carrying me down the hallway.

"Last room on the right," I said, my eyes glued on his mouth. I couldn't wait to have it on me again.

Alex deposited me on the bed and proceeded to strip off my clothes. His hands trembled as he opened the buttons of my blouse. I raised my body and shrugged it off before laying back on the bed.

I trembled under his intense gaze. "You're so beautiful."

With my help, he pulled down my pants, leaving me with just a bra and panties. Alex got off the bed and proceeded to undress, his gaze never leaving my body. He made me feel like a woman. A sexy woman.

The temptation to touch myself was almost overwhelming but that was not what I needed. I'd had enough of my hands and fingers in the last two years. I wanted his big hands on me. His shirt came off and I drooled as I took in his sculpted chest and massive shoulders.

Next to come off was his pants, leaving him in just his boxers. My pussy tightened at the sight of the tent that his erect cock made. Alex gripped the hem of his boxers and pulled them down. My throat went dry.

I couldn't see the details but I didn't need to. Even after two years, I could visualize his cock as intimately as if I'd seen it the previous day.

I moved to make space for Alex and he came to stretch out next to me. He slipped a hand around my waist and pulled me closer. Our bodies aligned with each other, Alex cradled my cheek and kissed me deeply.

I wrapped my hands around his neck and pressed my nipples against his chest. How had I lived without this for so long? Under his expert hands and mouth, my body came alive. I felt like a different person as Alex kissed me softly at first and then with a hunger that matched my own.

He pulled away from my lips and moved to my neck, trailing delicious kisses down to my breasts. He pushed me back gently to lie on my back and moved in between my legs. As he took a nipple into his mouth, I shamelessly rubbed my aching pussy against his thigh, the friction building a fire in my belly.

I writhed and arched my body as Alex pleasured me with his hands, tongue and body. The ache between my legs grew and when he moved further down, all it took was a single lick to my clit and the orgasm burst out of me.

"Alex."

He licked me until my body grew still, but another hunger was threatening to consume me. A hunger to have his cock inside me. "I want you," I said to him.

"Go on your knees," he growled.

I scrambled to my knees with my breath coming out fast in anticipation of having him back inside me. I envisioned his movements as he arranged himself behind me and caressed my ass. He parted my thighs and then ran his cock up and down my pussy, reminding me of how he had loved teasing me.

A nagging thought grew in my mind. Why had Alex wanted me in that position, facing away from him? Did he hate me so much that he couldn't bear to look at me?

That thought disappeared as soon as the tip of his cock prodded the entrance of my pussy. I closed my eyes as he slowly eased it in. A scream filled the air and it took a moment to realize that it was coming from me.

I wanted to cry from an overload of sensation. I whimpered and fisted the bedding as he pushed his cock deeper and deeper until he filled me completely.

ALEX

I was angry and I was taking it out on Charlotte, slamming my dick into her with a ferociousness that I'd never used before. Anger for what she had done to us consumed me as I pounded into her. Her screams of pleasure filled the air, and her words urging me on served to incense me further.

What right did she have to want me after walking out on me? It was a stupid question to ask because I should have been directing that question to myself. The obvious answer didn't do anything for my anger either.

Her lover had left her and Charlotte was a highly passionate woman. The simple answer of why she was having sex with me was lust, plain and simple. It hurt but I wasn't any better. I wanted her so badly.

It felt incredible to have her inner muscles squeezed around my dick, milking it. My anger dissipated as I lost myself in the sensation of being joined to Charlotte. Sweat dripped down my body as I kept an iron grip on my control, determined to make it last as long as I could.

"Oh God, Alex," Charlotte groaned.

I never thought I would ever hear those words from Charlotte ever again. She was almost coming. My thrusts became sharp quick jabs. Charlotte pushed back against me and then with a sound that was halfway between a scream and a cry, she orgasmed.

I held her in place as her body rocked with convulsions of pleasure. I thrust into her several more times. "Chaz." I groaned her name as my dick swelled and surged before I exploded inside her body.

We were both stunned when it was over. I gently withdrew and we both collapsed on the bed. Charlotte lay with her face buried in the bed and I stared up at the ceiling trying to come to terms with what just happened.

Where did this leave us?

Regret came over me quickly. I shouldn't have had sex with Charlotte. Things were complicated enough between us without throwing sex into the mix, however hot it was.

She was a cheat. She had pretended to be in love with another man, and had most likely been sleeping with both of us at the same time.

Charlotte was the first to move. She sat up and reached for her blouse which she held up to shield her breasts. "I need to go and get Kayden."

"I'll be dressed and gone by the time you get back," I said in a stiff tone that matched hers.

I kept my gaze averted to give her some privacy as she stood up and went to the bathroom. The sound of running water reminded me of the showers we took together that ended up as another sexual session.

A longing for what we had washed over me, leaving me sad and angry. I got up and reached for my boxer briefs. Charlotte left the bathroom and walked out of the room without saying a word to me.

It stung. It wasn't like I didn't have regrets over what had happened, but it was done and there was no going back. I finished dressing, went to the kitchen to pack my laptop into its bag.

I lingered longer than necessary, my heart filled with pain as I came to the decision that it was time to go back home to my own life.

Hanging on to the past had made me extend my stay but there was nothing between us anymore. The damage done in the past had been too great and to be honest, I doubt I could ever forgive Charlotte.

I had stayed with the hope of getting some answers but she had provided me with nothing and I knew she wouldn't. She had spelled everything out in the letter. What more did I need? Maybe closure, and I felt as if I had it now.

I grabbed my bag and headed to the front door. I paused. I couldn't leave without saying anything. I had to say something, even if it was in a note. I sat on the couch and fished out a notebook and pen from my stuff and wrote the note. I read it over once, signed my name and placed it on the empty coffee table.

I felt like a coward but I'd told her I would be gone when she got back. Neither of us was proud of what had just happened. I drove off feeling as if I had once again left my heart with Charlotte. I was a fool.

Back at the B&B, I packed my stuff, checked out and left. I glanced at the town of Woodfield one last time before driving down the road that would take me to the highway and away from Charlotte.

My chest felt as if it was being shredded into pieces. Had Charlotte felt the same way when she left me two years ago? I realized how ridiculous that comparison was.

Charlotte had been leaving to start a new, exciting life with her lover. She had left me behind as well as her best friend and her new family without a backward glance. I wished I could do the same thing but the sadness I felt refused to shift.

Over the years, I'd come to understand why she had decided to start a new life without her sister and best friend. If Amy had known anything, she would have told me and so would Helen. Their honesty and integrity would not have allowed them to be part of such a secret.

At first, we had emailed back and forth, mostly to figure out what had driven Charlotte to do such a thing. Amy had held on to the belief that she'd had a good reason. As soon as I got back, the first thing I would do was to email her to let her know that her worries and fears had been for nothing.

Charlotte was very well and raising a son in a small town surrounded by her new friends. Maybe then Amy would also move on.

Three and a half hours later of nonstop driving and I was home.

ALEX

Despite keeping up with my correspondences when I was in Woodfield, my inbox was still overflowing and I spent all morning returning emails. My dad popped in for a few minutes.

"You look tired son," he said, smiling indulgently.

"I'm fine Dad," I told him. No matter how much we both tried, we never got back the easy friendship we'd enjoyed before.

Trust had been lost and I still couldn't believe that my own father would resort to threats to force me into doing what he and my mother wanted.

"Maybe you should take some time off," he said. "Take Abigail somewhere beautiful. I'm sure that she would love that."

"I'm fine," I said. My cell phone vibrated on my desk and I almost groaned when I saw the caller. "Excuse me," I said to my father gesturing at the phone.

"Sure, go ahead and think about what I just said. We all need to recharge now and then. I'm lucky in that your mother forces me to. You've been at it hard for two years. Take a break."

I nodded impatiently and when he left, I pressed answer, inwardly bracing myself for Abigail's whiny tone. "Hi."

"I can't believe it. I had to hear from your brother-in-law that you were back," she said. "And you've been back for two days!"

Irritation came over me. I loved Richard like a brother, but I disliked how he mouthed off my personal stuff to Abigail.

"Yeah, I was busy," I said, ignoring the annoyance in her voice.

"Can we meet for lunch today?" Abigail said.

It was on the tip of my tongue to say no but Abigail was an item on my list of things to do. Seeing Charlotte had hurt deeply but it had made me confront my way of life and propelled me to want to make changes.

Abigail and I were wasting each other's time. Our breakup was long overdue. I agreed to meet for lunch at the club. I threw myself into work but thoughts of Charlotte kept intruding. I wondered how she and Kayden were faring.

Finally, as I was about to leave for lunch with Abigail, my need to find out overwhelmed me. I did what I had promised not to do. I called Charlotte. I paced my office while I waited for her to answer the call.

When she came on, she sounded rushed. "Hi."

"Hey Chaz, its Alex."

"Oh." She went silent. "I never expected to hear from you."

The sound of Kayden's cry came over the phone.

"Is Kayden okay?" I said.

"He's okay. Look, I have to go. I'm with Mrs. Horace. She got a call from her son. Her daughter-in-law fractured her leg and they need her help," she said, her voice sounding strained.

"What about work? Who will watch Kayden?" I said.

"I'll figure something out. We'll be fine. Bye, thanks for checking on us." She disconnected the call.

If Charlotte lost her job, she and Kayden would be in a lot of trouble. It shouldn't have been my problem but it was. Charlotte was part of my life, whether I liked it or not and so was Kayden. He was a sweet innocent child and he deserved stability in his life. He needed his mom to keep her job.

I was thoughtful in the cab on the way to the club. A solution came to me. Charlotte needed help with Kayden and I had a long vacation due to me. I would take time off and go back to Woodfield. My lunch with Abigail was a great idea.

I wanted to leave things totally settled so there was not an ounce of doubt that we were finished before I left. The past two days had rolled over each other in a stretch of boredom and longing for Chaz, but suddenly, color had been splashed into my life.

I shook my head as I got out of the cab. How dreary was my life that I was excited by the prospect of babysitting? I couldn't wait to leave New York and return to Woodfield.

I would drive down so that Charlotte and I would have a car to move around in. I made plans in my head. My secretary had a son about the same age as Kayden. I would send her to shop for toys for him. I smiled as I imagined his face lighting up when he saw a bunch of toys for him.

"You look pleased with yourself," Abigail said, standing up from her chair to kiss me. "You're late, but I'll assume that you were doing something important."

"I was," I said solemnly and sat down.

Abigail and I stared at each other and for the hundredth time, I asked myself what we were doing together. Maybe she also asked herself the same question.

"How have you been?" I asked her.

"Neglected," she said.

I nodded but I couldn't bring myself to apologize or say nice things. She was right. I had neglected her, but I didn't feel guilty about it. What I felt guilty about was that I had let it go on for so long.

"You don't seem to care," she said.

I met her gaze. "We're not working Abigail and I'm sure you know that too."

A panicky look came over her features. "We are just fine, Alex. We just need to spend more time together."

What was she talking about? We were two people who had made a mistake in thinking they could make it work. We had nothing in common and now, we had reached a point where we had started to grate on each other's nerves.

I shook my head. “I’m done.”

Tears filled her eyes.

“Come on Abigail. This is not like you.”

She sniffed loudly, attracting the attention of other diners. “Don’t make a rush decision,” she said. “Give us a chance. Please.”

“I’m really sorry, but I’m not the man for you, Abigail,” I said as kindly as I could.

CHARLOTTE

Kayden was enjoying the morning sun as I pushed his stroller back home from the grocery store. He was making happy noises and pointing at everything from passing cars to flowers by the sidewalk.

Everything in Kayden's world was perfect and I wanted it to remain so, but it wouldn't be if I lost my job.

I was a beat away from bursting into tears. Who knew how scarce child care was in my small town. It was my third day of staying home from work and as understanding as Hannah was, she was a business owner and she needed a full-time chef at the diner.

Not to mention I needed a job as well to keep a roof over my and Kayden's heads. The skin around my head tightened with tension. Nausea rose up my throat as I sifted through a list of possible babysitters.

I had called all the numbers that Lulu had given me. There was a lady who took on children two streets from mine but she already had four and that was the most she could watch. I had called a daycare but the owner had shut down six months earlier from low business.

I held back a scream of frustration mingled with fear. I thought about Alex. He was Kayden's dad and some of the responsibility was his. But what could he do from New York? Besides I hadn't yet decided when to tell him about Kayden or even whether to tell him.

Before we slept together, I'd more or less decided that I would tell him. Then we'd had sex and he had returned to New York leaving me a stupid note. I had read it so many times, its contents were ingrained in my mind.

Chaz,

It seems as if you and I were cut out to disappear from each other's lives. I'm grateful to have seen you again and met your awesome boy. You're a great mom and Kayden is lucky to have you.

Seeing you has brought me the closure I craved for so many years. I had so many questions and even though I didn't get any answers, it's fine. It doesn't matter now. All that happened is water under the bridge.

I wish you and Kayden well and I know you wish me the same. My number will be at the bottom. Don't ever hesitate to call when you need me. I'll always be there for you and Kayden.

Take care.

After that note, I had been so hurt by his sudden departure that I'd forgotten that I'd planned to tell him about Kayden. I'd felt used and then discarded. Not a good feeling. Then a voice had pointed out that it was the same thing I had done to Alex. Only worse. Much worse.

We had been married and in a ruthless letter, I'd wiped our marriage out like it had never existed in the first place. Sometimes, especially after seeing Alex, I questioned myself on whether I had made a horrible mistake. Done things the wrong way. But I reminded myself I was panicked and didn't want to destroy Alex's life and it was the right choice.

Every time I remembered that having sex with Alex had been what had driven him away, I bowed down my head in shame. What must he have thought of me, throwing myself at him like a woman in heat, which I was. I wished I could turn back the clock. I definitely would not have slept with Alex.

If I hadn't, things would have been different. Maybe Kayden would have finally had his father in his life.

Regrets were a waste of time and no matter how much I rearranged the past, it didn't change the fact that I was about to lose my job and my livelihood.

I rounded a corner and the first thing I saw was an unfamiliar car outside my barn house. The owner was nowhere to be seen and when I saw that the front door was slightly open, my heart galloped in my chest.

There was only one person who could enter my house without my knowledge or permission. Alex. With a lightness in my chest, I pushed the stroller to the front door, pulled it open and entered.

Alex was stretched out on the couch reading a magazine and when he heard the door, he looked up. A smile broke out on his face as he swung his long legs to sit up.

"Hey buddy," he said to Kayden. "Look around Kayden, Christmas has come early."

I finally dragged my eyes from his face to the living room floor. I gasped at the number of toys on the floor. It resembled a children's play area. Kayden had seen the toys too and in his unsuccessful quest to get out of the stroller, he'd started sniffling.

"Okay, I'll let you down," I said to him, glad to have something to do.

I couldn't even pretend to be mad at seeing Alex. All I felt was overwhelming relief to have someone in my corner. Because whatever happened between us, I knew that I could count on Alex. He was my friend, above all things.

We watched Kayden as he toddled over to his toys moving from one to the other and then flash me a toothless grin. His joy made me feel guilty at how few toys I had bought him. But we had needed to be careful with money and kept some for a rainy day.

"He's so happy," I said. "Thank you."

"It was nothing. It's nice to have a chance to do something nice for you and him," he said.

Feeling awkward standing, I plopped down on the couch next to him. "What are you doing here? Not that I'm complaining."

He laughed. He looked so relaxed.

"I'm on vacation and I decided I wanted to spend it here watching Kayden until Mrs. Horace came back," he said. "I'm already checked in at the B & B."

"You can't do that! What about your job?" I said, stunned at what he had done.

“I’ve worked like a dog for the last two years. My father was the one who shooed me out of the building.”

“That’s crazy,” I said. I wanted badly to accept his help but I didn’t want to take advantage of Alex’s kindness. A thought sprouted in my mind. Alex was Kayden’s father even if he didn’t know it.

Besides there was also another advantage to spending time with Alex. It would give me time to study him closely. I knew I could trust him with Kayden. That wasn’t the problem.

I needed to know that I could trust him not to take Kayden away from me when he learned that he was the father. I could just hear his mother telling him how unsuitable I was to raise Kayden.

CHARLOTTE

"Have you ever taken care of a baby?" I asked him, though by my tone, he had already deduced that I would say yes.

Not that I had a lot of options. Actually, I had none and finding Alex waiting for us felt as if I had won the lottery.

"Oh yes. I'm Ryan's favorite uncle," he said.

It took a moment to figure out who Ryan must be. "Oh, that must be Mary and Richard's son. How nice."

"He's a little older than Kayden but I've changed diapers, fed him and a lot of play in between," he said.

"Okay," I said. "You're hired on a trial basis. When do you want to start?" I was so happy and relieved, I wanted to scream.

"I've already started. I'll make dinner," he said.

I laughed at his enthusiasm. "When did you learn how to cook? From what I recall I did all the cooking."

"I had to learn."

The playful mood dissipated as we were both transported to another period before it all got so complicated.

"Let me put the groceries away and get dinner started," he said.

He kissed Kayden on the forehead before grabbing the shopping bags hanging from the stroller. Tears of relief filled by eyes. I dipped my hand into my handbag and pulled out my phone. I texted Hannah and let her know that I would be at work the following morning.

Her reply text came back almost immediately. She sent celebratory emojis and words to the effect that she was relieved to have me back. I popped into the kitchen to help Alex with dinner but he more or less chased me out.

I returned to the living room and plopped down on the floor to play with Kayden. With the sound of cooking in the background and myself and Kayden playing with toys, it was the kind of scene I had dreamed of years earlier and I'd almost let myself forgot what had derailed those dreams.

At six, I warmed Kayden's food and carried him clutching a teddy bear to the high chair at the small dining area at the far end of the living room. Alex joined us and watched as I fed him.

"He's a good eater," he said.

"Kayden's an all-round fussless boy," I said and kissed his cheek smeared with sauce.

We chatted easily, returning to our old friendship where we never ran out of things to talk about. After Kayden's dinner,

Alex helped me with washing him and then after a sippy cup of milk, we tucked him into bed.

"Does he like bedtime stories?" Alex asked me, eyeing a pile of story books that I'd bought when he was a baby with the plan that we would be reading together. Reading was tough for me and a strain but I didn't want to tell Alex that.

"He does." Every kid liked having someone read them a story.

"Do you mind if I read to him?"

Emotion rose up my throat. "Please do."

Kayden watched Alex's movements from his crib. "Boo," he said pointing at the books.

"That's right. You get a story tonight, my love," I said.

Alex turned and showed me the cover of the book. "Is this okay?"

I couldn't see a thing. "It's fine."

He plopped down on a rug beside the crib and showed Kayden the cover. Then he started reading. I sat on the floor and allowed myself to relax to Alex's deep soothing voice.

He acted out the character's voices, making us giggle, though I doubt Kayden knew why he was laughing. He probably just found the sounds that Alex was making funny.

I only realized after ten minutes that Alex's voice had gone very low. I peered into the crib and saw that Kayden was asleep. "He's out," I said to Alex.

We both went to the crib and looked down at Kayden's peaceful sweet face. I tucked the blanket around him and kissed his forehead, inhaling his sweet baby smells.

"You're very lucky," Alex whispered.

Emotion expanded my chest to almost painful proportions. I bit my lower lip to stop myself from blurting out the truth. I hated to doubt him but It was too risky to tell Alex now. I needed to know whether he was still the same Alex who could stand up to the right thing and to his parents.

I had woken up drenched in sweat plagued by nightmares of them taking Kayden away from me. I could survive many things, including the loss of my eyesight but not losing my son.

He was the reason why I kept moving forward even when things got tough.

ALEX

"I emailed Amy and told her that I'd reconnected with you," I said to Charlotte as we sipped an after-dinner glass of wine.

She went still before swinging her gaze to me. "You kept in contact with her?"

"Yes, we emailed back and forth a few times. She insisted from the first day you left that there was a mistake. That you must have had a reason for doing what you did. She wasn't ready to see the truth. Even now. She said she has to hear it from your mouth to believe it." I shrugged.

Charlotte didn't say a word. It was an uncomfortable topic for both of us but mostly for Chaz. She had sacrificed so much for him and then he'd left her. "What was his name?"

She gazed at me in confusion. "Who?"

"The guy you left me for," I said, my chest burning with a mixture of pain and jealousy.

"It doesn't matter now," she said.

There was a perverse side of me that wanted to know everything. What did he look like? What had she seen in him that had made her leave our perfect life and run away with him? Had he been a better lover than me?

That last thought made me feel as if acid had been poured down my throat.

"How are your parents?" she asked.

"They are well," I said. "Mother has mellowed since she became a grandmother."

"I can't imagine your mother as a grandmother," she said. "Or mellowed."

I searched her face and saw no traces of bitterness. She had every right to be after the way my family had treated her. They had rejected her when she had been so looking forward to being a part of a family.

I had toyed with that idea especially when Amy had insisted that there had to be another reason why she had left. That maybe she had left because of my family but that had made no sense. We had gotten married and things had been wonderful, more so when Chaz found her family.

There had been no other reason for her leaving except for the one she had expressed.

"Helen and her family are well too," I said. As with Amy, Helen and I exchanged sporadic emails. I hadn't told her the news yet.

"I miss them," she said, her voice thick with emotion.

"I understood why you didn't want contact with me but why them? Why lose your family and friends too?"

"Can we not talk about the past?" she asked after a moment. "Please?"

The anguish in her eyes was unmistakable. She had paid the price with her own heartbreak. Maybe it was time to permanently say goodbye to the past.

"It's getting late." Charlotte got up and carried the wine glasses to the kitchen.

When she returned, I was already on my feet. "What time should I come tomorrow morning?"

"Is ten thirty too early for you? Hannah, that's my boss, reduced my hours and I'll be starting work at eleven."

"Ten thirty is a breeze. I'm a lawyer, remember? We're used to starting work at crazy hours."

She walked me out to the car and I noticed when we were outside that she was moving even slower than usual. As though she was scared of falling.

"Are you okay?" I asked her.

"Yes, I'm fine," she said.

"If you like, you can use my car to go to work tomorrow morning," I said to her.

"I'm not comfortable driving these days," she said. "And I enjoy the walk to work and back home. It's my 'me time'."

There were so many things about Charlotte that didn't add up. She had loved driving in the past. How could that have changed in two years? I felt as if I was with her identical twin.

She lowered her gaze before looking at me again. "I can't tell you how grateful I am. I was in a bit of a fix and worried sick about losing my job. Thank you, Alex. I don't deserve your kindness."

Her words made my emotions rise to the surface. "You're welcome." I kissed her cheek. "I'll see you tomorrow."

There was one thing about Charlotte that had not changed. Her scent. I could be blindfolded and tell when Charlotte walked into a room. Her floral, musky scent followed me inside the car.

I waved goodbye and drove off, secure in the knowledge that I would be seeing her the following day. I whistled as I drove, something I never did back home in New York.

It was pathetic that the only woman who made me happy was the one who had dumped me for another man. Just knowing that I was easing her worries by helping her out made me feel ten feet tall.

I'd forgotten to mention to Charlotte that Amy had said she would surprise her one of these days. I didn't hold out much hope though. Amy had gone to work for her family's chain of restaurants in Cleveland after completing her culinary degree. I hoped that she would make it to come visit.

From what I'd seen of Charlotte's life, she needed her old friends.

Despite Woodfield having the usual small-town warmth, she didn't have particularly close friends. She hadn't mentioned anyone and no one had come to visit her and Kayden.

It was a choice she had made. She was a naturally warm person and she easily made friends but clearly, she had decided to keep people at arm's length. I had more questions now than when she left me two years ago.

I waved at the night receptionist at the B&B and went up to my room on the first floor. Maybe with time, a few of my answers would be answered. Most of them had to do with the mysterious man who had broken her heart and whom Charlotte still protected.

What kind of man fathered a child and walked away without looking back?

CHARLOTTE

There was so much to process after Alex left.

I returned to the house and poured myself a glass of wine. The tears I'd fought when he told me about Amy rose to the surface. She had known that the story I gave about meeting someone else was bull.

There was someone on the planet who knew me. Like really knew me. Knowing that made me feel special and guilty. I smiled through my tears. Still, I wasn't sure how I felt about Amy and me reconnecting. She would know that Kayden was Alex's son when she laid her eyes on him.

I wasn't ready for anyone to know about Kayden's paternity before I decided on the time to tell Alex.

Then there was Alex himself. How would I manage to be in such close proximity with him and still resist him? All evening, as we tucked Kayden to bed and had dinner, I'd been fixated on his perfect lips and his massive hands.

My panties had been soaked all evening as I watched him. Images of us in bed less than a week earlier tortured me. If only I had control of how my body reacted to Alex. If he had so much as touched me, I'd have fallen into his arms and bed.

It was as if he had a spell on me. I became his, with a mere touch. The power Alex had over me was frightening. I didn't want to even dream or hope that we could love each other again. I know how much pain I caused him and when he learned that Kayden was his son, that pain would triple.

I pushed away the disturbing thoughts. Alex was still too new in our lives. I wasn't ready to think about that.

After my glass of wine, I felt relaxed enough to go to bed. I rinsed my glass, turned off the lights and checked on Kayden. My son did everything else well, except sleeping. He was a restless sleeper.

I grinned as I tried to tuck a stray leg under the covers again. Not that there was any use. I was sure that ten minutes later, the covers would be on the edge of the crib and his body uncovered.

I kissed him softly and padded out of his room.

Minutes later, I was in bed too, thoughts of the future swirling in my mind. The fear that usually accompanied my worries of the future was gone. I hoped that Alex would prove to still be trustworthy and somewhere down the line, I could tell him about Kayden.

It felt good to know that my son's dad was now in his life even if it was on a temporary basis. I drifted off to sleep with a smile on my face.

~

At ten thirty, just as I tucked Kayden in the crib for his morning nap, I heard the sound of a car outside. Alex. I smiled, remembering how particular he used to be about time.

"Have a good day my little darling," I whispered to an already sleeping Kayden and tiptoed out.

I flung the front door open just as Alex was getting out of his car. Warmth spread across my chest as Alex strode towards me with a smile that could only be described as devastatingly sexy.

My heart pounded hard as he finally came to a halt before me, inches from my face. I swallowed hard.

"Morning," he said.

My eyes remained glued to his lips and all I could think about was how it would feel to taste him. Alex had a coffee scent in his mouth twenty-four seven. I wondered if that had changed.

"Morning," I finally said.

"May I come in?" he teased.

"Yes of course." I jumped to one side, ashamed at being caught staring. I was sure he could read the filthy thoughts going through my mind. "Coffee?" I asked after I shut the front door.

"Coffee would be great."

God, he smelled good. Edible. I led the way to the kitchen and I found myself swaying my hips just a bit more than usual.

"I've just put Kayden down for his nap," I said while pouring Alex some coffee. "He sleeps for about an hour and a half. I've stuck his schedule on the fridge." I was rambling.

"We'll be fine, don't worry," he said.

I liked his reassuring quiet confidence. I let out a breath and sipped my coffee. "The diapers are on the changing table in his room. I can't think of anything else but he's an easy kid."

"And you're only a phone call away," he said, pointing at phone numbers I'd stuck on the fridge.

Both were for the diner. I blushed at how psychotic I must have appeared to Alex. "That's just in case I don't hear my cell phone ringing."

"I doubt that very much," he said.

I drained the last of my coffee and carried my cup to the sink. "I have to go. Thanks for doing this."

I was a second away from crying.

He waved me away. "You're welcome. It can't be easy to be a single mom."

With a shaky smile, I turned to leave. I peered at Kayden one more time, grabbed my handbag from my room and moved to the front door where Alex was waiting for me.

"Are you sure you don't want to use my car?" he asked.

"No, I'm fine. Thanks."

CHARLOTTE

I should have been worried to have left my son with my ex-husband, whose capabilities of minding a toddler were questionable, but I wasn't. I was at peace while I chopped up vegetables and started the stews for the lunch time special.

As I worked, I experienced one of those moments of unexplained happiness and gratitude for my life. I loved my job. I enjoyed the creations we prepared which our customers enjoyed.

It was humbling to know that we were one of the most successful establishments in town and that people came from far and wide to eat at the diner. As I worked, my mind drifted to Alex and Kayden and a nice feeling swept over me.

Father and son were finally together and getting to know each other. As with all days in the diner, the day passed by in a whirlwind of activity, except for a small lull at four thirty. I texted Alex and he responded immediately, letting me know that they were fine.

Half an hour before my shift was to end, Lulu came to the kitchen as I was washing up my knives to let me know that someone was asking after me. Curious, I rinsed them off and followed her to the seating area.

As soon as I saw the silky red hair, I clamped a hand to my mouth and stifled a scream. Amy. She was facing away from me and when I got closer and stopped by her side, she glanced up and her eyes flooded with tears.

With a cry, she shot to her feet and grabbed me into a hug. We clung to each other, and just sobbed. No words could express the joy I felt at seeing my best friend again.

"I should punch you," she said when we finally drew apart.

"I deserve it," I said, sliding into the opposite seat. I wiped away my tears with the back of my hand and squinted as I peered into Amy's face.

She had kept one of my hands between hers and still hadn't let go. "I'm too happy to be mad though. I thought I'd never see you again. You just disappeared into thin air."

"I'm truly sorry," I said. "At the time, it seemed like the only option I had."

She cocked her head to one side. "You haven't changed much."

"Neither have you. Tell me everything," I said. "Are you married?"

A glint came into her eyes. "About to." She raised her left hand to reveal a gorgeous engagement ring, sparkling with diamonds. "We found each other in time. I'm getting married in two weeks."

"Oh wow!" I said. "Congratulations! That's so pretty. What's his name?"

"Ben Fox. He's great and I can't wait for you to meet him," she said.

Silence enveloped us as we stared at each other. The elephant between us grew bigger until Amy spoke.

"What happened Charlotte? Why did you run away? What were you running away from?"

A lump formed in my throat and I couldn't speak. I'd never thought of what I'd done as running away but that's what it had been. I'd been running away from my future life, not wanting to burden Alex or my friends with my problem. But they had found me now.

I had managed to fool Alex with hints that my 'boyfriend' had broken my heart but that wouldn't work with Amy. She knew me too well and would see through the bullshit.

I swallowed hard. "I don't know where to start."

"Start at the beginning," she said, in a voice that lacked judgement, only love.

"Okay," I said and started by telling her about my first visit to the eye doctor and the devastating results that I got.

"Oh no that's terrible," Amy said. "You haven't lost all your vision though?"

I shook my head and shivered. "Not yet. There hasn't been any change for months. I'm praying it stays that way."

"I didn't want to be a burden to Alex after everything he had sacrificed for me. Also I didn't want that he would have to take care of a disabled wife when he was so young" My voice was cracking.

Amy waited for me to regain my composure.

"So I run and wrote letters to all of you."

"I knew it!" Amy said. "I knew that story was bullshit as soon as Alex told me. But Charlotte, why would you think you'd be a burden. Illness is not a choice."

I bowed my head. How could I explain it in a way she would understand?

"Ah, I think I'm beginning to see where this is going," Amy said quietly. "You thought it was a punishment because of his family."

I fought to keep my tears inside my eyes but lost the battle and they dropped down my cheeks. I nodded.

"That's just like you Char to blame yourself for things which are out of your control. I'm so sorry I didn't look for you."

I laughed amid my tears. "You can't blame yourself for something like that. I didn't want to be found. I needed a new life from everyone I knew," I said. "Now that I think about it, my thinking might have been slightly flawed."

"Your thinking was fucked up," Amy said in her blunt way.

I was glad that she hadn't changed as her honesty was one of the traits that I loved and appreciated about her. Amy simply didn't know how to sugar coat.

Her features softened. "Alex told me that you have a little boy."

"Yeah." I fidgeted in my seat. "His name is Kayden and he's one year and three months old." I waited for the pin to drop.

When it did, Amy's eyes grew so big, I thought they would fall off.

"Oh my God!" she said. "Kayden is Alex's son."

I nodded. "Correct."

She narrowed her eyes and leaned forward on the table. "He doesn't know, does he?"

"No." Saying it aloud felt so wrong.

"Oh Char, you can't do that," Amy said. "He deserves to know."

"I know he does. I tried calling but he'd changed numbers. Then I called his mom and left a message with her that Alex should call me urgently. He didn't."

"Did it occur to you that she might not have passed on the message?"

"Now it has but then it did not," I said.

We were both silent again.

"What about now?" she asked.

"I'll will tell him but not just yet. I have to know that I can trust his family. What if they take Kayden away from me? They're lawyers, they could attempt to prove that I'm an unfit mother because of my medical issues, especially if they worsen" I said.

"Oh Char," Amy said and covered my hand with hers, and I knew she understood.

"Do you want to meet Kayden? How long are you in town for?"

She laughed. "Of course, I would. I'm going back tomorrow. How big is your house? I've not booked a B&B?"

"Big enough. I have a spare bedroom." Excitement coursed through me as we left the diner hand in hand. I was so happy, I wanted to cry.

"I love it here," Amy said as she unlocked her car.

"It's become home for us," I said and opened the passenger door. "Tell me about Ben," I said, desperate for a less emotionally heavy topic of conversation.

"He is sexy!" Amy declared. "And he has a heart to match. I can't wait for you to meet. Hey. Will you be my maid of honor? I'll happily boot my current maid of honor. That has always been your spot."

My chest filled with unshed tears. "Oh Amy. I wish I could say yes but particularly now I'm the most unsuitable maid of honor. With my eyesight loss not only will I trip on your train, I'll take you down with me. Can I just be a guest? Less pressure and all?"

She held my gaze and nodded. "Okay. Just keep in mind that it will be a whole weekend. In a lodge. It's going to be epic."

CHARLOTTE

"How can he not know?" Amy asked me after we'd tucked Kayden in and were back in the living room.

We had come home to find Alex and Kayden eating dinner. Amy had made silly faces and wormed herself into Kayden's heart. After our dinner, Alex had left and then it was just Amy and me catching up.

"He believed I had someone else and that someone dumped me, and I just kept that thought rolling since" I said and sipped my glass of wine.

Amy shook her head. "Men really are dumb."

"I don't blame him. That letter was pretty convincing," I said.

"I didn't buy it even then," Amy said.

I looked at her fondly. "No you didn't."

"He's a carbon copy of Alex," Amy said. "Even a blind per—"

I had to laugh. Amy looked so comically horrified. "Hey, relax, its fine. I know what you mean though. I can barely see and even I see the resemblance."

"Poor Alex," she said.

"Why poor Alex?"

"He never did get over you. Time just stood still for him. He's as in love with you now as he was then," Amy said.

"I don't think so," I said but I was remembering the night of crazy unbridled passion we had shared. "Too much has happened between us."

"You really are stupid when it comes to men, you know that?" Amy said.

"And you're a romantic," I said.

"What about you, do you still love him?"

"I don't want to think like that. I've forged a life for myself and Kayden here. We're happy and settled. I don't want any upheavals."

"And rejections," Amy said.

Pain gripped me, squeezing my heart like a vise. Being rejected by one's in-laws was an experience I never wanted to go through again. I felt sorry for the naïve version of me that I'd been.

I'd so looked forward to being part of a family. I'd believed that as long as I was a decent human being, they would accept me. Clearly things in New York worked differently and what mattered was who your family is.

"Don't forget that Alex picked you over being coerced by his parents. With the type of parents he has I thought that made him a pretty solid guy," Amy said.

"He was, and still is, I guess. But can you imagine living with that on your shoulders? Knowing that the reason that your husband doesn't see his family is because of you?" I shuddered.

"Sometimes you have to take a stand in life, and that's what Alex did," Amy said.

There was one person we had not talked about and I was dying to know how she was. "Did you keep in touch with Helen?" I held my breath as I waited for her answer.

She shook her head. "I tried but we sort of drifted apart with the person we had in common gone."

I had been so excited to finally have a sister but our time together had turned out to be short lived.

"She was devastated when you left. She wasn't sure what to believe. She hadn't known you long enough like I had."

My chest ached as I imagined the hurt she must have felt.

"Will you reach out to her?" Amy said.

I had thought about that a lot and it had been fifty-fifty. But knowing how badly I had hurt her, it wasn't fair to bulldoze my way into her life again. The kind thing to do was to leave her and her family alone. "I don't know."

We talked as easily as we had two years ago. No topic was too painful or too uncomfortable to talk about. We stayed up until midnight and by then we were both yawning every five minutes.

Instead of Amy sleeping in the spare room, we shared my bed like we used to back in college on the nights we went out together and staggered to my place or hers. Amy fell asleep before me and I stayed up a bit longer unable to quite believe that my best friend was back in my life.

CHARLOTTE

"You are too cute," Amy said to Kayden as they drove toy cars around the living room floor.

We'd just had breakfast and were just lazing around. "You never wanted kids, remember?"

"That was then," Amy said. "I was a girl with only one thing on my mind. Getting laid and having as much fun as I could."

"College was fun," I said wistfully, remembering those carefree days.

The morning went by fast and it was soon time for Amy to leave. I knew that the next two weeks were going to be busy for her with the wedding arrangements and all.

"I'd love to help in any way I can," I said to her.

"Thanks, I appreciate the offer. We have an awesome wedding planner so really there's not much to do. Just make sure you circle the date. You, Kayden and Alex will be special guests."

We walked her to her car and she hugged Kayden and me. Tears sprouted in my eyes and I had to remind myself that it was temporary this time. We could talk on the phone whenever we wanted to.

Still, I was teary as we stood waving goodbye. As we returned to the house, the sound of a car crushing gravel sounded and I turned sure that Amy had forgotten something.

Instead, Alex's SUV cruised into the compound and my stupid heart quickened in response. Kayden bounced on my hip and waved his little hands at Alex as he got out of the car.

"Hey buddy," he said as he came towards us. He took Kayden from me when he got closer and planted a kiss on my cheek. "Amy left already?"

"Just now," I said to him. We went into the house together.

"Someone is sleepy," he said. "Isn't it a little early for your nap?"

Kayden looked so sweet laying his head on Alex's shoulder. "He woke up earlier than usual and he and Aunt Amy played all morning."

It felt so good to say the words. Aunt Amy. For the first time in his life, my son was getting to know his relatives and his mother's close friends. I thought about Helen. I wish she could meet Kayden.

I went to the kitchen and made us some coffee as Alex tucked Kayden in his crib for his nap. Thinking about Helen and the chance I had lost of having an extended family made me teary again.

Alex returned to the kitchen just as I was placing the coffee on the island. I met his gaze with tears filling my eyes.

"Oh Chaz," he said and came to me. "What is it?"

I fell into his arms and he wrapped his big arms around me. A floodgate opened and a sob burst from me. Alex held me as I cried and when that avalanche of emotion left, Alex drew back to look into my eyes.

"I miss them all. Helen, Edward and Kacy." I couldn't even imagine how big my niece had become.

"We should go see them," he said softly.

I shook my head. "I can't."

He didn't pursue it and instead, pulled me into his arms again. Alex had always been the one person who had the power to still all my anxieties and that had not changed. I let out a sigh of contentment as I felt my body relax.

I raised my head to thank Alex but the words stuck in my mouth as I met his gaze. Awareness tingled through my bloodstream and my breathing went shallow. His gaze dropped to my mouth and one or both of us moved and in the next second we were kissing and my world was righting itself.

I clung to his shoulders as he plundered me with his tongue. I gave back as good as I got. No matter how much I tried to deny it, the magic between us was still there. In a matter of seconds, he had reduced me to a moaning, helpless woman.

Even though I had not been looking, no man could come close to what Alex was. He filled me with joy and splashed color in my life. My body responded to his touch and his kisses as if I belonged to him.

I slipped my hands under his t-shirt and ran them over the hard ridges of his stomach and his sculpted chest. He pulled the t-shirt over his head, leaving his top half, gloriously wonderfully, naked.

The bulge of his cock pressed against my thigh as Alex nibbled on my lips and then took my lower one and held it captive. I reached into his pants and dipped my hand into his boxers. I moaned as my fingers wrapped around his hard cock and squeezed.

I moved my hand from his cock to his balls. Alex groaned into my mouth and when I pumped his cock, he reached into his boxers and pulled my hand away. I let out a murmur of protest.

"If you keep doing that, the show is going to be over before it begins," he growled.

I laughed softly but the laughter soon died on my lips when he slid his hands under my t-shirt and cupped my breasts. I arched my chest into his hands, wanting more of his hands on me.

He pulled my bra cups down and I pushed his head down to my nipples. He thumbed one and took the other in his mouth. My legs turned to jelly as arrows of sensations shot to my pussy.

Cries filled the air and when I realized they were coming from me, I bit my lower lip and reminded myself that Kayden was napping. I'd missed the things he did to my breasts. Missed was not quite right. Craved. For two years, I'd remembered the feel of his large hands on my breasts.

He shifted his attention lower, to my belly, circling my navel with his tongue. I whimpered and pushed his head further down to my achy pussy. Alex pulled down my shorts and hoisted me onto the island. I threw my legs apart, not caring at how needy I looked.

I was beyond the point of caring. I would face the consequences afterwards. I stopped breathing when Alex dropped his head between my legs. I threaded my fingers through his hair, my whole body tight with nervous sexual tension, waiting to be relieved.

His tongue swept over my folds and I let out a scream. I forgot that I had a sleeping toddler in the house as I arched my hips forward. "More," I purred.

Alex pried my hips further apart and continued teasing me with his mouth and tongue. He found my clit and flicked his tongue over it until I couldn't take it anymore.

He pushed a finger inside my pussy and I thought I'd go insane from pleasure.

A cry broke through my lusty haze and I froze when it came again and I realized that it was Kayden. Oh God. I opened my eyes. Alex withdrew his finger just as Kayden let out another long cry.

ALEX

"Where do you get your energy, buddy?" I asked Kayden.

His response was to bang the table from where he sat on his high chair.

"It's a good thing that your mom is not here to see us," I said, taking in Kayden's sauce smeared face and the front of my t-shirt which looked like it had been dipped in spaghetti sauce.

I wondered how much lunch had ended up in Kayden's stomach. Most of the spaghetti was on the floor and on the table. Kayden looked up at me and the biggest grin came on his face.

And something struck me then. He reminded me of someone. My heart pounded hard in my chest as the answer came to me. Kayden reminded me of myself. For a few seconds, I couldn't breathe as I contemplated the remote possibility that he could be mine.

I cocked my head and searched his features. He had blue eyes like mine but it had never crossed my mind to even suspect that there was a possibility that Kayden could be my son. I lifted my gaze to his hair. It was sandy colored and curly. Just like mine.

Sweat broke out on my skin and my heart galloped in my chest. It couldn't be. But the evidence was staring at me. Why hadn't I seen the resemblance between Kayden and myself before?

Something else I hadn't considered popped into my brain. What if her boyfriend resembled me? That would explain Kayden's resemblance to me.

"Give me a minute to prepare your bath buddy," I said and gave Kayden his favorite toy car to drive on top of the table.

The thought would not leave my mind though. As I cleaned the tub and half filled it with water, I kept going back to the possibility that he was my son. But then again, Charlotte wouldn't do something like that. She would not have kept my son away from me.

No matter how much I tried to dislodge it, it wouldn't leave my mind. Maybe it was a man thing, wanting a child. It wasn't even about love because I loved Kayden just because he was Charlotte's son.

I couldn't love him more if he was my son.

If Charlotte had been pregnant before she walked out of our marriage, what reason would she have not to tell me? None of it made any sense. The only thing that did was that Kayden was not my son.

After his bath, I cuddled Kayden on the couch as he drank some water from his sippy cup. I kept thinking that there was a slight chance that he was my son and I have to admit, I wanted that to be the case.

Kayden's favorite play activity after the toys was running outside. The compound was extensive and shaded by trees. I carried a ball with us and for the next half an hour, Kayden and I played with the ball, throwing it as far as he could and running after it.

I found myself studying his movements, searching for more similarities between us. Then there was the attachment I'd felt to Kayden when we met. That had to be caused by something right?

From my experience with children, they did not often take to strangers but Kayden had. The afternoon flew by and Kayden had his second nap. By the time Charlotte got home at twenty past six, Kayden and I were relaxing, watching TV.

As soon as I looked into Charlotte's eyes, I knew that Kayden was not my son. There was a lot I didn't know about Charlotte but I knew she would not lie about something like that. She had known how much I had wanted a child.

"I missed you," she said to Kayden and cuddled him and then aimed a kiss at my cheek.

I shifted my head and her lips landed on mine. Charlotte's cheeks reddened, no doubt remembering the heavy make out session in the morning before Kayden had interrupted us.

"How was your day?" I asked.

Our gazes met and the atmosphere changed. Electricity sizzled between us. I lowered my gaze to her lower lip and imagined nibbling on it softly. I shifted on the couch to hide my growing hard on.

Being around Charlotte was like a lesson in self-control. A lesson that did not work. She excused herself to take a shower and I distracted Kayden by driving trains on the floor with him.

Charlotte returned from the shower wearing a pair of shorts that showed off her shapely legs. My hands ached to feel the softness of her skin.

"You look beautiful," I said, staring at the curves of her body hungrily.

"Don't say such things," she choked.

"Why?" I growled.

She didn't answer. Instead she lifted Kayden from the floor and carried him to the kitchen for dinner. The right thing should have been for me to leave but I couldn't. I was so fucking hard for Charlotte. I knew she was feeling it too.

We went through the motions of the evening and anytime our hands or bodies accidentally touched, raw need raced through me. Dinner time was quiet and I couldn't tell what she was thinking either.

"I should go," I said to her later, after we'd cleaned up the kitchen and put Kayden to bed moving back into the living room.

"How are things at work?" she asked, moving closer. She squinted as she stared at my face.

"I suspect they're good. I haven't spoken to anyone. They know I'm fine." That wasn't quite the truth. I'd switched off my cell phone but I had let my parents know that I was fine and would be off the radar.

"Are you sure this is okay? If you've changed your mind about babysitting Kayden, I understand. It's a tough job," Chaz said.

"Are you serious? I enjoy being with him. Kayden's an easy guy to take care of." All I thought about was when to feed Kayden and how to entertain him. After dealing with complex legal cases in the last two years, I was enjoying the simplicity of my days.

She smiled. "Thank you." She moved effortlessly into my arms for a hug and as soon as my hands slipped around her waist, all my blood supply dropped to my cock. There was no way to hide the steel rod in my pants.

ALEX

Charlotte's nipples hardened and pressed into my chest. Her breath became short gasps. I drew back and slipped my hand along her jaw and neck. I inhaled her floral musky scent before touching my lips to hers. She trembled slightly as I held her in my arms.

I teased her lips by nibbling on them and capturing the lower one between my teeth. The rest of the world ceased to exist and it was just me and Charlotte. My hands stroked her back and hips and then rested on her perfect ass.

She parted her lips, inviting me deep into the heat of my mouth. She tasted of coffee and something else that was sweet and indescribable. A solely Charlotte taste.

I'd kissed only Abigail after Chaz, but no one affected me the way Chaz did. Kissing her was more than two mouths coming together. It was a connection of two kindred spirits. It was finally reaching home.

Even as those thoughts raced through my mind, I knew how dangerous it was. I was playing with fire. Charlotte had damaged me before. I couldn't afford to let myself go back there again. It would just be sex, I told myself. None of that mushy stuff.

With that, I slipped my hands under her hips and lifted her. I kissed her as I carried her to the bedroom and kicked the door behind us. I lay her on the bed and undressed as I hungrily watched her. Her eyes were hooded and I wasn't sure where she was looking.

I tossed away my shirt and pulled down my pants, quickly followed by my boxer shorts. Stark naked, I moved to the bed and Charlotte took my hand and pulled me to lie on the bed beside her.

She palmed my chest and stroked my man nipples. I cupped her face and brought my mouth to hers. A surge of love came over me as I kissed her. The very thing I'd promised myself to steer clear from.

I emptied my mind and focused on the gift before me. "I need you naked," I growled at her.

She helped pull the top she wore over her head. I inhaled sharply at the sight of her breasts encased in a lacy bra. Unable to wait, I took a nipple in my mouth and teased it with my tongue over the lacy material. I moved to the other one, licking and sucking it.

Charlotte raised herself from the bed and reached behind to unclasp her bra. She shrugged it off and fell back onto the bed.

"I want you," she murmured.

I moved over her and braced myself on either side so that my weight was not on her. As much as I wanted to be inside her,

I needed to touch her some more. I played with her breasts, teasing the hard peaks until Chaz was squirming under me and arching her body for more.

I trailed kissed down to her navel and further down to the waistband of her shorts.

"Impatient," I said when Charlotte grabbed the waistband of her shorts and tugged it down. She pulled her panties down as well, with me helping her the rest of the way.

I sunk my face between her welcoming thighs and feasted on her sweet pussy.

"Alex."

I loved the sound of Charlotte's voice when she was heady with arousal. No woman had ever caused me as much pain as Charlotte had but when we made love, none of that mattered. She penetrated a part of my soul that no other woman could.

Her nails dug into my skull as I flicked my tongue on her clit. She whimpered and threw her legs further apart. She tasted so sweet and I licked off her juices as they flowed out. I pushed a finger in and then another. Her muscles clamped down on my fingers hard as I pumped in and out.

Moments later, Charlotte came hard on my tongue and fingers. I draped my body over hers as her breath returned to normal. I stroked her hair and smoothed it back from her face. "You okay?"

"No."

"What is it?"

"I want you inside me," she said, the words coming out like a moan.

All air left my lungs at the blunt declaration. My dick did a dance of its own. I gripped it and brought it to her entrance. I slowly eased it in until it was buried to the hilt.

"How does that feel?"

"I think I'm going to die," she replied.

I laughed and drew back and fell into a slow rhythm that allowed me to enjoy watching her face as it contorted with pleasure. Chaz wrapped her legs around my waist, gripping me tight and almost bringing me to orgasm too fast.

I shifted my mind from the heat of her pussy and the walls that clenched me tighter and tighter. I picked up the speed of my thrusts as Chaz urged me on with squeezes of my legs. I lost control and slammed into her. Hard.

"Alex," she moaned.

"Come my love." The words left my mouth before I could stop them. I hoped that she was too far gone to have heard.

"Oh yes," Chaz cried, her nails digging into my shoulders.

I'd missed how responsive and inhibited Chaz was in bed. There was no holding back for her.

"More. Please," she said.

I looked down at her and almost came. She looked so gorgeous with her eyes half closed and her lips slightly parted.

Convulsions came over her body and her walls clenched around my dick as she rode the wave of ecstasy, taking me along with her. Chaz screamed and I felt as if all air had been knocked from my lungs.

"That was out of this world," I said to her as I lay facing her.

She smiled. "It was for me too. I'm not sure it's a good idea though. What are we doing Alex?"

"Enjoying each other's bodies as we used to."

"It can't be more than that," she said. "Our ship sailed a long time ago."

ALEX

Sadness came over me. I still didn't understand. How could she have given up what we had with the stroke of a pen. Why had she written that damn letter instead of talking to me face to face?

Why hadn't I moved on? Looking at Charlotte as she lay staring at me with her wide gorgeous eyes, I knew that I loved her as much as when we had been married. Nothing about my love had changed.

It almost felt like a punishment to love a woman who had betrayed you by leaving you for another man. I wanted to ask her about Kayden's dad. I would have liked to see a picture but that wasn't the kind of thing you asked a woman you were in love with.

Can I see a picture of your ex?

Yes, that would be weird. I was becoming weird. And jaded. And sad. I wished I could turn back the clock. Go back to when we both loved each other.

"We've been invited to a wedding," Chaz said.

"Amy's?"

"Yes. In two weeks. Do you want to come?"

I should have said no, but I wasn't ready to part ways with Chaz. I told myself it was to relieve my itch. I hadn't had enough of her body. That was all I wanted from her. I would always love her and I was slowly going to have to come to terms with that.

But I would never commit myself to Chaz again. "Sure, why not?" I said, keeping my tone as casual as I could.

"Good. Amy said it'll be from Friday to Sunday at a lodge in the mountains. She'll send me a virtual invitation."

She sounded so happy to have reconnected with Amy. When they came home together, I was surprised that Amy was sleeping over and even more so that they had ironed out their differences.

I'm ashamed to say that I'd been envious of Amy. They had been at ease with each other, just as though that two-year separation had not happened. She had probably told Amy the truth about what happened between her and the guy she had been with.

As desperate as I was to know, I was not going to ask Amy and put her in an impossible position of needing to be loyal to an old friend and a newer one.

"You seem so deep in thought," Charlotte said. "What are you thinking?"

"Tell me about Kayden's dad?"

We had so many lies and secrets between us. Even though I had broken up with Abigail, I hadn't mentioned her to Charlotte. As for Charlotte, she had so many secrets, I doubted she would have known the truth if it would have bit her on the ass.

The air visibly tensed between us.

"What do you want to know?"

"Are you completely done with him?"

She raised her head to look at me. "What do you take me for?" Her eyes flashed.

I met her gaze with a raise of the eyebrow. She had the grace to blush.

"What else do you want to know?" she asked.

"What does he look like?"

She inhaled sharply. "He has dirty blonde hair and blue eyes."

I stopped breathing. She had fallen in love with a man who resembled me. "What kind of sick shit is that Charlotte? Why did you want someone who looked like me when you had me?"

A lid went off. The anger and pain of the last two years exploded inside of me. I sat up on the bed. What was I doing in Charlotte's bed? I was fooling myself that she was a good person.

She was a cold bitch. The only reason she was interested in me was because I had come at a convenient time. She needed me and she had no man at the present to warm her bed.

I cursed under my breath. I couldn't think. I needed some fresh air and space. I grabbed my boxer briefs and pulled them on.

"Are you leaving?" she asked.

"Yes, but just to the B&B. Unlike you, I fulfil my commitments. I promised to take care of Kayden until Mrs. Horace comes back and that's exactly what I'll do."

"You don't have to, Alex. Kayden is my responsibility," she said in a small voice.

I refused to let it get to me. I ignored the swell of a weird emotion in my chest.

"What would you like me to do? Write a letter and run away? Sorry, I don't roll like that." I finished dressing and stood over her. "I'll see you tomorrow morning."

She sat up. "We need to talk, Alex."

I shook my head. I had reached the end of my rope with Charlotte. There was nothing she could tell me that would make me contemplate opening my heart to her again.

"I don't want to hear it." I stalked out of her bedroom and her house.

I was a fool. Outside, I punched into the air. She thought I was an idiot but even idiots wised up after some time. Nausea rose up my throat as I visualized Charlotte with a guy who looked like my twin. She was sicker than I thought.

CHARLOTTE

It was my favorite kind of summer evening, with a soft warm breeze blowing and the trees swaying gently in the wind. I should have been happy that it was Friday and I had the whole weekend free.

Instead, I dragged one foot in front of the other, dreading the moment when I would get home to Alex's painfully polite welcome. Since he had walked out that evening after making love.

I'd known that walking out of our marriage would hurt him, badly, but I'd honestly believed that after he went back to New York and his family he would eventually get over me. My chest squeezed painfully when I remembered the bitterness in his voice. It hurt terribly to know that I had turned Alex into the angry man who had walked out of my house that evening.

It was easy to believe that I carried bad luck with me when I remembered the carefree young man Alex had been the day we met. I remembered his smiling open face. His excitement as he spoke about working at his father's law firm. He rarely spoke about it and I wondered if he was happy there.

I rounded the corner and saw them at the front of the house and I slowed down to watch them. Alex was pushing Kayden on his tricycle in circles. They looked so serious and so alike and at that moment I knew that soon I needed to make a decision.

Maybe I would tell him when we went for Amy's wedding. Cowardice, I knew. There, we would be surrounded by people and I wouldn't have to face Alex's anger. He was an awesome dad and he enjoyed teaching Kayden new things. He would feel cheated and betrayal but I hoped that when I explained all of it, he might be able to understand. Forgiveness that was something else.

"Hi," I said and strolled towards them.

I tensed as I waited for Alex's reaction.

He looked up and nodded at me politely as if I was his employer. And an unfriendly one at that. I bent down to kiss Kayden.

"Mama," he said grinning. He gripped the tricycle handles tighter. "Bike."

"And you're riding it!" I said and clapped for him.

Kayden let go of the handles and clapped along. That cracked a smile from Alex who joined us in clapping and cheering.

"How was your day?" I asked.

"It was good. We had a ball, right buddy?"

"Ball," Kayden said and scrambled off of the tricycle and waddled into the house in search of a ball.

We laughed and followed him.

"Coffee?" I asked when we entered the house.

"Why don't I make the coffee and you can give Kayden his milk and see if he'll nap," he said. "I think I might have excited him too much with the tricycle."

"It doesn't matter. That smile on his face is worth a delayed nap."

I washed my hands, prepared Kayden's cup and managed to carry him and his ball to the couch. We settled down and within seconds of starting to drink his milk he was dozing and I had to keep jolting him awake to finish his milk.

Alex returned with the coffee as I was placing the empty cup on the table. He chuckled at the sight of Kayden falling asleep clutching his ball. "Do you want me to carry him to his crib?"

"Okay, thanks."

He gently lifted Kayden from my arms and carried him to the bedroom. As I watched them disappear, I was flooded by gratitude for Alex's presence in my life. He had been a rock at a time when I needed one.

That one week had both saddened me and at the same time brought joy into my life. Joy because Kayden was lucky to have a dad like Alex. Patient, loving and playful. The kind of daddy that every little boy should have.

My sadness came from the wall that had grown between us. I'd tried making conversation but Alex was not interested. I missed the conversations we had in the evenings and, I know this made me a shallow person, but I missed making love with Alex.

I ached to have his strong arms around me and his lips on mine, kissing me with everything he had. Alex returned to the living room as I was squeezing my thighs together to keep the heat from spreading.

"I should go," he said.

"Please stay, I'm making steak for dinner." I swallowed hard.

He contemplated it for a few seconds, his cobalt blue eyes intense and trained on me. I trembled as heat whipped through me. I really, really wanted him to stay. As aroused as I was, the main reason I wanted Alex to stay was because I owed him an apology.

I had caused a lot more damage to the man I loved the most on the planet. It didn't matter that my reasons had been noble and well intentioned. I knew now that I had broken his heart.

But even worse, I had kept his son from him. I could have tried much harder to find him. And now, I was just plain scared to tell him. I was frightened of his reaction and I was afraid of losing my Kayden. I couldn't think clearly enough to make a decision.

Maybe when we went to the lodge for Amy's wedding, I would tell him then. The more I thought about it, the more appealing the idea became. We would be surrounded by people and I wouldn't have to face Alex's wrath.

One thing was for sure, he was going to be mad and rightly so.

"Can't say no to a steak," he said and collapsed on the couch.

"Long day?" I asked with a giggle.

He chuckled. "He's so tiny and so much work. But I'll have Kayden any day rather than a day at the office."

"I'm really grateful—"

Alex raised a hand to cut me off. "You already said."

We exchanged a smile. I drained the last of my coffee and as I reached out to place the empty cup on the table, I missed the edge. The cup fell to the hard wooden floor, but other than bouncing around it didn't break.

"Fuck."

"Its fine," he said, diving after the cup. He sat back down and held my gaze. "I've noticed that this kind of thing happens a lot. Is there something wrong with your vision?"

CHARLOTTE

Oh God! I should have known that Alex would notice. How much was I going to tell him? "Yes, my vision is bad."

"Why don't you wear glasses?"

"Don't like them. I'll look terrible," I said flippantly.

Alex stared at me. "That's not like you Chaz. You've never been vain. I refuse to believe that's the reason you don't get glasses."

Tears flooded my eyes and threatened to spill. "I need to marinate the steaks and make Kayden's dinner." I grabbed the cup and fled to the kitchen.

Alex was so right. I was not hung up over my looks. If ten inch glasses would help me see better, I would happily wear them. It felt good to hear him say that he did not believe me. But it also made me question why he had not had the same reaction when I walked out of our marriage.

Why hadn't he reached into himself to know that I wouldn't have fallen in love with another man, let alone run off with him?

It wasn't long before Alex joined me but by then I had regained control of my emotions.

"Put me to work," he said.

I gestured at the island stool. "Sit there. Your job is to keep me company."

We chatted easily as I worked. When I was done boiling Kayden's potatoes and peas, Alex insisted on mashing them while I placed our potatoes in the oven.

"Have you spoken to Mrs. Horace?" he asked.

"Not recently, no," I said. "I'm sure she's fine. I'll give her house a cleanup. I'm sure it's dusty."

"That's kind of you," Alex commented.

"It's nothing. She's been so kind to Kayden and me."

Comfortable silence fell between us.

"I wish I'd been there for you," he said.

"How could you when I'd walked out of our marriage?" The words slipped out of my mouth before I could filter them.

I stopped dicing lettuce and faced Alex. "I'm really, really sorry for the pain I caused you. You didn't deserve any of it and if I could turn back the clock, I would."

I was apologizing for so much. For fleeing our marriage, for keeping his son away from him, and for destroying our dreams. I remember how happy and simple our lives had been and I wanted to cry.

We had such a short time together, but it had been the happiest period of my life.

"It was the happiest period of my life," he said, echoing my thoughts.

"Tell me about your life back in New York?" I said. "I remember how excited you were to work at your father's law firm. Was it everything you wanted it to be?"

"It's a job," he said. "I don't mean to pile on the guilt but you asked, so I'll tell you. All those dreams meant nothing when you left. They were important to me only if we would do it together."

Pain sliced through me. I didn't know how to respond. The raw honesty and pain in his voice almost brought me to my knees.

"I can practice law anywhere," he said. "What about you? What happened to your dreams of opening your own sandwich shop?"

Mine was easy to answer. "Life happened. Responsibilities took over."

"Kayden?" he asked, as we both returned to our tasks.

"Yes."

"I would be happy to loan you the money you need to start. I've made piles of money to be honest and I've spent very little of it," he said.

I stared at him, shocked that he would even make such an offer. "You can't spend your hard-earned money like that."

"I can spend it anyway I like. Then of course there's my trust fund money. Following your logic I can spend it how I wish, since, I haven't worked hard to earn it."

"No, Alex," I said.

"The offer is open. You can change your mind anytime. You mean a lot to me Chaz. You always will."

ALEX

It was Saturday Morning and I stayed in bed and caught up on my subscriptions most of which were law magazines. I kept thinking about Kayden and Chaz. It was almost ten and depending on what time Kayden had waked up, it was almost time for his morning nap.

The weekend stretched out before me and I contemplated asking them to do something fun together. Like taking Kayden to the zoo. I'd done some research and there was one about twenty minutes away in the next town.

I picked up my phone to text Charlotte and then it hit me that I'd never seen her texting. Was her eyesight that bad that she couldn't text? My phone vibrated as I was still musing over Charlotte's vision problems.

I looked down and was surprised to see Charlotte's name flashed across the screen. It reminded me of the time we had been married. We'd been so close that we had fallen into the habit of finishing each other's sentences.

I swiped a finger across the screen to answer.

"Morning, I was just thinking about you."

"Morning to you too."

I could hear the smile in her voice. Charlotte was one of those people who was perpetually happy irrespective of time. She never had a bad day or woke up feeling down. The Charlotte I remembered viewed each day like a gift to be savored.

"What were you thinking?" she asked.

I could visualize her cradling the phone. Kayden's voice sounded from the distance and I found myself smiling and wishing that I was home with them.

"I was thinking how nice it would be to go to the zoo with you and Kayden this afternoon."

She sighed. "That's actually what I was calling you about. Michael, the chef who is on duty today called to cancel. He has some sort of emergency so I have to go in."

Chaz sounded so uncomfortable asking, I jumped in to save her the trouble. "I'll be there in twenty minutes."

I could hear her sigh of relief over the phone.

"You're a lifesaver. Thanks so much Alex. And yes, to the zoo date. Kayden and I would love to go. Tomorrow."

I grinned like a fool. "Great. See you soon."

I powered off my laptop and shut it. I took the fastest shower in the history of man and when I was done, I stared at my face critically. There was no time to shave and I wondered if my day-old stubble was too rough.

Kayden was fascinated by my slight moustache and liked to play with it when I was holding him. I hoped that my stubble would not hurt his fingers. I hurried out of the B&B, down to the parking lot.

One of the many advantages of living in a small town was the absence of traffic. Twenty minutes after Charlotte and I spoke, I was parking my car in front of her house.

"That was super fast," she said smiling when she flung the door open.

My male senses perked up when I took in her appearance. She was dressed in a loose maxi dress that clung to her curves when a gust of wind blew.

"You look beautiful," I said.

Her cheeks colored. "This old thing?"

"You'd look beautiful in a sack," I said.

"Mama," a voice said behind Charlotte and tiny hands rested on her legs and tried to shift her out of the way.

"Okay, okay Kayden, you'll get your turn." Charlotte laughingly moved out of the way.

I squatted and Kayden flew into my arms. His little hands went around my neck and for a few seconds, the world was perfect. There was something about children that melted my heart but with Kayden, it was more than that.

He'd stolen my heart and I couldn't help but wish he was my son.

"I missed you, buddy," I stood up and carried Kayden into the house with me.

"His lunch is in the fridge and snacks are in the usual place," she said, picking up her bag from the couch. "Dinner is ready too but I'll definitely be back by then."

"Hey, relax," I said. "We're good."

She inhaled deeply and smiled. "Okay. Thanks—"

I put a hand to my lips. If only she knew how much pleasure it gave me to make her life easier. As for Kayden, he was just a great kid. "Let's walk Mommy outside and get some sun."

ALEX

My cell phone battery must have died at some point. After I laid Kayden down for his afternoon nap, I checked it and found it turned off. I left it charging and cleaned up the mess Kayden and I had made in the afternoon.

With the house back in order, I made a cup of coffee and settled on the couch to check my messages. Abigail had taken to calling and texting, demanding to know when I was coming back home.

I found five text messages from her, most of them ending with at least three question marks. I hit call. It was easier to call her.

She answered the phone on the second ring and went right into it. "I don't understand what you're doing in some town in the middle of nowhere. People are starting to suspect that you've gone off the rails again," she said.

I went still. "Off the rails? Because I was devastated when my wife left me, I was classified as insane?"

She laughed nervously. “It was a joke.”

It wasn’t a joke. I hated the gossip that was rife in our circles.

“People who are in a committed relationship spend a lot of time together,” she said.

“How clear do I have to be that I’ve uncommitted myself?” I asked, irritated with the conversation.

She was quiet for a few seconds. A completely un-Abigail behavior. “You can’t do that.”

“Excuse me?” I said.

“I said you can’t do that. I’m pregnant.”

“It’s not possible.” The chance of me impregnating her was next to nil.

“Don’t be dumb. Of course it’s possible and I am,” Abigail hissed. “So if you want to ever see your son or daughter, you had better hightail it back to New York.”

I disconnected the call. I didn’t know what games Abigail was playing, but I wasn’t going to play along. I had barely slipped the phone into my pocket when it rang again. I smiled when Charlotte’s number flashed on the screen.

“Hey,” I answered with a smile, my sour mood forgotten.

“Hi.” The background was noisy and I imagined her in the kitchen looking cute with her hair tucked into a chef’s top hat.

“I’m going to be late coming home,” she said, sounding rushed. “We’ve just gotten a booking for a large group for dinner. I’m sorry Alex.”

"What are you apologizing for?" I asked her. "Kayden and I are cool. When he wakes up and eats his snack, we'll go out for a game of soccer. Then dinner and a bath. We're good. So quit worrying."

She sighed. "I owe you big time. Have to go. Give Kayden a big, noisy kiss from me."

"I will," I said and disconnected the call.

For the next hour or so, I used my cell phone as a hotspot and responded to the messages that my secretary had marked for my attention. My father may have been right when he said I was suffering from burn out.

I couldn't bring myself to care about the legal world that I'd left behind. What I cared about at that moment was how Kayden and I would occupy ourselves in the afternoon.

My life now revolved around Kayden and Charlotte and the small town they called home. I knew that when Mrs. Horace came back and resumed her duties as Kayden's nanny, I would need to figure out my life.

I loved the predictability of my days with Kayden. He woke up from his nap energized and ready for more play. After a snack, we took a walk around Mrs. Horace's extensive property. Her place was wooded, secluded and surrounded by acres and acres of land. It was gorgeous.

The walk exhausted Kayden and after a bath, we settled down on the couch to read story books. I acted them out for him and got rewarded with giggles and shrieks.

An hour later Kayden was fed and ready for bed. I held him in my lap as he drank his milk. Before the milk was done, he had grown heavier in my arms. It felt good to hold him and I delayed taking him to bed as long as possible. When I finally took him, it was eight and Charlotte was not back home yet.

I stretched out on the couch to wait and watched TV. I was as exhausted as Kayden had been and my eyelids struggled to stay open. Just for a minute, I said to myself and gave in to the pull of sleep.

CHARLOTTE

"Thanks for the ride," I said to Hannah as she brought her car to a stop in front of my house.

"You're welcome and sorry for keeping you so late. I hope your sitter isn't mad," she said, her voice filled with concern.

"It's fine. See you on Monday." I got out and stood waving until she left.

It was about nine and I knew Kayden was already asleep. It was the first time that he had ever fallen asleep without me there to tuck him in and kiss him goodnight.

The anxiety I expected to feel was not there and Alex was the reason. He was great with kids and he and Kayden had taken to each other, as if they instinctively knew how connected they really were.

I opened the door slowly to keep the noise down in case Kayden was not completely asleep. Deep snoring filled the air and I stifled a giggle at the sight of Alex deep asleep on the couch.

I tiptoed past him to Kayden's bedroom. Unlike his dad, he was sleeping quietly for once. After dropping my handbag in my bedroom, I padded back to the living room but paused to peer into the kitchen. It was spotlessly clean as was the rest of the house.

Alex's mouth was slightly parted and a hint of a smile tugged at the corners of his lips. I sunk to the floor and stared at him. His face was so close that his warm breath fanned my face. My chest swelled with love and other emotions that I could not define.

He had put a pause on his own life to help a woman who had abandoned their marriage two years earlier to run away with another man. Alex was simply a good human being. The best there was.

My gaze dropped to his sexy mouth and unable to resist, I bent down and brushed my lips against his. He groaned and a hand shot out and went around my neck, holding me captive.

As the kiss deepened, the heat between my legs intensified and spread to the rest of my body. I needed to feel more of him. I drew away.

"Where are you going?" he asked.

"Just getting comfortable," I said, moving on top of him and aligning my body with his. "I thought you were asleep." I peppered kisses around his mouth.

"I still am," he said and wrapped his hand around me, pulling me against his bulging cock.

I laughed softly and shifted my body and pushed my pelvis against the bulge of his cock. I rocked against him, creating delicious friction that built a fire in my body.

Alex, never one to lie still, took charge, thrusting his tongue into my mouth and engaging my tongue in a sweet dance that had me moaning softly. His hands cupped my ass and squeezed, and I let out a cry of pleasure.

"I want to see you naked," Alex growled into my mouth. He broke the kiss and moved to a sitting position shifting me to his lap.

I wrapped my legs around his waist and he stood up with me, his hands cupping my ass as he walked. I trailed kisses down his neck, longing for the moment when we would be skin to skin.

In the bedroom, he lowered me to the floor and as if my mutual agreement, we stripped off, our eyes glued to each other. When I threw the last piece of clothing, I stood before him, naked and aching.

"You look beautiful," he said, closing the gap between us.

I shivered as he raised his hands to my breasts and cupped them, his thumbs automatically stretching to flick my nipples. He lowered his head to take a taut nipple into his mouth.

I threw my head back and reveled in the sensations that coursed through my body. I threaded my fingers through his silky hair. He circled my nipple with his tongue, teasing it for a few seconds before taking it into his hot mouth.

He shifted his attention to the other waiting achy nipple, sucking and licking until I was begging for more. I pulled him up and guided him to the bed. My pussy was drenched and I was desperate for Alex to be inside me.

He sat at the edge of the bed and I straddled him. He cupped my breasts and played with my nipples as our mouths met for another spine-tingling kiss that sent waves of pleasure straight to my pussy.

His groans and trembles made me feel powerful. As if, I alone had the power to make Alex feel like that. I raised my hips and gripped the base of his steel hard cock. I squeezed my eyes shut as I lowered myself onto his cock. It parted my folds and pushed its way in aided by Alex' hands on my waist.

"You feel so fucking good," he said, looking up at me.

I giggled. "So polite."

"If you want polite you have the wrong man," he said, his cobalt eyes wild and passionate.

My heartbeat changed to a gallop at the intensity in his voice. Alex and I were kidding ourselves. We could never keep it as just physical. The love we'd had was too strong, too explosive. Already, I knew that my feelings had waked up from hibernation.

They consumed me when I thought about Alex and this time, I knew that I would not be the one doing the walking away. How would I survive when he went back to his life in New York?

I pushed away the thoughts threatening to invade on my pleasure and instead concentrated on the pleasure that came from having Alex fill me completely. I rocked up and down on his cock, breasts swaying with every movement.

He had always loved my breasts and now his eyes were glued to my chest and I arched my back to give him a better view. I moaned and rocked as his cock hit sensitive spots deep inside me.

Alex flicked his tongue over my nipples every time they got within reach. We fell into a rhythm and I lost myself to the magic that Alex and I were creating. His cock throbbed inside me and I clamped his cock with my muscles, needing him to come at the same time as I did.

My insides grew tighter and tighter, until my body started to convulse and the surge of my orgasm lifted me like a wave and then exploded, sending pulses of pleasure to every part of my body.

Deep growls rose from Alex's throat and his quick jabs and grunts told me that he was coming. He gripped my hips harder as he pumped his essence into me, filling me with his sweetness.

Alex held me tight against his body and when our breath returned to normal, he pulled down the sheet and gently laid me on the bed. He entered after me and folded me into his arms.

CHARLOTTE

I woke up to Alex's heavy hand draped across my waist. For a few seconds, I was transported to our previous life. I woke up thinking that it was one of our lazy Saturday mornings and joy swept through me.

A baby's whimpers slammed me back to the present. Disoriented, I sat up shifting Alex's hand away from my body. My surroundings started to make sense. The baby's whimpers grew louder. Kayden! I scrambled out of bed and quickly pulled on a t-shirt and shorts.

Guilt flooded me as I hurried to his room. In those few seconds, I'd forgotten that I had a child. What good mother did that?

"Morning baby," I crooned as I lifted him from his crib.

I held him close to my body and savored his warmth and scent. His hands went around my neck and he held me fiercely. Every part of my body swelled with love, to almost the bursting point. My little boy held my heart in his hands.

"Mama!" he murmured and burrowed his face deeper into my neck.

"My darling," I said and after a few minutes of cuddling, I lay him down on the changing table for a change of diaper and clothes.

I spoke to him as I prepared him for the day. "Do you know what today is?"

Kayden nibbled on his favorite soft toy, a lilac worm that rarely left his side. He looked at me with interest, his cobalt blue eyes reminding me so much of his dad.

Was it right for me to keep them from knowing the truth? Alex deserved to know that he had a son. He had more than proved himself. I made the decision there and then to tell him about Kayden. When we went to Amy's wedding.

A sheen of sweat formed on my forehead at the thought of telling Alex but I was not going to give in to fear. I carried Kayden to the kitchen and grabbed his already prepared milk bottle from the fridge.

While he drank most of his liquids from a sippy cup, he had refused to make the switch when it came to his morning milk. I enjoyed it as well as it gave us a chance to cuddle.

"I missed you last night," I said to Kayden as he drank his milk.

"He missed you too." I hadn't heard Alex enter the living room.

My breath hitched when I lifted my gaze to him. He was clad in low hanging shorts and nothing else. He looked deliciously hot. My body heated up from the memories of the previous night.

"Morning," I said, wishing my vision was not so blurred so that I could see his washboard abs that narrowed to a 'v' down his shorts. "I'm sorry I was late. It took forever to clean up."

"I'm the one who should be apologizing for falling asleep on the job." He placed his hands on his hips and grinned.

My heart stuttered and I felt as if I was free falling into an endless abyss. I shouldn't have been surprised at how much Alex affected me. He was my one true love. The last two years had proved that. Not one man had held my interest. My heart, body and soul belonged to Alex.

I allowed myself to think about what would happen if we got back together. It was wistful thinking and I knew it. It was one thing to have sex and fool around, but a relationship was a whole other thing to Alex.

He had admitted on more than one occasion that he'd never gone through the kind of pain he did when I left him. His heart was sealed off from that kind of a relationship. As hard as it was to accept that, I couldn't blame him. There was only one person to blame, and that was me.

Kayden raised a hand and Alex kissed his forehead and murmured some endearments. "I'm going to grab some coffee. Do you want some?" he asked me.

"Sure," I said, staring at his tight sexy ass as he walked away.

I was making up for the two dry years we'd been apart. I couldn't get enough of him. Kayden wriggled in my lap like an earthworm, wanting to be set free. I hadn't noticed that he had long finished his milk.

He waddled off to his corner where we kept his toys and sat down on the rug.

Alex was wearing a t-shirt when he returned with the two coffees. I swallowed a lump of disappointment. Coffee with a view of a barrel of a chest. Yum.

"You're very thoughtful for a Sunday morning," he said, sinking onto the couch next to me.

I pulled my mind out of the gutter. "Just looking forward to the day. Kayden has never been to the zoo."

Alex frowned. "Why not?"

I shouldn't have shared that particular piece of information but I was excited about seeing Kayden's reactions when he saw the animals. It wasn't just the zoo either that he hadn't been to. It was also swimming and other activities that required my vision to be a hundred percent.

Going to the grocery with him was the best I did and I was comfortable with that because I knew the route like the back of my hand. Plus it was within walking distance from home.

"Chaz?" Alex prompted.

I had no choice but to tell him the truth. "I'm frightened I might drop him or lose him. My vision is worse than I told you." The admission left me feeling as if I had stripped off all my clothes in a busy supermarket and everyone was staring at me.

"And yet you won't get glasses?" he asked.

I had no response for that. I'd rather he thought I was vain than that I was close to blind. I'd hate to hear the sympathy in his voice.

"What time do you think we should go?" I hoped that he would go along and not pursue the issue of glasses. If he pressed, I would bow under pressure and tell him everything. I wasn't ready yet.

"I think its better we go in the morning before it gets too hot and crowded. I'll go to the B&B for a shower and change of clothes after this coffee." He yawned and stretched his long legs.

I shifted my gaze to his very muscular thighs. While he had been pretty fit when we were together, now he had become buff. He obviously spent a lot of time in the gym back in New York.

A pang of exclusion came over me when I remembered that Alex had a whole new life back home. Maybe even a lover. I'd seen him huddled over his phone several times and I must admit the thought that he had someone in his life, left me with burning jealousy.

A feeling I had no right to. I had given up any rights to Alex when I signed the divorce papers. I wondered how long it had taken for him to sign them.

He drained the last of his coffee and stood up.

An idea popped into my mind. "Hey, do you want to move into the spare room? It seems silly for you to stay at the B&B when I have a spare room." I held my breath and fisted a hand.

I wanted him to say yes so badly.

He grinned and my heart melted. “I feel as if I passed a test.”

I let my gaze move over his body to settle on the bulge in front of his shorts. I liked that I affected him the same way that he affected me. “You did.”

“God Chaz,” he said, sounding tortured. The swell in his pants increased in size. My thighs trembled and heat whipped across my body.

“Why do you do this to me?” he asked.

I giggled. “It’s mutual. You didn’t answer my question.”

“Yes, and thank you. It’ll be easier for all of us,” he said and blew a kiss at me and kissed Kayden.

That was it. I had offered him the spare room because it would save Alex time, plus I owed it to him after how much he was helping me. Who was I kidding? I liked having Alex in the same house even if it was going to only be for a short time.

I could even pretend that we were a real family.

ALEX

"What's all that?" I said to Charlotte as she carried the bags from the house to the car trunk.

"Going anywhere with a baby is like moving houses. Trust me, everything I've brought will come in handy. Where's Kayden?"

I held the back door open. "Come and see."

Kayden was secured in a brand-new car seat I'd picked up the previous week. He was happily kicking the air.

"Hey baby," Chaz said and then faced me. "You shouldn't have. You can't spend that kind of money on us. Besides, we won't use it again after you leave. We don't have a car, remember?"

"I can leave you mine," I said.

Chaz stared at me. "You're too generous but no thank you. I won't take advantage of your generosity."

"I would give you and Kayden everything I had to make your lives comfortable."

Her eyes filled up. "Thanks."

"Okay, let's get this show on the road," I said and opened the front passenger door for Chaz.

"I'm so excited," Chaz said as we drove onto the highway. "Did your parents do such things with you?"

"Not all families spend a lot of time together," I said. "My dad was always at the office and Mom; well you know how she is." My mom's interest has always been charity work and when Mary and I were younger, we were left under the care of nannies.

If only my parents knew what they had been missing. That was probably one of the reasons why my sister had given up a promising career as a lawyer to stay home and raise her children.

"That's sad," Chaz said.

In the back seat, Kayden made happy noises, already understanding the day would be different from his set routine.

Chaz sang nursery rhymes and I joined in when I knew the song. Kayden sang too, if you could call the loud noises he was making singing. Being a family felt like that. As if you belonged. What if Charlotte and I tried again?

The skin on my forehead tightened as I remembered the last two years. For the first six months, I had moved like a zombie. I'd gone through the motions of living but I'd been dead inside. Then the pain had come and the realization that my dreams of a family and life with Charlotte were over.

Then I remembered the last couple of weeks. Spending the day with Kayden. Showing him stuff as only a father could and I wanted it so badly. My longing for a family overrode the fear I felt over being hurt again.

It was a real fear. What if Kayden's dad came back into his and Charlotte's lives? Where would that leave me? Confusion swirled in my mind. There were so many what ifs.

Could I trust Charlotte with my heart again? What if she met someone and fell in love? The beginnings of a headache were forming. I gathered those thoughts and stored them in a compartment to be examined later. I was determined that it would be a good day, especially for Chaz and Kayden. They deserved one of those.

We got to the zoo in twenty minutes. Like I'd predicated there were not many people at that time of morning.

"I'll carry him," I said and took the front facing carrier from Charlotte and fastened it on myself.

Chaz slid Kayden into the carrier and as soon as he got comfortable, he started kicking his legs in delight. He kept it up as we strolled around the zoo.

"He's so excited," she said.

The baby elephants excited him the most and he bounced up and down in the carrier. At one point, I took Charlotte's hand into mine and she didn't complain or remove it.

That was what I wanted for my future. To be with the woman I loved and to have a family together.

Charlotte had brought a blanket and after an hour of walking around, we took a break. As fun as the carrier had been for Kayden, he was glad to be back on solid ground.

After feeding Kayden a snack and some milk, Charlotte brought out some sandwiches and a flask of coffee.

"You're an angel," I said as I took the mug from her. "Who knew that the zoo could be so exhausting."

"But fun," she said, a twinkle in her eye.

"Do you remember the walks we used to take along the river bank?" I asked her.

She laughed softly. "We started off well enough, but we were always in a rush to go back home afterwards."

"I don't think that has changed," I said, my gaze dropping to the lines of her body.

Charlotte's cheeks reddened. We had always had out of this world physical chemistry. All she had to do was say something or look at me in a certain manner and my dick rose to attention.

"There's no way I'm not seeing the rest of the zoo," she said.

"We will," I said. "If Kayden wakes up."

He'd fallen asleep lying on his stomach. Charlotte reached out and rubbed his back in gentle round circles.

"Do you miss New York?" she asked abruptly.

"Not one bit."

"That's weird considering that New York is your home," she said.

"Home is usually where your heart is."

She looked away.

"Tell me something. How bad is your eyesight?"

ALEX

She bit her lower lip. "Pretty bad. I was actually diagnosed with a condition in which the eyesight deteriorates."

I was heartbroken by her words and I asked her more questions but at the end of it, I wasn't satisfied that she had not gotten a second and maybe even third opinion.

"With the technology these days, I'm surprised they couldn't do anything about it. When were you told?"

"Not too long ago," she said.

I knew when Chaz was being evasive. I let it go. It didn't matter. What mattered was that she needed to see a top ophthalmologist and get a second opinion. I knew there was a top guy in Cleveland. I just had to dig for his name and address.

"There's a top Ophthalmologist in Cleveland. I'd like to schedule an appointment for you," I said.

"The eye doctor who diagnosed me seemed pretty confident," she said.

"I'm not doubting his expertise but even doctors are people and like lawyers they can make mistakes. Besides what will it hurt to have them checked again?" I said.

"Okay," Chaz said "I can't say no to a chance of seeing better," she said.

"I'll see if you can get an appointment next week," I said and then frowned when I thought about Kayden. We couldn't go with him. It would be too exhausting.

"You're frowning," Chaz said.

"Yeah. I'm thinking about Kayden."

"Lulu can watch him. She's my colleague at work. She has a boy who is Kayden's age and they've played together a few times."

"That's settled then," I said and shifted my thoughts to Chaz. So many things made sense now. Her refusal to drive. It wasn't a matter of vanity as I'd suspected. It was that she couldn't see.

"How much do you see?" I asked her.

"Blurry. I can't see details in a person's face except for people I knew before my eyesight deteriorated." She laughed softly. "Those ones have their faces ingrained in my brain."

A thought came to me that also filled another hole. "Is that why he left you? Because of your eyesight?"

Chaz dropped her head. That was enough of an answer. I folded my right hand into a fist and wished the loser was here so that I could slam it into his face. What kind of man left his woman when she got sick?

"I'm so sorry, Chaz," I said, fighting to control the anger in my voice. "He was a loser. Any man who can leave his woman because of an illness should not be called a man."

She never spoke.

Kayden woke up after half an hour, energized and ready to continue with the zoo adventures. My earlier joy had disappeared and I felt both angry and guilty about Chaz's eye illness. I was angry at her lover who had hightailed it when she got sick and also for Kayden.

How could you abandon your pregnant lover in her hour of need? It baffled me and no matter which way I looked at it, the man was an asshole.

I felt guilty that I'd believed her when she implied that she didn't want to wear glasses because of her looks. That wasn't Charlotte. She was beautiful in a way that could stop traffic but she had never been obsessed with her looks in any way.

The monkey enclosure was the last one and I was glad when it was time to go home. I was eager to get on my laptop and do some research. The sooner I got Charlotte that appointment the better I would feel.

"I wish you would have gotten in touch with me when you were diagnosed," I said to her as we drove back. "Or even later when Kayden's dad left."

"I did," she said.

"What?"

"You had changed cell phone numbers so I called your parents' house," she said. "I left a message with your mom."

Fresh anger gripped me. "She never told me."

"Yeah, I have since figured that out," she said, her voice casual.

I gripped the steering wheel harder. How could she not have told me? I loved my mother but I disliked her interference in people's lives! This time, it had cost Charlotte a friend when she desperately needed one.

"I'm very, very sorry," I said.

"Hey, don't be upset." She patted my shoulder. "It was a long time ago and I did manage after all."

"I'm just glad that my mother's not here."

Back home, Chaz carried a tired but still awake Kayden into the house while I carried the bags and carrier. I helped Chaz prepare Kayden's bath and then left to go check myself out of the B&B.

I packed all my stuff while my mind came up with a plan. Finally, I decided on the people I needed to call. First on my list was Sam. He was an old friend and his father was a renowned ophthalmologist.

He promised to speak to his dad and call be back pronto. If Sam didn't work out, I would call Lisa, another old friend. Her mother was also in the eye medical field.

Sam called me back after ten minutes. It turned out that his father and Dr. Mueller were friends and Chaz had an appointment to see him on Monday.

"Sweet," I said to Sam. "I owe you man!"

That settled, I grabbed my two suitcases when a switch suddenly turned on in my mind. A thought so clear and so shocking that I dropped them and sat back down on the bed.

My chest rose up and down as I stared straight ahead unseeing him. Kayden. He was my son. Thoughts jumbled in my brain. Memories. Snippets of conversations. Amy's words.

Charlotte must have had another reason. She loved you.

Even her sister, who had not known Charlotte for long, had insisted that there must have been another reason why Charlotte left and not the one she said.

I searched my memory for another instance that was significant. I searched and sieved until I found it. Charlotte losing her balance a lot and walking into things in the last few months before she left.

The first time I'd seen it had been when she tripped over the ledge outside our old house and fell. Amy and I had been puzzled. The ledge was big enough to see and it had been from the beginning.

Pieces of the jigsaw fell into place. She must have gone to see an eye doctor after that. Guilt gripped me by the throat. What sort of husband had I been that I had not noticed my wife's failing eyesight?

Chaz must have made the difficult decision to leave me when she was told that her vision would deteriorate. I was the bastard who had left her when she was given the sad news. I had never bothered to even come looking for her.

Emotion overwhelmed me and I covered my face with my hands. What was wrong with me that she could not tell me about her illness? Was I such a perfectionist that she thought I would not want her if she wasn't perfect?

Charlotte had said earlier that day that she had called me. It didn't take a genius to work that out why she called me, it was about her pregnancy. I punched into my other hand.

My mother had unknowingly kept me away from my son but I couldn't really blame her. Charlotte had not tried very hard. If you wanted to tell your ex that you were expecting his child, you would find a way to.

She had not tried very hard. Or even at all. That made me sad and angry. I understood that she was dealing with a difficult situation with her eye illness but there was no excuse to keep a father and son apart.

The fact that she was ill made it even worse. Charlotte was not in touch with any of her relatives or anyone from her past. What would have happened to our son if God forbid, something happened to her? He would have been taken into foster care, and all because Charlotte had been too proud to look for me. I was not mad. I was seething.

CHARLOTTE

"Is something the matter?" I asked Alex, ten minutes into the drive to Cleveland.

He had been different since the previous day when he returned home after checking out of the B&B. I'd hoped that we would spend the night together, making love, but he'd been silent and brooding. At bedtime, he had said good night and gone to the guest room.

I'd stood outside his door contemplating whether to go in or not. Courage had failed me and I'd spent a long, sleepless, horny night alone. Alex's sour mood had continued in the morning, which led me to believe that he did not want to be in the same house with me.

"No," he said.

"You know, it's okay if you want to continue staying in the B&B," I said.

He glanced at me. "It's not that."

"So there's something."

"Drop it, okay?"

I swallowed my hurt. In the years we had been married, nothing had been off-limits to talk about.

"We'll talk about it after your nappointment," he said.

I fiddled with the radio and searched for a station with soothing music because clearly, we would not be conversing. I gave up on trying to figure out what was bugging him.

As we got closer to Cleveland, my thoughts shifted to the appointment with the ophthalmologist. I didn't want to get my hopes up and then have them crushed. But a tiny seed of hope had grown. Maybe in the last two and a half years, a new treatment had been found.

With the wisdom that comes from hindsight. I should have gone for a second opinion but I'd been young and naïve. And then I panicked and all I could think about was what a burden I would be to Alex.

Would he understand when I explained all that as the reason why I didn't tell him about Kayden?

"Here we are," he said, easing into an empty parking space. He turned off the ignition and turned to me. "Whatever happens, I'm here and I'll always be. Okay?"

The anger was gone and all I saw was love in his eyes. My heart ached with so many things that I wanted to tell him but which I'd forfeited the right to.

I love you. So much.

I need you. I want you back in my life.

I tried to remember how my life and Kayden's had been before Alex came back and failed. All I saw was darkness. He had splashed color back into our lives. Kayden was flourishing with the attention from two adults.

I tried but, on some evenings, I was too tired to play with him. When there were the two of us, one person was always ready to play with him.

"Okay," I said softly.

We got out of the car and walked to the entrance of the building. It was nothing like the time I had gone to get my results after the eye tests. This time, even though I was nervous, I was bearing it well. I had Alex with me and I knew that whatever the outcome, unlike before I knew I had someone in my corner.

How I wish I'd not let my thoughts become so irrational back when we were married. I wished I'd given Alex a chance to be there for me. To fight with me. Instead, I'd focused on how much of a burden I would be and run.

But worse than that was keeping Kayden away from Alex. That was unforgivable.

The offices of doctors occupied half of the third floor. We walked up to the reception desk and introduced ourselves.

"Oh yes," she said. "Doctor Mueller is waiting for you. He said to show you in as soon as you got here."

Alex turned to me. "Do you want me to go in with you?"

"Yes please," I said, my belly twisted in knots.

We followed the smartly dressed middle aged lady to a door on the other side. She held it open and beckoned us in.

I couldn't see his features well but I could make out his graying hair and I made him out to be in his early sixties or so. He stood up and introduced himself. Alex introduced us then he and the doctor caught up about mutual friends.

"Please sit down," he said.

He got right into it, asking me questions and jotting down some notes.

"We're going to treat this like a new problem without considering your past diagnosis. That means that we'll do a myriad of tests and take it from there. How does that sound?"

He had a reassuring manner about him. An authoritative yet gentle voice and a manner that made me feel that I was in safe hands. "Sounds good."

The next couple of hours passed by behind machines and eye drops. None of the tests were invasive and I was relaxed throughout. When we were done, Dr. Mueller told us to return on Thursday for the results, which was perfect as we were leaving for Amy's wedding on Friday afternoon.

"I liked him," I told Alex on the way back. "Thank you I really appreciate your help. I know it must have been difficult to get an appointment that fast."

"You're welcome," he said.

We talked about the wedding a little. I admitted to Alex how excited I was and nervous.

"Why nervous?" he asked.

"Amy emailed me last night. She decided to invite my sister and her family at the last minute and she'd accepted the invitation."

I loved Amy but sometimes I wanted to strangle her. I wasn't sure whether a wedding was the right place to reconnect with my sister. I'd hurt her deeply and I didn't know how she would react to seeing me again.

I didn't deserve a second chance with her.

"Good. You need to be surrounded by people who love you," he said.

Are you one of those people? I knew that he loved me as a friend, but what I craved was to be loved like a woman. I'd missed that side of my life.

CHARLOTTE

Back in Woodfield, we stopped by Lulu's place to pick Kayden up. Alex went with me to the door and when Kayden saw him, he shrieked and ran to him. Alex grabbed him and lifted him up and held him close.

He kissed Kayden's forehead and then held him close again. My heart galloped in my chest. Had he somehow found out?

I thanked Lulu for keeping Kayden and also took the opportunity to ask her about the following Thursday. As always, she refused my offer to pay for the two days.

"We moms have to help each other out," she said and handed me Kayden's bag.

In the car, nausea swirled in my belly. I wracked my mind and tried to remember how Alex had behaved that morning when he came to pick us up. I'd been busy making sure that I'd packed everything Kayden would need for the day so I hadn't paid much attention.

"We're home, son," he said and my heart stopped.

I turned and met his gaze. I was the first to move. I grabbed the door and opened it. The nausea rose up my throat. I sprinted to the side of the house, away from view and bent down to throw up.

Oh God! How had he figured it out? The only person who knew was Amy and I knew her loyalty was to me first. Even if she did tell Alex, she would warn me first. Alex was a smart guy. I'd been fooling myself that I could hide Kayden's paternity for long.

As a lawyer, he was used to putting parts of a puzzle together. I wanted to kick myself for not telling him before he found out by himself. Now, he would never believe that I had planned on telling him.

Alex and Kayden were already in the house and I followed them in and headed straight to the bathroom to rinse out my mouth and then to the bedroom to freshen up. I could hear Alex and Kayden's voices coming from the bathroom.

Kayden loved bath time and his dad never tired of blowing bubbles off his skin, making him giggle. When I'd changed into comfortable clothes, I went to the kitchen and warmed Kayden's food while getting our dinner started.

I refused to meet Alex's eyes while I brought Kayden's dinner to the table.

"Did you enjoy your bath with…" I wasn't sure what to say.

"Dad?"

I took a deep breath. "Dad." It felt terrifying but good to say the word aloud.

"Daaaad!" Kayden said, over and over again, as if getting his tongue used to forming the word.

But it was the smile on Alex's face that made my heart stop. The only way to describe it was pure, unadulterated joy. Fresh guilt smashed into me. I was a horrible, selfish person. How did I ever let myself think Alex was anything but a fantastic guy. A guy I really did not deserve.

"I'll feed him," he said and pulled a chair next to Kayden's high chair.

I was cooking chili for our dinner and kept myself busy enough so that I didn't have to sit down with Alex. But I couldn't escape the conversation forever.

Kayden went to sleep and then Alex and I sat down to dinner. We ate silently and when we were done, we sat facing each other.

"Were you ever going to tell me?" he asked.

A lump grew in my chest, spreading until it filled every empty space and then expanded further, making it painful to breath. "Yes." My voice was a whisper.

"When Kayden was eighteen years old?" he asked, his voice harsh.

"I'm sorry," I said.

"Start from the beginning and this time, I want the complete truth. No lies either by omission or out-rightly."

I cleared my throat and started at the beginning, my words taking me back to a simpler, happier time. Tears interrupted my explanation and I had to stop to gather my composure before continuing. I told him all of it and left nothing out, including my conversation with his mother.

I dwelled a lot on not wanting to be a burden to him but it seemed to go over Alex's head.

"Was there something I did to make you believe that I would not be there for you?" he asked, his voice raw with pain.

I shook my head. "It was not about you. I'd brought so much heartbreak into your life and I was determined not to heap more into it. I took you away from the family that you loved so much."

"That's bullshit!" Alex thundered. "They rejected you and in doing so, they disrespected my choice. Love means accepting someone's right to make their own choices."

"Alex I wasn't thinking straight at the time. I can't tell you how many times I've wished that I'd done it differently."

"What about Kayden? He's my son Charlotte! I deserved to know. I've missed so much of his life," he said.

I preferred the anger to the sadness in his voice. Tears filled my eyes. What did you say to something that was true? "I'm truly sorry." It sounded so inadequate to say sorry. It wasn't going to bring back the time Alex had lost with Kayden.

He would never experience the joy of hearing Kayden's first word or see his first step. So many firsts that he would never experience.

"I didn't try very hard. After I left the message with your mom, I told myself that you had chosen to ignore me and thus Kayden and I made myself move on."

"And this time? When we met at the diner? I couldn't leave Woodfield fast enough as far as you were concerned," he said, a trace of bitterness in his voice.

I bowed my head. Shame came over me. He was right. I'd wanted him to leave and leave me and Kayden to our lives. All I cared about was maintaining the status quo of my life.

I'd decided to be honest with Alex, even when making some admissions was painful. I raised my gaze to his. His cobalt blue eyes bore into me, questioning, wondering, nursing pain.

I had made so many bad decisions all of which had ended up hurting the person I'd loved the most in the world. I made a decision right there and then. No matter how painful, I was never going to lie to Alex ever again.

We were joined together by Kayden and we would always be in each other's lives, in one capacity or another.

I cleared my throat. "I was frightened that when you found out about my vision problems, you'd take Kayden away from me."

His eyes widened. "Oh Chaz. You know me better than that. I would never do that. Not in a million years. You know that?"

I was too choked up to speak. I nodded.

ALEX

No matter how much I wanted to be angry at Charlotte for not telling me about Kayden, I couldn't. She had done it for the right reasons, as misguided as they were. Besides, there was a part of me that would always blame myself.

In the years we had been married, I hadn't made her feel secure enough to know that I was a permanent feature. I was not only around for the good times but for the bad as well. Especially for the bad. That was what marriage was.

The one lesson that I'd learned from my parents was that marriage was a lifelong commitment. It was easy to heap the blame on Charlotte but I shouldered almost as much blame as she did.

"I should have tried to find you," I said to her. "I'm sorry that I never had the faith in you like Amy did. I should have known the contents of that letter were bullshit."

She smiled. "I was pretty convincing."

"But Amy knew," I said.

"It's easier for a friend to see through the lies. It was you whom I'd supposedly betrayed," she said. "You were angry and hurt as I knew you'd be."

"Why that?" I said, remembering the nights I'd lain awake consumed by jealousy as I imagined another man making love to Charlotte.

"It was the only way I knew to make you hate me enough to go back to your old life," she said.

She knew me well, except for one thing. "There's nothing you can do that would make me hate you."

"Unless it involves hurting Kayden," she said.

"Correct but that would never happen."

"Never," she said fiercely. "He kept me going when I thought I'd reached the end."

"He's an awesome kid," I said. "And it's all thanks to you Chaz. You're an awesome mom and he's lucky to have you."

Silence fell between us. The way forward was so hazy and so unclear.

"What happens now?" Chaz said.

"I don't know. What I do know is that you and Kayden are stuck with me. I don't know how we'll make it work but we will."

"A day at a time, for now," she said.

"A day at a time."

I loved her so much. Her and Kayden and to know that we

were a real family and no man was going to walk into our lives and claim Kayden as his son. That made me feel as if I could fly. And happy. And home at last.

So much had changed with the knowledge that Kayden was my son. I had to tell my family when I went back home. I had to update my wills and such and include Kayden. I'd never removed Charlotte as she was still my legal wife. I wondered how she would take that news, but it wasn't the time to talk about that.

I covered Charlotte's hand with mine in a moment of complete understanding between us. I didn't know how the future would unfold, but I was at peace. The relief of having my questions answered was indescribable.

Charlotte hadn't stopped loving me. I couldn't imagine how much it had taken for her to walk away from the man she loved. From her husband and the father of the child she was carrying in her belly.

I ached to hold her in my arms. To shower her with my love all night. "Let's go to bed."

"Mine or yours?" she asked, her tone playful.

"I don't care where, as long as you're with me." And that there was the bottom line.

The past didn't matter. I wanted to be with Charlotte and Kayden. I wanted us to be a family. But I wasn't naïve enough to imagine that we could bridge the gap of two years in a single night, week or even a month.

Despite knowing and understanding the reasons that had led Charlotte to leave, it still hurt and it would take a while for me to trust her wholly again. What if she ran into another setback, would she flee?

It was the same for her as well. She needed to know that she could depend on me at all times. That I would be there. That her happiness and Kayden's meant everything to me.

ALEX

We turned off the lights and went to Chaz's room hand in hand. We shut the door and took off our clothes while soaking in each other's presence. All the walls between us had crumbled and we could see each other clearly for the first time in over two years.

When we were both naked, we slipped into bed and she moved naturally into my arms. Our lovemaking that night was filled with a tenderness that had been missing before. A sweetness, tinged with the knowledge that we shared something precious. A son.

Charlotte had to go into work the following day. She was a little shy with me in the morning and it was a little awkward for me too. We were learning how to be a family.

She fed Kayden his breakfast while I cleaned up the kitchen and then made us some coffee. We went out to play in the grass with the ball while Chaz showered and got ready for work.

Kayden's favorite outdoor game was soccer. He grinned and laughed when he managed to kick the ball and then run after it.

"You boys have yourselves a good day," Chaz said, coming outside with her bag.

"We will," I said.

We kissed and then she lifted a resisting Kayden into her arms. "Traitor," she said and I laughed.

"Say bye to mommy," I said to Kayden.

I had so many decisions to make but first I had to play soccer with my son. There would be time to figure out the next step. After half an hour, Kayden was ready to go back to the house for a drink and his morning nap.

In the afternoon, I decided to take Kayden to the nearby park, seeing how much he loved going places. I fastened him into the car seat and double checked his bag again. A blanket to relax on, more diapers than I thought he would need, two cups of milk, snacks and water.

"Daddy and son's day out," I said to him as I jammed the key into the ignition.

It was a beautiful afternoon to be out. Not too hot with a breeze that kept the air cool. The park was only a five-minute drive away and, on the way, Kayden made happy noises and kept his gaze focused on the passing landscape.

We reached the park and I got the bag out and shoved it under Kayden's stroller. I lifted him from the back seat and fastened him into the stroller. After locking the car, we entered the park and strolled along the walking path that meandered through the trees and grass and a small manmade lake.

"Daddy!" Kayden said, pointing at ducks floating gracefully on the lake.

Time lost meaning as we strolled in the park and finally stopped in the play area. I unfastened Kayden from his stroller and walked with him to the slides. He wasn't ready to slide at first and was more fascinated by the bright colors of the playground equipment.

"Your first born?" A mom with a little boy who looked to be in the same age bracket as Kayden, asked.

"Yes. Only child." My chest swelled with pride as I said the words I never once thought I would say.

"Mine too," she said.

We chatted easily as we helped the boys navigate the swings and then the slides. I wished I had my phone to take a picture of Kayden when he agreed to a slide. He wore a look of wonder and pure joy. And he wanted to do it over and over again.

I lifted him from the slide to give him his sippy cup of milk and as soon as he was done, he wiggled out of my lap and waddled over to the slides. I wished that Chaz was here with me to see it.

When we finally made it out of the play area, it was because Kayden was so tired that he could barely keep his eyes open. He fell asleep as soon as I fastened him into his car seat.

I chuckled softly as I drove him, impatient to regale Charlotte with tales of our afternoon. As I turned the corner, I caught sight of Charlotte outside the barn house, pacing up and down. When she heard the car, she sprinted towards us and my heart dropped to my feet, sure that something horrible had happened.

"Where is he?" she screamed as I slowed the car to a stop.

"Who?" I said, thinking that Charlotte had lost her mind.

"Kayden! Where's my baby?"

She gripped the passenger door and flung it open. When she saw Kayden peacefully sleeping in his car seat, her whole body slumped. "You're okay." She covered her face with her hands.

"What's going on Charlotte?" I said.

"I thought you took him," she said, uncovering her face to reveal tears streaming down her face.

"You thought I stole Kayden?"

CHARLOTTE

I stole a glance at Alex's profile and I wanted to punch myself. What was the matter with me? Why did I always mess up when it came to Alex? What had he done to make me so mistrustful? How could I think that he would steal Kayden after he had more or less promised that he would never do something like that?

It was easy to say that I trusted him but when I was tested, I failed. I had come from work bearing a pie I'd bought at work for our dinner and when I found Alex's car missing, panic had set in. I'd dashed into all the rooms in the house calling Kayden's name and when I saw that it was empty, my panic went up a notch.

All sorts of crazy thoughts had run through my mind. Alex knew about my eyesight. He had taken him to New York and I would never see my baby again. He would fight for custody with the full support of his parents and win because I was an unfit mother. He would bring up my past and how I was raised by a drug addict mother.

My life was over. When Alex drove onto the farm, I'd been pacing rapidly like a woman possessed. Just remembering the sight I must have been, made my toes curl up in shame.

The atmosphere between us in the last two days had been horrible. We had barely exchanged a dozen words and only when it had to do with Kayden. I understood why he was hurt. Shame filled my insides. What right did I have to mistrust him when I was the one who had left him with only a letter for an explanation?

We drove to Cleveland in silence. I waited until we reached our destination and when Alex was about to get out of the car, I touched his arm. A current of electricity zipped between us.

"I'm really sorry about what happened," I said, pleading with my eyes.

He let out a deep sigh and sunk back into his seat. "Is it so difficult to trust me? I can't believe you'd think such horrible things about me. From the very first day we met Chaz, I've done nothing but show you that you can trust me."

I swallowed hard. He was so right. That first day on the train, he said that he would be waiting at the next station and even though the next train had been delayed, he had been where he had promised to be.

Then there was the confrontation with his parents. I'd been afraid that he would do what his parents wanted and leave me for a more suitable girl. All along he had promised that nothing would ever come between us. And it hadn't.

"I'm the problem, not you," I said to him. "In my heart, I know you'd never take Kayden away from me. I just default to thinking the worst any time something happens."

He was quiet for a few seconds before he spoke again. "Do you think you can reconfigure your settings to think positive things first, at least when it comes to me?" A hint of a smile played on his lips.

"What I can do for sure is promise to work on it," I said.

He nodded. "That's good enough. Let's go."

Alex took my hand into his, engulfing it in his big strong one, making me feel warm and safe. I inhaled deeply as butterflies rolled in my stomach.

"Nervous?" he asked in the elevator.

"A bit," I admitted.

"Don't be. Whatever the doctor says, we'll face it together." His confidence was contagious and I found myself relaxing.

This time, the doctor still had a patient with him and we had to wait for fifteen minutes before we went in. I tried to read the doctor's facial expression as we exchanged pleasantries but he gave nothing away. He was just as pleasant and friendly as the last time.

"What's the verdict doctor?" Alex asked when we sat down.

"It's not as bad as Mrs. Turner was told by her doctor two years ago, I think," Dr. Mueller said. He smiled.

I stifled a giggle. Mrs. Turner sounded like Alex's mom. He'd automatically assumed that we were married and Alex didn't correct him.

My heart rose with hope. I tried to tell myself to calm down. Not to set myself up for disappointment but the thought of going completely blind terrified me. I never came to terms with it.

"A lot of things have changed in the optometric world and treatments these days have come a long way. The good news first. I won't bog you down with the treatment details for now, but we can restore Mrs. Turner's eyesight to at least eighty percent," Dr. Mueller said.

My jaw dropped. I pressed a hand to my chest, tears sprouted to my eyes. Eighty percent? "Oh my God, that would be…." I fumbled for the correct word. "A gift."

"Charlotte was told that her eyesight would deteriorate until she went completely blind," Alex said.

"Yes. Without this treatment, it will."

"When can she get it done?"

"It's an expensive procedure," the doctor said delicately.

Alex waved an impatient hand away. "She's covered by my insurance."

The doctor smiled, clearly relieved. "In that case we can schedule it a week from now. My secretary will give you the details."

Alex asked for more details about the procedure. I couldn't concentrate enough to understand. All I kept thinking was that I would see every little change that would happen with Kayden as he grew up. I would know my son's face.

My body trembled as I tried to wrap my mind around this unexpected gift. We wrapped up with the doctor and Alex and I left and went to the reception area. Alex filled out the forms as Dr. Mueller's secretary secured an appointment date for us.

CHARLOTTE

The procedure was to be done in a nearby hospital and she would do all the bookings necessary. All I needed to do was to show up. She mentioned the figure of the whole procedure and my jaw dropped. The euphoria cloud that had enveloped me fell away. What was I thinking? I couldn't afford that kind of money.

I waited until we left the office. I gripped Alex's arm, bringing him to a stop. "Alex, you can't pay that kind of money for me. I just won't allow it."

"It's not me paying Chaz, it's my insurance. You're covered and so will Kayden once I update my information."

I frowned. "I don't understand. I didn't think insurance companies covered ex-wives?"

"They don't but you're not my ex-wife. I never signed the divorce papers," he said.

My insides turned to water. *We were still married?*

"Let's go," he said, taking my hand. "It's lunch time. Let's go have lunch and celebrate. I know of a nice restaurant not far from here."

As the shock wore off, I looked at Alex with new eyes. He was still my husband! I wanted to pinch him to make sure that everything was real and that I wasn't dreaming.

At the back of my mind, I'd always worried in case some medical emergency came up and Kayden needed to be hospitalized. Insurance had been on my list of goals for the year. I wanted to cry with the relief of knowing that whatever happened, Kayden would be taken care off.

And me too. I knew I didn't deserve any of it. Overcome by emotion and unable to control myself, I broke down in the car. Loud, noisy sobs wracked my body. Alex snapped open my seatbelt and his arm went around me, pulling me close. I lay my head on his shoulder as my body shook uncontrollably.

"It's okay Chaz. Everything will be fine," he said.

"I feel like a real adult," I said to Alex as I sipped a glass of chilled water and reveled in the buzz of muted conversation around us at the restaurant.

"You don't need to have lunch in a restaurant to feel like an adult. You're an adult every day, being Kayden's mom and going to work to provide for him."

Warmth flowed through me. "You say the nicest things Alex. You always did."

“That’s because they’re true,” he said. “How do you feel about the treatment?"

"I can't wait," I said. “I feel as if I’m about to have a new beginning. None of this would have happened without you. Thank you.”

“You’re welcome,” he said and then a twinkle came into his eye. “You almost collapsed when I told you that I never signed the divorce papers. I’m hoping that it was good news?”

Shyness came over me. I smiled to cover it up. “Definitely good news.” Everything was too new for me to question it. I didn’t know whether Alex wanted to remain married or we would divorce after my treatment.

It was crazy to imagine that all along, he and I had been married.

The waiter brought our food and I made appreciative noises as the smell of roasted chicken and potatoes wafted up my nose.

“You always did love your food,” Alex teased then the waiter withdrew.

“Me and you both,” I quipped, feeling carefree and young. For the last two years, weighed down by the need to survive and provide for my baby son, I’d always felt ten years older.

It felt good to be my age again. To laugh and to enjoy a meal in a classy restaurant.

“You spoilt me when we were living together,” he said. “I don’t remember ever cooking,” he said.

I laughed. "I'm glad I did because now you do most of the cooking."

We shared a fond look as we remembered the past. This time without pain. My phone shrilled from the handbag hanging on the chair. I reached for it and looked at the huge name across the screen. Mrs. Horace.

I'd had the settings on my cell phone changed to make everything on the screen extra-large.

"I have to get this one," I said to Alex and swiped to answer. "Hi Mrs. Horace."

Her time with her son and daughter-in-law was almost up and she was probably calling to arrange to have her house cleaned up. Dust gathered quickly in our part of the world.

We exchanged pleasantries but mostly she wanted to know about Kayden.

"I miss that sweet boy and I'm sad I won't get to see him start school," she said.

I went still. "Why is that?" A sinking feeling came over my belly.

"I'm moving here permanently Charlotte, that's why I'm calling you. My son and his family need me and they've built the sweetest cottage for me by their property."

"Oh." I didn't know what to say.

"I'm so sorry, I know how much you need me," she continued.

That snapped me out of my shock. "Don't worry about it. They're family and you have to do the right thing by them. Kayden and I will be fine. Don't worry."

She cleared her throat. "There's something else. We decided to sell the property. My son is actually down in Woodfield to see to it. I feel terrible but maybe the person who buys it will want to continue renting out the barn to you?"

That was truly bad news. But there was no use taking it out on Mrs. Horace. It wasn't her fault. It was no one's fault. It was just part of the ebb and flow of life. I would find another place to live and life would move on.

I reassured Mrs. Horace but as soon as I disconnected the call, my brave face fell.

"What happened?" he asked.

I told him about Mrs. Horace and the house.

"We'll figure out something," he said. "Everything usually has a solution, as long as we don't panic."

I laughed nervously. He'd read me correctly. I'd started panicking and imagining the worst.

ALEX

We picked up Kayden from Lulu's place and drove back home. It hadn't taken a lot of thought to decide that it would soon be home. At least for Charlotte and Kayden. If they would have me, it would be my home too. A plan was slowly forming in my mind.

There was nothing in New York for me. As I'd told Charlotte once, home was where your heart was. And my heart was firmly with my wife and Kayden. I was beginning to believe that we could make a go of it and this time we would succeed. We had gone through so much but through it all my love for Charlotte had not gone away one bit.

If anything I loved her more than I ever had.

When we got home, I excused myself saying I needed to get some stuff from town. I settled my family and then drove to town, to the B&B. I assumed that was where Mrs. Horace's son was staying.

I was right. The B&B wasn't strict about giving information concerning their guests. The crime rate was practically non-existent and I had ceased being a stranger, especially when word got out that I was staying with Charlotte.

"He's at the restaurant," Jeanette who manned the reception said.

"Thanks," I said. "I'll join him there."

It wasn't difficult to find a man having breakfast alone in the B&B dining room.

"Mr. Horace?" I said, standing at a respectful distance.

"That would be me but most people call me Charles. Mr. Horace was my late father." He had a friendly face and manner.

"Sorry to intrude on your dinner." I introduced myself and told him why I wanted to see him.

He stood up. "I'm having an early dinner. Will you join me?"

"Thank you but I'll say no to the dinner. I had a late lunch," I said.

"So you're interested in the property?" he asked.

"Very much so," I said. "And I'm willing to pay cash for it." I wasn't being a smart negotiator but I didn't care. I was so excited to be able to buy the property for Charlotte and Kayden.

It meant that whatever happened between us, they would always have a home. My family would always be taken care of. There was more I needed to do in New York but this was an important first step.

I ordered a coffee as Charles and I compared ways of life in Virginia and New York. The waiter brought my coffee and we went straight into business.

Because I was paying cash, Charles reduced the buying price which pleased me. We agreed that his lawyer in town would draw up the paperwork and the following week, after the necessary inspections were done, I would sign the paperwork.

We shook hands, both of us pleased with the outcome of the meeting. I sat in my car and turned on my cell phone. There were the usual messages from Abigail, but more threatening. I deleted most of them without reading.

There were messages from my father and a voicemail from my mother, asking me to return home as there were things we needed to discuss. I immediately knew what it was about.

I had a thought. Today was Wednesday. Charlotte had the rest of the week off and we had both looked forward to spending Thursday together before leaving for the wedding on Friday.

But she would understand. I could catch a late flight to New York and then come back early on Friday morning. Yeah that could work. I called my secretary and had her book a flight for me.

It felt off to text my mother to tell her I'd be home for dinner that evening. For the last few weeks, I'd eaten dinner with Charlotte every day. It felt so real, while my life back in New York felt unreal, like it belonged to another person.

"I'm back," I said as I entered the house.

"We're in the kitchen," Charlotte called, reminding me of the earlier days when I'd come home from work and she would call out from the bedroom or kitchen.

Kayden grinned at me from his high chair, his face smeared with spaghetti and sauce. He raised a plastic spoon in the air. "Daadd."

I grinned like a fool. I always did when he called me dad. "You're feeding yourself! Good job."

Charlotte made a face. "Most of it is on the floor. He won't let me feed him."

I laughed. "That happened to me too. Sometimes, Kayden thinks he's a little adult who doesn't need help."

"Did you get what you wanted?" she asked in a poor attempt at finding out where I'd been.

I kept a straight face. "Yeah, I did." I wasn't going to tell her about the property just yet. I planned to tell her when I had the deed in my hand. "But I'm going to fly down to New York this evening."

Her face fell and that pleased me. It was nice to know that she would miss me.

"Kayden will miss you," she said.

I went to her and wrapped my hands around her waist. "Just Kayden?" I asked as I nibbled on her neck in a spot I knew to be extra sensitive.

She giggled. "Okay. I'll miss you too. Happy?"

"Very happy. I'll miss you too but I'll be back early on Friday, and then we can drive up to the lodge."

“Kayden and I will go shopping for clothes tomorrow. We feel like going out to celebrate,” she said, turning around to face me. She draped her hands around my neck.

“I’ll leave you my credit card,” I said.

“No, you’ve done so much. I’m not exactly a pauper,” she said.

“I know.” I lowered my head to kiss her. “I just want to spoil the two of you to make up for the time I wasn’t around.”

“You already have.” Charlotte returned my kiss with fervor, prodding my lips open with her tongue.

My dick pulsed to life in my pants. I groaned. “I’m tempted to cancel my flight.”

She laughed. “Don’t. I know it must be important.”

“It is,” I said and reluctantly stepped back. I went to Kayden and kissed his forehead. “Next time we’ll all go together.”

“That would please your parents,” she said.

“They’re not the same people you knew,” I said. “They’ve seen how unhappy I’ve been without you. I can’t wait for everyone to meet Kayden. Time to freshen up.”

I took a quick shower and dressed. I didn’t bother carrying a bag as I would get fresh clothes from my apartment. When I was ready, I found Charlotte and Kayden in the living room driving toy cars round the carpet.

Charlotte stood up and gave me a suggestive hug, pressing her body against mine. Her nipples pressed against my chest emitting another groan from me. I cupped her ass and pressed her against my erect dick.

"I can't wait for you to come back," she whispered into my ear.

"I can't wait to be back."

We drew apart and I lifted Kayden from the floor. As if sensing that I was leaving he clung to me and refused to get down. My heart felt like it was splitting in two.

If I'd had any doubts over what I planned to do, they ended when my son wouldn't remove his hands from around my neck. I was done with New York. I would fly back over the coming weeks to wrap things up, but my life there was finished.

I belonged here with Kayden and Charlotte. An opportunity for work would come up. Maybe I would open my own practice. There was no rush and I had a lot of time to decide what I wanted to do with the rest of my life. All I knew at that point was whatever I decided, it would be in Woodfield or the nearby towns.

ALEX

I got home in time for dinner. Nina opened the front door and hugged me as if I'd been gone for months instead of weeks. To be honest I felt the same. So much had happened in such a short time. I'd found Charlotte and discovered that I was a dad.

I was in the process of buying a home for Chaz and Kayden. I had made up my mind to leave New York. My life, which had seemed so dull, was now full and the future excited me to no end. I was even contemplating reversing my vasectomy. Maybe Charlotte and I would try and add to the brood.

There was so much to be excited about.

"Welcome home," Nina said. "You know where everyone is."

"Everyone?"

"Yes, your sister and Mr. Richard are here," Nina said.

A lightness came over my chest at the thought of seeing my nephews? "The kids are here too?"

"No, just the parents," Nina said.

"Okay."

"Hello stranger," Richard said when I walked into the drawing room.

"Hey."

"Don't get overexcited to see your family after going MIA for three weeks," my sister said, her voice dripping with sarcasm.

"It's nice to see you too Mary." I kissed her cheek and shook Richard's hand.

"Alex," my mother said, as I kissed her cheek.

I shook my father's hand and compared our greeting to mine and Kayden's. I hoped that he would always throw his hands around me and give me a bear hug, even when he became an adult.

I grabbed the bottle of wine from the ice bucket and a glass and poured myself some and then sat down.

"I'm glad you made it," my mother said. "We have a lot to talk about."

My mother didn't believe or practice small talk. If there was something she wanted to talk about, she dove straight into it.

"Starting with your child!" My father boomed. "Congratulations, son!" He grinned and stared at me proudly.

"It's not the ideal way to do it, but I'm sure we can arrange a quick wedding," my mother said. "I suggested it to Abigail and she's fine with it."

"I'll have a sister," Mary squealed.

"It's about time our kids had cousins," Richard said.

I shook my head in disbelief. Damn Abigail! If she thought that she could coerce me into a marriage by getting my family to pile on the pressure, she didn't know me very well.

"I'm not marrying Abigail and she's not pregnant with my child. She lied to you."

Silence descended in the room.

"Why would she do that?" My mother asked.

I shrugged. "That's something you're going to have to ask her."

"Are you sure son?" my father said.

"A hundred percent."

"Well then, we can forget about that," he said, surprising me as well as everyone else.

"James," my mother said but before she could continue my father interrupted.

"If Alex says, he is not the father, then I believe him and so should you. I'm done interfering in his life. He's an adult and we'll respect his decisions from now on."

I stared at my father, stunned.

"Fine," mother said, the words clearly forced out.

I can't explain how it felt to have my father finally recognize that I was a man capable of my own decisions. "But I do have some news which I know will please you." I turned to my mother.

"Do you remember when I came back home after Charlotte and I parted ways?"

"Yes," she said.

"She called the house and you spoke to her, right?"

She shifted in her seat and looked visibly uncomfortable. "She said she wanted to talk to you but I didn't want her to cause you any more pain."

"That was not your decision to make mother," I said. "It was mine." I met everyone's gaze before returning to my mother. "She called because she was pregnant with my son. She wanted to let me know."

"Oh God," my mother cried out and covered her mouth with her hand. For a moment I felt sorry for her but her stubbornness and refusal to accept Charlotte had cost us a lot of lost time and I wanted her to know the impact that not informing me had.

"His name is Kayden and he's almost sixteen months old." I couldn't keep the smile from my face.

"Oh Alex, that's wonderful," my sister said. "I can't wait to meet him."

"Do you think Charlotte will let us see him?" my mother said in a voice that tugged at my heartstrings.

"Tell her we know we've made mistakes in the past and we'd like to rectify that," my father said in a gruff voice.

It was the closest to an apology he would offer but it was good enough.

"Charlotte has gone through a lot in the last couple of years" I told the whole story and ended with the scheduled eye surgery the coming week. My mother and Mary dabbed at their eyes.

I told my father about my decision to move to Woodfield.

"Why don't you open a branch of James and Alex Turner LLP in Cleveland?" he asked.

"Really?" I said, unable to believe what I was hearing. I hadn't dared to believe that my father would want to continue working with me when I left the firm.

He stood up and so did I. He offered his hand and I gripped it. "To a successful partnership."

"To a successful partnership."

"This calls for more than wine," my mother said. "I'll go and get a bottle of champagne."

CHARLOTTE

A knock came on the door as I was cleaning up the kitchen, the only chance I had after Kayden napped. I frowned. It was rare to get an unexpected guest. It was Thursday, so it couldn't possibly be Alex who was still in New York. Besides, Alex never knocked, after all, he was living with us.

I dried my hands on my apron as I moved to the front door. Woodfield was safe and I can't remember ever checking the peep hole before opening the door. I flung it open. A dark haired, obviously from the city woman, stood there smiling at me.

"Hi," she said. "You must be Charlotte."

My vision was bad but I recognized people I'd met before. I had never seen the woman before. "Have we met?"

"No we haven't, but I've heard of you and am sure you have heard of me. My name is Abigail. I just flew in from New York."

My blood turned to ice. New York meant Alex. She had a connection to Alex and that's how she knew me. I fisted my hands to keep them from trembling.

"May I come in?" she asked.

"Sure." I moved to one side to let her in.

She was fashionably slim and tall. Not curvy and messy like me. I could feel her eyes on me as we sat down opposite each other.

"I'm Alex's fiancée," she said. "I'm sure he told you that."

I blinked several times like an idiot. Fiancée. *Oh God.* I was going to be sick. "I don't understand."

"He never told you about me, did he?" she continued in a smooth, calm voice, making me feel like a blubbering idiot.

"No," I whispered.

I thought about the nights we had spent making love, whispering sweet nothings to each other. I'd believed that Alex was mine. Nausea rose up my throat.

She moved her hand to her belly. "Did you imagine that he's been alone all this time. We more or less live together."

Yes, I had imagined that he was alone. That he still loved me. I wanted to cover my eyes and cry. I felt like such a fool. I hadn't thought that Alex was capable of such deceit. I deserved it too, after the way I'd left our marriage.

But he knew the reasons why and he had said he'd understood and forgiven me. Why then hadn't he told me about Abigail? Why had he slept with me and pretended that he was available to try again? He had cheated on his fiancée.

"We're expecting a baby and Mrs. Turner wants us to get married as quickly as possible." Her voice hardened. "I don't know what hold you have over Alex, but I came to ask you to leave us alone. You had your chance and you messed up. Let Alex move on and have a chance at happiness with us."

She stood up, but my legs refused to move.

Even after she left, I stayed rooted to the spot, losing track of time. I only realized that I was crying when my vision became too blurry to see. Alex was a cheater. The Alex I'd been married to would not have done something like that.

He had turned into someone I didn't know.

Another disturbing thought popped into my mind. Alex had said that we were still married. Was that true or had he lied to me about that too? He couldn't have, I decided thinking about the insurance.

Why was he doing all those things for me when he had another life with someone else? I didn't understand any of it. All I knew was that I wanted no part of it. I didn't want to be responsible for messing up his life again.

I wiped away my tears with the back of my hand. Alex was returning the following day. This time there was no panic. I just couldn't bear to see him. I would drive to the lodge earlier and leave a note for him. That way, we could each move on with our lives and this time, for good.

CHARLOTTE

The view on the drive up the mountains was gorgeous. In the sunlight, the peaks appeared as if they were dressed in gold. Beside me in the cab, Kayden was silent, as if he knew that our lives had changed once again.

I ached with sadness. For a few weeks, my dream of a family and love had been resurrected. I had fallen in love all over again with Alex. He had made me believe that we could work.

I had so many questions and no one to answer them. How could I have allowed myself to be so gullible? Alex was a catch. He drew attention everywhere he went. He was everything that a woman wanted in a man.

I had deserted our marriage. It had been naïve of me to think all that time he had been brooding over me. We followed a winding road until we got to the picturesque lodge.

It was picture perfect and the ideal location to have a wedding. I tried to be excited about the ceremony but all I could think about was Alex. If only he hadn't come back into our lives but even that was lying. He was an awesome dad to Kayden and my little boy deserved to have his dad in his life. Despite all I couldn't deny him that.

The cab came to a smooth stop in front of the scenic rustic lodge. After paying the driver, I lifted Kayden out of his car seat and a friendly concierge helped me unbuckle the car seat and carry it together with our bag to the lobby.

The lobby was beautiful with a shiny wooden floor and curved seats arranged around a wooden table,

I gave my name to the lady at the check in.

"Oh, you must be with the wedding party. Miss Amy booked the family suite for you. It has a master bedroom and a smaller bedroom," she said.

My chest ached at the reminder that we should have been here with Alex. I forced a smile. "Yes, thank you. That's perfect."

After I'd checked us in, we followed the concierge down a hallway that took several turns before we reached our door. As I waited for him to open the door, I heard footsteps and then a familiar voice.

"Charlotte, is that you?"

My mother's voice reincarnated in my sister. Helen. A cold sweat broke out in my skin. After Abigail's visit the previous day, I'd not thought of anything else except Alex. I'd forgotten that Helen was going to be at the wedding. What was I going to tell her?

How would I deal with her anger? The concierge had already opened the door and was carrying in our things. The temptation to follow him in and shut the door was strong but that was the coward's way out. I was done with behaving like a coward.

I breathed in deeply and whirled around.

"It is you," she whispered and closed the gap between us. "Oh Charlotte, Amy told me everything. I never thought I'd ever see you again." Tears fell from her eyes.

She took my hands and held my gaze. There was no judgement in her eyes. Just pure love.

"Oh Helen," I cried, and wrapped my hands around her as best as I could with Kayden in my arms.

"Mom," a voice said behind Helen and we broke apart.

Helen moved and Kacy came forward, looking at me quizzically but when she shifted her stare to Kayden, her pretty little face was wreathed in smiles.

"Oh my goodness, Kacy, you're so big. You must be four and a half now," I said.

She nodded. "Yes. You look like my mom."

"That's because I'm her sister and this is your cousin Kayden. He's almost one and a half."

"He's so handsome," Helen said.

Edward and I exchanged a hug then he excused himself, leaving me with Helen and Kacy.

"Let's go in," I said and led the way into the suite.

Seeing another kid, Kayden was eager to get out of my hold. I lowered him to the ground in the small living room of the suite.

"This is just like ours, mom," Kacy said. "Can Kayden and I explore?"

"Yes, you can but don't go into the bathroom, okay?" Helen said.

"Okay mom," Kacy said and took Kayden's hand who looked up at her as if she was a real life princess.

I laughed. I'd never thought I'd ever see the two cousins together. I'd thought about Kacy a lot over the years, wondering how she looked and how she talked. "Kayden is already in love with his cousin."

"He's beautiful," Helen said and then moved seats to sit next to me. She took my hand in hers. "Amy said you'd be here but I didn't know whether to believe her or not."

I swallowed hard. "I'm sorry Helen."

She shook her head. "Don't be. I knew from the very beginning as did Amy, that there had to be a compelling reason why you did what you did. We were right. Amy told me the whole story."

A sob broke out of me. Understanding was difficult to take. It made me feel shittier and undeserving. It would have been easier to deal with her anger.

"I'm sorry you went through so much alone," she said. "Amy told me but I want to hear it from you."

And so I told her. She squeezed my hand as I spoke. I didn't stop where Alex found me. I told her everything up to and including Abigail's visit the previous day.

"Did you speak to him at all?" she asked me gently.

"There is nothing to talk about," I said.

Helen stared at me without speaking. "May I be your big sister right now?"

"I'd love that," I said with a nervous laugh.

"Give Alex a chance to tell you his side of things. Don't jump to conclusions. Your past rush to imagine the very worst caused you so much pain. You don't want to make a harsh judgement without facts. What appears to be is not always the reality."

Her words sounded familiar. All air left my lungs when the memory came to me. It was the conversation that Alex and I had when I thought he'd stolen Kayden and taken him to New York. His words came to me as if he was right there speaking them.

Is it so difficult to trust me? I can't believe you'd think such horrible things about me. From the very first day we met Chaz, I've done nothing but show you that you can trust me.

But this was different. A woman was pregnant with his child. A woman that he had proposed marriage to or at least promised that they had a future together.

"She couldn't have lied to me!" I said.

"How do you know? The only person you know is Alex. A man who refused to be bullied out of marrying you by his family. I've never seen two people who loved each other as you did. From everything I know there must be a rational explanation to this," Helen said.

"I wish I was more trusting, like you," I said. Fear coursed through my veins as I spoke. What if I did as she suggested and gave Alex another chance and he broke my heart?

But what if, like Helen said, there was an explanation for it? Alex had asked me to trust him. I squeezed my fist together. I wanted to take that leap of faith so badly. I stood on the edge of the cliff, frightened to make that leap that would lead me to calling him. To open my heart to him.

Before I could make up my mind, a rapt knock came on the door before the knob turned and the door swung open. The subject of our conversation appeared, his face tight in barely suppressed anger. Alex looked like he was about to pounce on someone.

CHARLOTTE

"Hello Helen," he said tightly.

"Nice to see you too," Helen said and jumped to her feet. How about I entertain the kids in my suite while you two talk."

"Thanks," I said.

She shepherded Kayden and Kacy out, amidst Kayden's protests after seeing his father. The door shut behind us and Alex came and stood in front of me.

"I don't get this Charlotte. What did I do this time?"

I raised my gaze. I needed to see his reaction when I told him about Abigail. "Your fiancée came to see me."

"I don't have a fiancée. How can I have a fiancée when I'm already married?" he asked without flinching.

"Abigail. Will you deny knowing that such a person exists?" I said.

Alex sighed and sat on the chair, his shoulders slumping. "I know you have trust issues Chaz from your past or whatever but please don't do this anymore."

"Do what?"

"You said you'd try and stay before running off. I do know Abigail and we *were* in a relationship, but the rest of it is not true. If she's pregnant it's not with my child, and we are not getting married."

I wanted to believe him so badly. "Why would she say such things?"

"That's something you're going to have to ask her. The reason I know that she's not pregnant with my child is because I used my own condoms every single time and had a vasectomy. If I wasn't going to have a child with you, I was never going to have one with anyone else. Least of all her."

I felt as if I'd been punched in the chest. "You did?" I closed my eyes and willed the pain in my chest to dissipate.

"I shouldn't have agreed to a relationship with Abigail in the first place knowing that I was still in love with you and always would be. I thought maybe it would help me move on from the hurt. It didn't so I ended it. She chose to ignore that and concocted this story about being pregnant and then went about telling anyone who would listen."

"What do your parents say about all this?" I asked.

Abigail was the sort of woman they wanted their son to marry. The way she spoke, the way she held herself, she was obviously from their circle.

“I told them the truth and they never want to see Abigail again. They’ve changed and all they care about is that I’m happy. And you and Kayden make me happy.”

His face lost the tight look. He smiled “They really want to see you and to meet Kayden.”

That made me feel warm inside and tingle with anticipation. Nervousness threatened to overwhelm me as I asked the next question. “What about you?”

“I want to be with you but I don’t know if we can do this Chaz. You keep running away and to be truthful, I’m tired of chasing you. I’m tired of being prosecuted and judged without being given a chance.”

“I want to stop,” I said. “And I will. Just tell me there are no more nasty surprises.”

“There are no other surprises but life comes up with its own nastiness. What do we do then?”

“I won’t run, I promise. If I have to handcuff myself, I will.” I inhaled deeply.

“I put in an offer to buy Mrs. Horace’s property and her son accepted. We should finalize next week,” he said.

Joy exploded inside me. “So Kayden and I don’t have to move?” I was going to cry.

“Not only that but, the deed will be in your name Chaz. The property is yours,” he said.

I covered my face and cried. I heard movement and then Alex’s hand taking me into his arms. I draped my hands around his neck and clung to him.

"I feel like I've passed a test," he said, later.

"I don't know what to say. I've never owned a property. We should have it in both our names," I said.

"No, I'd rather it was in your name. It's my genius way of ensuring you don't bolt. Property ties you down," Alex teased.

I cupped his cheeks. "I do hate myself you know for always doubting you and I don't know what I did to deserve you, but I'll take it."

"I love you and Kayden so much. You're my whole life," he said.

"I love you so much Alex and I trust you."

He chuckled and angled his mouth over mine to kiss me. "Let's go get our son."

EPILOGUE

Alex

Six months later

"I think we should swap," my father said after I'd given him a tour of the James Turner and Son LLP offices in town.

Rather than set up offices in Cleveland which was a good two hour drive away from Woodfield, an opportunity had arisen when the only attorney in town decided to close shop and retire to tour the world with his wife.

The location of his office was ideal. It was walking distance to the court house and home. Sometimes I went weeks without using my car unless Charlotte, Kayden and I were going out of town.

Business had quickly picked up and my father's name brought clients from as far as Cleveland which worked out perfectly for me. I'd even brought in two lawyers fresh from law school and together with a secretary, there were four of us at the office.

There was enough work to keep us busy and I got to live the lifestyle that I wanted. Most importantly I had time to be with my son and to help my wife with her pursuits. Charlotte had resurrected her dreams of opening her own sandwich shop.

She was working part time at the diner and spending the rest of the time looking for the perfect location and working on recipes. Meanwhile, Kayden and I were enjoying being her tasting guinea pigs.

"You should be in New York and I should be here," my father said and I got the feeling that he was not teasing.

I laughed but he had it wrong. Woodfield was where I belonged. I felt part of a community and I felt as if I was really helping people. I also liked the fact that I was establishing friendships with my clients. I could imagine decades from now, doing the same jobs for their children.

I liked the sense of community and who knew maybe Kayden would want to be a lawyer too, here in Woodfield or in New York. Or he could want to be a chef. Whatever he wanted to be in the future, I would be his biggest supporter.

"I like the slow pace," he said when we left my office and went back to the street.

"Afternoon Alex," Jonathan from the hardware store said as he went past. I'd worked on his parent's estate after his father passed on.

I exchanged greetings with a few more people as we walked back home.

"See what I mean. Everyone knows you and vice versa," my father said. "You made a good choice son."

Life for me had never been about belonging to the right clubs and having the right circle of friends. Good people were found in all walks of life.

My mother and Chaz were seated on rocking chairs on the porch watching Kayden ride his brand-new bicycle that was a gift from his grandparents. It was a good thing that they were far away and only visited once every two months otherwise, they would spoil him rotten.

"Dad, Grandpa, look!" he said.

"You're looking good, son," I said, and my dad echoed my sentiments.

Kayden had brought out a softer, more relaxed and loving side to my parents and dismantled some of the preconceptions that could have lingered in their minds. My dad even played soccer with him. My amazement made Chaz laugh but she hadn't known the kind of serious man my father had been when Mary and I were growing up.

Chaz was smiling but I could see her eyes behind the dark glasses she had been prescribed after the surgery on her eyes. They were a continuation of her treatment to try and bring up her vision from eighty percent to ninety. She could now drive and do everything a normal sighted person could.

"You're right on time for lemonade," Chaz said, getting up.

My mother stood up too. "I'll help you," she said and followed Chaz into the house.

I was proud of my mother and Chaz. Despite the terrible beginning they'd had, they had managed to patch things up and forge a relationship that was quickly turning into a real friendship.

We spent the afternoon hanging out together and just being a family. My parents were in Woodfield for three days before they left on Sunday.

"I can't believe I'm saying this but I'm going to miss your parents," Chaz said as we stood on the porch waving goodbye to them as they drove off in a cab, headed to the airport.

"They grow on you," I said to Chaz. "And they love you and Kayden."

"We love them too," she said.

I turned to face her and pulled her into my arms. I lowered my head to her neck and nibbled it. "I have an idea."

She laughed softly. "Let me guess. Does it involve a bed and the fact that Kayden is asleep?"

"You're a smart lady," I said, breathing in her sweet feminine scents. "You drive me crazy, you know that?"

She sighed sweetly. "You drive me crazy too husband."

I kissed her deeply before pulling away and taking her back into the house. In our bedroom, conveniently located at the end of the hallway, away from Kayden's room, I peeled off her clothes, leaving her gloriously, beautifully naked and proceeded to worship her gorgeous body.

That was all I'd ever wanted from that first day I met Chaz at the train station. To spend my life with her, loving her and raising our family together.

The End.

SAMPLE CHAPTERS...

No Boss Of Mine

Chapter One
Finn

I lean against the balcony wall and take a long pull from the cigarette I bummed off my Grandpa's lawyer. The last time I smoked was when I was nineteen, but today is bad, crazy bad. I've been out here on the balcony for what seems like a lifetime, and I'm almost done with my cigarette, but it's done nothing to calm me down.

I shake my head, partly in disbelief, and partly in anger. My lips twist into a smile. It's not the sort of smile that reaches my eyes. It's bitter. After ninety years on earth, the old man couldn't just let go and enjoy heaven or wherever he has gone.

"You've really fucking done it this time, Grandpa," I mutter under my breath.

I look out over the carefully cultivated grounds of my parents' home, trying to stop the thoughts of my grandpa, who, it seems, has excelled himself and found a way to fuck with me even from beyond the grave.

The wind picks up, rustling the leaves of the tall trees around the edges of the huge lawn. The gardener is cleaning the massive Romanesque marble fountain my father had imported from Italy as a wedding gift for my mother. She is very proud of it.

I caught hell off her for squirting a whole bottle of dish soap into the water when I was seven. I was delighted with the result. I thought it looked magical with bubbles and suds everywhere.

My mother, not so much.

I straighten and take one last drag of the foul cigarette, then crush it out in the ashtray on the glass table behind me.

I should have known something like this was coming. Obviously, not this exact thing, I never could have predicted this one in a million years, but I should have known there would be something. My grandpa has always challenged me, pushed me to be the best version of myself, even when I resisted him, but this? This one is completely, totally, utterly from left field.

Throughout his entire life, he never did anything without a reason. When he asked me to run his company for him seven years ago, I should have guessed there would be a catch, that it was only the first phase of his plan for me.

I guess I was naïve, but when he told me he had terminal cancer and he wanted me to take the helm, I thought maybe I had finally done it. I'd impressed the unimpressible man enough to have him take a back seat and leave me to it. But no, I hadn't. We were at loggerheads the whole time. Ninety-five percent of the time he was wrong, but it was worth the stress for the five percent when he had the better solution.

He's finally done it now though. He's set me a challenge he thought I wouldn't be able to rise to.

"You underestimated me, Grandpa. I see your challenge and I fucking raise you the final victory," I say to him, wherever he is. Then I head towards the doors leading back into the house.

I step back inside the house, and walk through the cooler, air conditioned air of the interior. I make my way quickly towards the large, elegant dining room, which is where my mother, my dad, and Andrew Garfield, my grandpa's lawyer and the executor of his will, are waiting.

My mother usually looks young for her age, but today, her face shows the strain of this meeting. My dad is as stoic as ever, hiding his fury behind a stony mask of neutrality. Anyone who knows him well though, will not fail to see the little tic above his jawbone, a sure sign that he's tightly holding himself from blowing a gasket.

Thank God, he got his share of Grandpa's fortune without having to jump through the hoops I'm having too. Grandpa played it clever. He knew it's not about the money for me. If it were, I'd have walked away a long time ago and told him to stuff it. He's made it about something I feel is mine. Something I've spent the last three years building to the exclusion of everything else.

Hell, I've poured everything I have into this business.

I can't just let go of it, and he fucking knew it. It's my life. Especially not now, when I'm just about to transition it into the next level and turn it into something amazing.

As I step into the room, Andrew looks at me expectantly. I ignore his eyes and stop off at the dresser to pour myself a glass of iced water from a jug. I don't want the water. I want a very large glass of whisky, but there you have it. I compose my face as I pour the water, then I saunter over to the long table and retake my seat. "Okay, Andrew. Run this thing by me again," I say.

He does it with pleasure. After all, he bills clients, in this case, my grandpa's estate, at five hundred dollars an hour, so he's in no hurry at all.

As he drones on, I start tapping my fingers on the table.

Finally, he gets to the dreaded part. He clears his throat and gets it out, "In order to inherit your grandfather's shares and gain full control of the company, you'll have to marry Ashley Winters, the granddaughter of Walter Winters, who co-founded the company with your grandfather." Andrew stops and watches me over the top of his silver framed glasses.

This had been the point I had walked out of the room before... in furious shock.

"And if I don't?" I ask quietly.

"Then the shares go to the board, being shared equally between them, giving you no voting rights, although your job as CEO will be safe, of course."

My grandpa knew how I would view this. What's the point in being the CEO of a company if you can't make any important or risky decisions? I had gotten the company this far because I'd made decisions other men wouldn't. This deal would suit some people, but I am not one of those people. And Grandpa knew this.

I had begun to take the company in a completely new direction, one my grandpa allowed to happen, but it was clear the board seemed wary. They still are. Given half the chance, they would crash all my hard work and just keep the company ticking along at its present state. They don't understand that if the company doesn't grow now, it will be a dead duck in today's digital world.

Andrew looks at me calmly.

The choice is simple. Marry Walter's granddaughter or stand back and let all of the work be for nothing and watch from afar as the company slowly disintegrates until there's nothing left of it. "And this Ashley. She's agreed to this?" I ask.

"Not exactly," Andrew mutters, looking uncomfortable for the first time since he arrived here in his expensive car and his expensive suit. "Ms. Winters has no idea she is part of this clause."

"What?" I explode.

"You'll have to... um... talk her into it."

"I don't fucking believe this," I mutter and shoot to my feet. "So what's in it for her?" I demand. "Why would she agree to this—this— madness?"

"I'm afraid I can't help you with that one, Finn. Your grandfather's answer when I asked him the same question was that you'll use your natural charm."

"Oh well, that should be easy enough then," I say sarcastically.

"Financial inducements do help," Andrew suggests delicately.

The truth is, he could be right. If I agree to this, and get this Ashley girl to agree to it, then I can make Ashley the sort of financial offer she won't be able to refuse.

"Mr. Garfield," my mother burst out, ever formal, even though Andrew has told her to call him Andrew a hundred times. "This is completely ridiculous. The terms are archaic and are just a sign of that old fool trying to control not just Finn's life, but the life of this poor girl's too. It's not realistic and there must be some way around it."

"There isn't," Andrew says. "I'm afraid Finn's grandfather made this particular specification watertight, Helen. He's even closed the senility loophole by getting a certification that he was of sound mind from a psychiatrist."

"We'll go to court. Fight it. No court will uphold such a silly clause," my mom fumes fiercely.

Andrew looks a little surprised, although he hides it well, covering the tiny flash of emotion by clearing his throat and pushing his glasses up his nose. "You could try it, but I guarantee you will lose. The will is clear and has been through all of the correct channels. And even if you do win the case, there will be nothing left to win."

"What do you mean?" my father asks.

He's been silent throughout the rest of the meeting and we all turn to look at him.

"The terms are clear," Andrew explains. "If the will is contested, the company is to go on the market immediately and be sold for one hundred thousand dollars and it cannot be bought by any of the family or by any proxy of this family."

"What?" my mother cries in disbelief.

"But it's worth three hundred times that," my father exclaims.

"Actually, it's worth three hundred and seventy nine times that." Andrew nods. "And that's the point. The company will be sold for one hundred thousand dollars, and by the time the fees and taxes are paid, Finn will stand to inherit around two thousand dollars."

"Well damn," my father says, shaking his head. He tries to hide it, but there is grudging admiration in his voice at how truly wily the old man was. "He's really got this sewn-up, hasn't he?"

"So it would seem," Andrew replies.

"Look Mr. Garfield, I know the man was my father-in-law, and I hate to say this, but he was clearly insane when he wrote this will. Finn has worked so hard bettering this company and quite frankly, he deserves better," my mom states.

"I'm not here to debate what your son deserves, Helen," Andrew replies. "I'm here to see to it that your father-in-law's will is adhered to. He wasn't insane when the will was drafted, as three separate psychiatrists attested to, in the event you tried to pull that card." He turns his attention back to me. "The choice is simple Finn. You remain at the company as an employee with a big office, an obscene salary, and a fancy title, or you marry Ashley Winters and run the company as you see fit. That's really all there is to say on the matter. I'll leave you my card and you can call me when you have made your decision. You have three business days to decide, and if I don't hear from you within that time frame, then the company goes on the market."

"Three days," my mother gasps incredulously. "That's not enough time to bake a fruit cake."

"I'll do it," I say. I never had any real doubt in my mind. I would do it. I would show my grandpa I am worthy one last time and I would keep the company I'd turned around with my blood, sweat, and tears, if it was the last thing I ever did.

"Finn, you don't have to do this," my father cautions. "Those aren't the only two choices. You can walk into any firm in the city, and get a real job where you have real power and real responsibilities. Better still, you can start your own. Between you and me, we have enough."

"I know that, Dad, but it wouldn't be the same. I can't walk away. Not after I have given everything to this company. I can't see it fall into the hands of a board who knows nothing about the current market trends and watch them run it into the ground."

"But you've never even met this girl," my mom cries.

I shrug. "It will only be a marriage of convenience." I don't add on the rest of what I'm thinking. It'll be a quick wedding, a quiet affair no one needs to know about, followed by a few months of pretense, and then an even quicker divorce.

"But you two might hate each other," my mom adds unhappily.

"So what? That's how most marriages end up anyway."

My mother looks totally dismayed and my father hangs his head.

I stand up. "I guess I'd better arrange a meeting with Ashley Winters and – how did Grandpa put it again? Ah yes – use my natural charm on her."

Then I leave the room before anyone has the chance to try and argue with me, or talk me out of my decision. Not that anyone could.

Chapter Two

Finn

I've seen some pictures of Ashley when she was younger. Long, chestnut brown hair, glasses, bad skin, and chubby cheeks. I also had a private investigator do a bit of digging into who she is. He found out she'd turned her back on the corporate world and dedicates herself to running a charity that helps get homeless kids off the streets, but I can't believe she works here.

To say the area is run down would be an understatement. I hardly dare to leave the car. Partly, because I'm expecting to be mugged the second I get out, and partly because I suspect my car will be gone when I get back outside.

Ok, so I'm exaggerating a little bit, but this place has bad vibes written all over it.

I was expecting… I don't know… something that at least looked inviting. The place is anything but inviting. It's a one story building nestled between a grubby looking greasy spoon and a boarded-up newsagent. It hardly screams 'I know how to make money work for the people I'm trying to help.'

I check the address on the text Andrew sent me one more time, sure I must have the wrong place, despite the faded sign hanging over the entranceway telling me I'm exactly where I'm supposed to be. The address checks out, as I knew it would. I sigh to myself and get out of the car. As the car locks engage and the red alarm light flicks on, I look around me warily. I'm trying my best not to be judgmental, but it's hard when my car is probably worth more than some of the buildings around here.

Maybe my grandpa wanted me to marry this girl because he felt sorry for her, stuck working in a shithole like this. God, couldn't he have just left her some money? She could certainly use the money, and my chances of reaching an agreement with her were getting better with every passing minute.

I think it would be easier to get donations if her charity was based somewhere slightly more flashy.

I imagine my grandpa watching me, laughing at my discomfort, taunting me from beyond the grave. The thought of him enjoying my discomfort forces me inside the building.

The lobby is tiny, but thank God, it's nicer inside the building than outside. Everything still screams cheap though. The chairs for visitors to wait on don't match each other and the table placed next to the chairs is far too low for the height of the chairs. But I have to admit it also looks scrupulously clean and tidy. Even the floor is shiny. And the air smells of freshly brewed coffee, always a good sign in my book. A large vase of artificial flowers stands at one end of the reception desk.

Behind the desk is a woman who looks to be in her early twenties, pretty with curly blonde hair and perfectly applied makeup. She's wearing a tight fitting black polka dot top. She looks up and flashes me a friendly smile.

I feel a spark of hope. If this girl's attitude is anything to go by, maybe Ashley will be easier to persuade than I'm thinking. I flash back a smile and move towards the desk. "Hi," I say. "I'm looking for Ashley Winters." I wait for the girl to smile again, maybe even blush a little, as she tells me I've found her.

Instead, she nods curtly towards her left. "Down the hallway, third door on your left," she huffs sourly.

Oh well, looks like Ashley is not popular with her. I start down the only hallway I can see. It occurs to me that this is part of my grandpa's plan. Ashley is probably one of those hippy types who doesn't shave her armpits and refuses to shower until there's world peace or some shit like that. My grandfather always seemed to want to throw me into the worst situation. He thought it was good for character building, but he wouldn't choose anyone too far outside what he considered feminine and socially acceptable.

Or would he?

My grandfather had always been interested in making money, lots of it, not the scene that went with it. It was my mom's side of the family who'd been interested in impressing society. Grandpa was self-made and he instilled a sensible work ethic in my dad and a furious one in me. I think he picked me to succeed him a long time ago. My mom was old money, more interested in how she was perceived than anything else. Maybe my grandpa who never got on with her has chosen a tree hugger type just to horrify her.

I guess I'm about to find out because I've reached the third door on the left. The hallway is far from fancy. There's no carpet, just ugly, cracked floor tiles. The walls are painted a disturbingly bright white. Let me put it this way. If there'd been the smell of boiled cabbage in the air, I'd be hard pushed not to imagine it belongs in a third-rate hospital or a prison. But I guess if you're homeless, then this would seem like heaven.

The door to Ashley's office is ajar and I tap on it, then step into the tiny room. It has a threadbare brown carpet and the same brilliant white walls. They must have gotten the paint cheap in a job lot or something. Not only on Ashley's desk but all around her on the floor is stacked with files and papers and I honestly cringe at the sight of it. I'm a minimalist. I hate mess and excess. How can she work in that kind of chaos?

She is on the phone and waves me towards the lone chair opposite her.

I take a moment to study her.

She is twenty-seven, but she looks more like a teenage boy. Petite, thin, seemingly flat chested and around five foot three at a guess. NOT my type at all. I'm a simple man, I go for chesty, blonde girls with mile-long legs. Ashley looks so thin I imagine a good hard fucking would break her in half, something I tend to avoid in women. I don't want to take a woman to bed only to have to hold back in case I hurt her. Anyway, we won't be fucking so that's a relief.

Also, her dark brown hair is in what I think is called a pixie cut. I instantly hate it. The style is unflattering and not in the least bit feminine. Admittedly, some women can pull off short hair. Unfortunately for Ashley, she's not one of them.

I take in her face. She has lost her glasses which is a good thing. She has full red lips and warm brown eyes, and granted, she's not completely unattractive, but would it kill her to wear a bit of makeup? It's like she has no interest in how she presents herself to the outside world, which for me, is a major turn off.

She's wearing a blouse that looks a little bit too big for her, and I know without even having to look that she will be wearing shapeless trousers and sensible shoes. Maybe she thinks by trying to look masculine, people will see past her small, delicate frame and think she's a force to be reckoned with. However, with the way she has started yelling into the phone, I don't think she needs to dress like that to be taken seriously.

"Just get it done," she snaps and hangs up the phone.

I move to the chair she had indicated and pick up a stack of papers from it. I look around for somewhere to put them, but of course, there is nowhere. Giving up on finding any empty space, I sit down and put the papers on my lap.

She looks at me properly for the first time since I came into her office. If she recognizes me, she doesn't let on. She smiles, and her eyes light up, making her look almost radiant.

Okay, so maybe she's not totally masculine.

"I swear the red tape in this country gets more ridiculous every day," she condemns. "It's like the government wants kids to feel hopeless. Anyway, what can I do for you?"

"I'm here to fix your computer," I say.

"Excuse me?" Ashley asks, with a slight frown. "I think you might have the wrong building. Our computers are fine."

"They work properly?" I quiz.

She nods.

"Ah! I gave you the benefit of the doubt and assumed they were broken when you ignored all of my emails. I guess you're just rude."

"I'm rude?" Ashley snaps. "I think you'll find it's considered rude to barge into someone's office then sit and check them out like they were a piece of meat hanging in a butcher's shop."

I can't help it, the words trip out of me, before I can hold them back, "Oh honey, you wish."

She blushes bright red, and clears her throat. "Actually, I wish you'd just leave. I can't believe Rachel let you in here with that dumb story."

I assume Rachel is blondie. "I didn't tell her that story," I say. "I just asked for your office."

Ashley rolls her eyes with irritation. Obviously, there's no love lost there. "So, I assume you're here to tell me what your emails say rather than just moan about me ignoring them? Although, I must warn you, if I ignored your emails, they obviously weren't interesting enough for me to want to respond to them, so you're probably not going to like my response."

I grin charmingly. "And here I was thinking you were just playing hard to get."

She frowns darkly.

I get to the point, "I emailed you to invite you to lunch."

"*That* was you?" Ashley asks, her frown deepening ominously. "The charming email demanding I present myself at some pretentious restaurant to discuss a mutual interest?"

Clearly, she's using the word charming sarcastically, but I decide to play along. She's easy to fluster, and it's turning out to be kind of fun watching her become more and more incredulous. If she doesn't watch it, she might pop right in front of me. "I'm glad you thought it was charming. Personally, in hindsight, I think it was a little arrogant, but now we're back to you being rude. You clearly got my email and ignored it. Even if you didn't want lunch, would it have been so hard to send back a quick 'no, thank you'?" I pause.

Well, she doesn't disappoint. She blushes bright red. Another reason she should make the effort and wear a little makeup, her emotions are too easy to read. "Of course, I ignored it," she huffs. "I don't take well to being ordered around by anyone, least of all a total stranger."

"I'm not a total stranger, but that's not the point. You do realize now that because of your stubbornness, we're going to have to eat lunch in this neighborhood, a place I can only describe as unsavory."

She laughs then, a confident, gorgeous laugh. "Oh honey, if you scare that easily, then I was right to ignore your email."

This catches me by surprise. I expected her to maybe take offense at my observation, but I thought she would try to defend her choice of getting an office in the middle of a slum. Instead, she's judging me. Someone with that haircut judging me is just—well, wrong. Something about this girl just rubs me the wrong way. From the moment I laid eyes on her, I've been doing and saying things I would never normally dream of saying to a girl. "I didn't say I was scared. I just don't fancy eating somewhere where the cleanest guests are probably the rats in the kitchen," I shoot back.

I know I've gone too far when Ashley's face clouds with real anger.

"Get out of my office," she shouts.

I've come this far, I might as well keep going now. I shake my head and smile.

"It wasn't a request," she adds. "Get out and don't come back here. Oh, and by the way, you're far too old for that preppy schoolboy outfit."

Despite myself, I can't help but glance down at my khaki slacks and shirt. It's neither preppy, nor school boy. "I'm not about to take fashion advice from someone who looks like she dumpster dives for her clothes."

"Oh, you're one of *them*," Ashley leers, nodding to herself.

She doesn't elaborate, and although I know I am playing right into her hands, I have to ask, "One of what?"

"One of *them* who will wear anything with a designer label. Because if Ralph Lauren or Gucci tells them it's acceptable, then it must be. I think the word for that is clone," she finishes with great satisfaction.

I don't know whether to be angry that she thinks I actually have no style of my own, or impressed because she is so feisty.

Before I decide, she smiles sweetly at me. "This meeting is over. Have a good day." She flips open a file sitting in front of her, dismissing me. Very likely, she has no idea which file it even is.

It's a dismissal tactic I've used several times myself over the years, but I'm not one to be dismissed. "So you're not interested in hearing about the proposition I have for you?" I ask coolly.

Ashley glances up from the file and shakes her head. "Nope. I have zero interest in anything you have to say."

I shrug my shoulders and stand up. "It always strikes me as a shame when people running charities let their emotions get in the way of what could amount to a sizable donation of sorts, but never mind. There are plenty of charities who could use the money."

"Wait," Ashley calls as I turn away.

I turn back, one eyebrow raised.

She swallows hard and tries to smile. "Donation? I guess I could spare five minutes."

Just then, something odd happens inside me. I want to make it hard for her. I want to see her beg me to rip her ugly skirt off, open her legs, and fuck her hard on her desk. *Jesus!* Where the fuck did that come from? The stress must have gotten to me. I am literally going insane. Slightly disorientated by the unwanted images inside my head, I sit back down. I rub the back of my neck to compose myself, then meet her eyes. "I told you earlier I'm not a total stranger, and that's true." I extend my hand over the desk.

Ashley takes it, eyeing me somewhat warily.

"I'm Finn Jagger, Arthur Jagger's grandson."

Her eyes widen slightly as she releases my hand.

I go on, "And you're the granddaughter of Walter Winters, my grandfather's business partner, correct?"

Startled and confused, she nods. "Yes, but I haven't spoken to my family in years. Not since I decided I didn't want to marry a monkey in a suit."

I shift uncomfortably in my chair. This is going to be even harder than I thought.

"It's funny," she carries on, "how I was the golden child of my family until I decided I wanted to do something worthwhile with my life," she admits, bitterly. She catches herself revealing too much, and gives her head a little shake.

I decide to gloss over the moment and try to take away a little of her discomfort. "It's okay. Some people just aren't cut out to marry into the corporate world. It's hard. It takes a tough woman to put her needs after her family," I say.

Her face clouds again.

I realize I've said the wrong thing again, although it was unintentional this time. I was actually trying to sympathize with her because I wouldn't want to give up my precious time to care for others either.

"You sound just like my grandfather. He didn't get it either."

"Get what?" I ask.

"That this isn't easier," she replies.

Before I can even open my mouth to reply she goes into a passionate rant, "You think it's hard to be married to some rich guy? Then try sitting here with a fifteen-year old boy who has run away from his abusive father and been on the streets for six months. Try making that kid, who has been shat on by everyone in his life who was meant to help him, trust you. Try making that kid see that you're not like the rest of them. That you're not going to throw him away like trash. Try making that poor kid see his worth. Then you'll know how hard this choice is compared to being the pampered wife of a rich man."

I swallow hard, uncomfortable suddenly. Ashley is turning out to be someone very different from who I thought she would be. "I-I couldn't do that," I say honestly.

She raises an eyebrow, waiting for the punchline.

I shake my head. "I'm serious, Ashley. I talk in facts and figures. I wouldn't know where to start with a kid like that."

She sizes me up for a moment, and she must see that I'm not patronizing her because she relaxes slightly. "So what? You looked my charity up and decided to appease some of your corporate guilt by throwing money my way?" She pauses and smiles, a genuine smile. "Not that I'm above easing your guilt in that way."

I find myself returning her genuine smile. "It's a little bit more complicated than that. It seems that somewhere along the way, before your grandfather sold his shares to mine, they decided we would be good together."

Ashley frowns.

I rush on before she can interrupt and close me down completely. Like what I would have done if someone came to me with that ridiculous story, "My grandpa passed away a couple of weeks ago and ..."

"I'm really sorry for your loss," Ashley murmurs.

I nod and go on quickly, "I'm here about a clause in his will. To get his shares in his company, a company I have spent the last three years of my life pouring everything I have into, I have to marry you."

Ashley stares at me for a few seconds then throws her head back and laughs.

It's not the reaction I'm expecting at all, so I just sit here in silence, watching her for a moment.

She sees the way I'm watching her and the laughter dies in her throat. "Oh, my God, you're serious, aren't you?" She asks incredulously.

I nod grimly.

She shakes her head at me. "This is just typical of my grandfather. He dangles a bit of money in front of you and expects you to sell your soul for it."

"Marrying wouldn't exactly be selling your soul."

"Wouldn't it?" She asks archly.

"Maybe it wasn't your grandfather. Maybe my grandpa thought you could change me, make me do something good with my life. Join you in the charity business." Even as I say it, I know it's not true. I don't know exactly what he wants to achieve except make my life awkward, but he definitely wouldn't want me to sell out and go into the nonprofit sector. I know what he thought of those guys.

"You really believe that?" Ashley asks, her head tilted to one side.

I shake my head.

She smiles again. "Good. Then you're not as stupid as I thought. I still don't know why you're here though. Are you thinking that giving some sort of a donation will be a way of getting the last laugh over your grandpa?"

I shake my head slowly, trying to work out how to word this.

Ashley's jaw drops. "What? You're actually considering marrying a complete stranger to get his company!" She gapes at me like I'm crazy.

Maybe I am, this might just be the most insane idea I have ever considered.

Her jaw drops even further. "And you're thinking I might consider it too. Fucking hell, is this a... proposal?"

"I am considering it," I say cautiously. "But it's not a proposal in the way you think it is. It'll be a business arrangement. I would donate a huge, very huge initial sum of money to the charity, then we'll draw up some sort of contract so the charity gets a percentage of the profits each month. We can really make this work for both of us."

She's still staring at me like I'm insane. "God, Finn. Are you hearing yourself? This... this arrangement of yours is completely, utterly, and totally preposterous. Let me save you some time. Don't bother working out any details, or drawing up any contracts, and certainly don't even think about buying a tux, or roping in a best man. There is no way in hell I'm letting my grandfather map out my future for me in this way. The answer is never."

"Hang on—"

"There are no buts or hang ons with this one," Ashley cuts me off. "This is a firm no for me. I don't care how much money is in it for me the answer is no. No. No!"

I hold up my hand. "I can see that you are feeling very emotional about this. But remember your life need not change in the slightest bit. The only change will be a marriage certificate, which you can put away in a dark cupboard and forget about. You don't even need to see me. After a very short while, we can initiate divorce proceedings. Think how many of those fifteen year boys you can save with all that money."

She takes a deep breath. "I don't want to sound horrible or anything, but let me make this crystal clear for you. I would rather be buried alive than marry someone like you."

"I dread to think what you would have said if you were trying to be horrible." Weirdly, I'm kind of impressed she didn't lay down for the money. I don't know a single woman who would have said no to me and my extremely generous proposal.

I stand. Not because I've given up, but because I know I need a different strategy.

"Believe it or not Ashley, the idea of being married to someone as stubborn as you isn't exactly my dream either. But I can see the benefit of it for both of us." I fish into my pocket and pull out one of my business cards. "Here is my card. Just in case you decide to start putting the charity before your own personal prejudices."

I hold the card out.

She takes it and looks at it.

For a second, I think she might be starting to reconsider the idea.

Ashley looks over it and then she drops it into the waste paper basket. "Goodbye, Finn."

Read more here:
No Boss Of Mine

CONTACT RIVER

Thank you so much for reading!
Please click on the link below to receive info about my latest releases and giveaways.
NEVER MISS A THING
and remember
Or come and say hello here:

ALSO BY RIVER LAURENT

Cinderella.com

Taken By The Baller

Daddy's Girl

Dear Neighbor

The CEO and I

Kissing Booth

The Promise

Dare Me

Single Dad

Accidental Rivals

Too Hot To Handle

Sweet revenge

www.ingramcontent.com/pod-product-compliance
Lightning Source LLC
LaVergne TN
LVHW041107080826
845145LV00007B/1718

* 9 7 8 1 9 1 1 6 0 8 4 5 5 *